Exiles in the Garden

Books by Ward Just

NOVELS

A Soldier of the Revolution   1970
Stringer   1974
Nicholson at Large   1975
A Family Trust   1978
In the City of Fear   1982
The American Blues   1984
The American Ambassador   1987
Jack Gance   1989
The Translator   1991
Ambition & Love   1994
Echo House   1997
A Dangerous Friend   1999
The Weather in Berlin   2002
An Unfinished Season   2004
Forgetfulness   2006
Exiles in the Garden   2009

SHORT STORIES

The Congressman Who Loved Flaubert   1973
Honor, Power, Riches, Fame, and the Love of Women   1979
Twenty-one: Selected Stories   1990
    (reissued in 1998 as *The Congressman Who Loved Flaubert: 21 Stories and Novellas*)

NONFICTION

To What End   1968
Military Men   1970

PLAYS

Lowell Limpett   2001

EXILES
IN THE
GARDEN

WARD JUST

HOUGHTON MIFFLIN HARCOURT
BOSTON   NEW YORK
2009

For information about permission to reproduce selections from this book,
write to Permissions, Houghton Mifflin Harcourt Publishing Company,
215 Park Avenue South, New York, New York 10003.

www.hmhpub.com

Library of Congress Cataloging-in-Publication Data
Just, Ward S.
Exiles in the garden / Ward Just.
p.   cm.
ISBN 978-0-547-19558-2
1. Photojournalists—Fiction. 2. Psychological fiction. I. Title.
PS3560.U75E95 2009
813'.54—dc22   2008049572

Book design by Brian Moore

Printed in the United States of America

DOC 10 9 8 7 6 5 4 3 2 1

As always, *To* Sarah

and to John and Symmie Newhouse

and to Jon and Genevieve Randal

and special thanks to Larry Cooper

PART ONE

PART ONE

THE PHOTOGRAPHER

ESPECIALLY when he was alone Alec Malone had the habit of slipping into reverie, a semiconscious state not to be confused with dreams. Dreams were commonplace while his reveries presented a kind of abstract grandeur, expressionist canvases in close focus, untitled. That was how he thought of them, and not only because of the score in the background, German music, voices, trumpets, metronomic bass drums, and now and again the suggestion of a tango or a march. The reveries had been with him since childhood and he treated them like old friends paying a visit. The friends aged as he did, becoming increasingly abstract now that he had begun to lose sight in his right eye, a hole in the macula that began as a pinprick but was now the size of an *o*. That eye saw only the periphery of things with any clarity. The condition was annoying, not disabling, since sight was a function not of one eye but of two and Alec's left eye was sound. However, driving at night was an adventure. He did not permit himself to drive in fog because objects had a way of vanishing altogether. And there was some amusement — when he closed his left eye and looked at a human face with his right, that face appeared as an expressionist's death's-head, an image very like Munch's *The Scream*.

Alec had the usual habits of one who lived alone: a fixed diet, a weekly visit to the bookstore, a scrupulously balanced checkbook, and a devotion to major league baseball and the PGA Tour. He worked when he felt like it. He described himself to himself as leading a chamber-music sort of life except for the Wagnerian reveries. They were neutral fantasies, meaning they had nothing to do with the life he wished he had led — Alec was quite content with the one he had — or might lead in the future. He did not count himself a prophet. He returned often to his childhood but rarely lingered there. His childhood was so long ago that the events he remembered most vividly seemed to him to have happened to someone else and were incomplete in any case, washed-out colors side by side with ink-black holes, a half-remembered country governed by a grim-faced man with a long nose, a figure from antiquity, perhaps a *bildnis* from Dürer's sketchbook. Alec considered the long-nosed man a family heirloom, grandmother's silver or the pendulum clock on the mantel, the one whose ticks and tocks sounded like pistol reports. He lost his footing in those early years in which the domestic life of his own family was usurped by the civic life of the nation. That was the life that counted. The Malone dinner table, his father presiding, was a combination quiz show and news conference.

Quick now, Alec. How many congressional districts in Iowa? Which nations were signatories to the Locarno Pact? Who wrote "Fear of serious injury cannot alone justify suppression of free speech and assembly. Men feared witches and burned women. It is the function of speech to free men from the bondage of irrational fears"?

What was Glass-Steagall? Who was Colonel House?

Where is Yalta?

Question: What's the difference between ignorance and indifference?

Answer: I don't know and I don't care.

Hush, Alec. Don't disturb your father when he's talking to Mr. Roosevelt. Don't you know there's a war on?

À la recherche du temps Roosevelt. The president inhabited the house in Chevy Chase like a member of the family or a living god, present everywhere and visible nowhere. Alec's father called him the Boss. The Boss wants this, the Boss wants that. The Boss sounded a little tired today but he's leaving for Warm Springs tomorrow. In his reveries Alec conjured the president in his White House office, talking into the telephone in his marbled Hudson River voice, commanding an entire nation — its armies, its factories and farms, all its citizens great and small. Yet Alec had no sense of him as a man — not then, not later — and when he tentatively asked his father, the reply was bromidic. He was great. He was the greatest man his father had ever met, and he had met many, many of the highest men in the land, shaken their hands, spoken tête-à-tête, worked with them, worked against them. The Boss was different. The Boss lived on a different level, deriving his strength and his courage from — and here his father faltered, uncomfortable always in the realm of the mystical. Finally he said, His legs are useless, you know. He can hardly walk. But he likes a martini at the end of the day just like the rest of us, and there the comparison ends. Alec, I'd say he's Shakespearean. That's the best I can do.

Alec nodded, wondering all the while which of Shakespeare's kings his father had in mind — Macbeth, Richard III, Coriolanus? Henry V, no doubt, though that comparison did not seem apt. Shakespeare's kings suffered the consequences of their will to power. The will to power was the evil in them, not that they did not have ample assistance from others — wives, false friends, rivals, the Fates. When the president died Alec's father was inconsolable. Washington was suddenly a darker, lesser place. Then he was summoned by Harry Truman — they had never gotten along — who extended his hand and asked for help, not an easy thing for him to do. Mr. Truman was a prideful man, often vindictive. Of course Senator Malone agreed to do whatever Mr. Truman wanted done. There was a war on. Each man did his part willingly. But it wasn't the same.

For years Franklin D. Roosevelt figured in Alec's reveries but eventually faded as Alec drifted upward, forward to his young manhood and early middle age and beyond, what he considered his meridian years — when he was out of his father's house, out of his orbit, out from under, married to Lucia Duran and working in what his father dismissively called "snapshots" but which everyone else called photography. His father wanted his boy to follow him into politics, commencing a dynasty; state attorney general, his father thought, then governor, and after that anything was possible. The Boss had been a governor.

No, Alec told his father.

But — why ever not?

I don't believe in dynasties, Alec said, which was the truth but not the salient truth. The salient truth was that the civic life of the nation held no attraction. He preferred Shakespeare's life to the life of any one of his kings or pretenders, tormented men always grasping for that thing just out of reach. Deluded men. Men adrift on a sea of troubles, some of their own making, some not. In any case, the Fates were in charge, part of the human equation along with ambition and restlessness. Alec was satisfied with his photography and his reveries, including the mundane, the look of ordinary things and the time of day, what the weather was like outside and who was present at the occasion, a cat slumbering in a splash of bright sunlight, red and yellow roses proliferating. Life's excitement lay just outside the

6

frame of reference, grandeur felt but not seen yet grandeur all the same. Alec's reveries were his way of bringing life down to earth, so to speak.

It is reliably reported that the people of Milan, where Verdi lay dying in the winter of 1901, put sheaves of straw in the street outside his hotel to deaden the sound of horses' hooves so that the great composer might have peace in his last days. Alec liked to believe that Verdi was composing a melody up to the end, another opera or requiem, surprised that his street was so quiet; annoyed, perhaps, because he was accustomed to commotion, shouts, arguments, even a burst of song. Alec imagined the residents of the neighborhood laying straw before dawn, even the children. Verdi honored the Milanese by choosing the hotel and they would repay the honor. If God granted him another month he would give them one last opera, but if that was not God's plan, then at least the maestro would have silence. That was the least they could do. Verdi had given them much pleasure, many occasions for laughter and tears, cries of Bravo! And his own life had been marked by terrible tragedy, his wife and young children dying within a few years of one another. Verdi found happiness and repose in his music. The *Requiem* alone was sufficient for any man's creative life on this earth.

Alec was thinking of the musician Verdi because his thoughts had turned once again to his father, slipping away at last at a private hospital in the Virginia countryside. His father was a composer of sorts, a maestro in his own way. He would describe himself as a composer of laws. A law needed allegro here, adagio there; no crescendo if it could be avoided. Legislation was ensemble work. Soloists had their place, but the ensemble came first. The ensemble enabled the soloist. He had been a senator for nine terms, fifty-four years, retired now for a decade and still alert on good days. The old man was well content at Briarwoods, with its cheerful staff, well-stocked library, four-page wine list, and relaxed attitude generally.

The hospital was situated atop a low rise approached by a road that worked through farmland and hardwood forest and stands of cherry trees in furious bloom this April afternoon. The mansions and outbuildings of gentleman farmers, their barns and stables, tennis courts and swimming pools, were well off the main road and were not visible except for a chimney or flagpole. Horses moved about in fields bounded by whitewashed fences. A mile or so from the hospital a small cemetery enclosed by an iron fence appeared suddenly and Alec pulled off the road to look at it, as he often did when the light was good. The grounds were deserted, as they often were. Here and there flowers were placed next to gravestones, causing him to wonder if survivors arrived at night or early in the morning, paying their respects in a private fashion. Confederate dead from Second Bull Run were buried there along with local residents. At the far corner a statue of an infantryman, eyes north, his Sharps rifle at port arms, stood guard. From that distance the infantryman's attitude was one of truculence but up close his face was blank, unreadable below the visor of his forage cap. He was a muscular young man, his forearms balancing the Sharps as if it had the weight of a feather. His name was Timothy Smith, no rank or unit, his dates given as 1845–1863. *Beloved son of Andrew and Constance Smith.*

Alec focused and shot two pictures but he thought the light was not correct and lowered his camera. He wondered if the Smith family still lived in the region. Probably not; there was no sign that anyone had ever visited the boy's grave. And then he saw a spent cartridge, twelve-gauge from the look of it. Someone had used the boy's statue as a blind for bird-shooting. Far away Alec heard the rat-a-tat-tat of a woodpecker. He stood for a few minutes more, looking at the cartridge and listening to the bird but thinking again of his father and wondering if he contemplated a statue as a gravestone, the old man standing at his desk on the

Senate floor, his hand raised, an accusing finger pointing skyward, an image from the nineteenth century, Daniel Webster or Henry Clay denouncing perfidy — but no, his father rarely rose on the Senate floor except to deliver an encomium to his state and its many sound-minded hard-working God-fearing citizens. He was a cloakroom man, his arm around someone's shoulder, a whispered confidence, a promise, often a threat. Ensemble work, hard to capture successfully in limestone or marble — though *Time* magazine once published a profile titled "The Violinist" with an inspired cartoon of the Senate as an orchestra, Senator Malone the concertmaster whose bow was attached by threads to all the instruments of the ensemble, the old man smiling benignly as he sawed away. Alec could see in his mind's eye the words on the plinth: *Erwin Harold "Kim" Malone, 1905–200-, United States Senator.* The old man had been called Erwin until he was five, when his mother became enthralled by Kipling's daring lad. She began to call her son Kim, and the name stuck.

The hospital's slate roof was visible beyond the cemetery. Alec thought it tactless to build a hospital so close to a graveyard. Old people were superstitious. But while the hospital was visible from the graveyard, the graveyard was not visible from the hospital. The old man's doctor made the point quite forcibly. The architects knew what they were doing. They promised a secure and cheerful environment and that is what they delivered. Rest assured, Mr. Malone. The view from your father's window will be pastoral, a comforting vista for him to contemplate in his last days, however many there are. Alec squeezed off one last shot of the Confederate sharpshooter and returned to his car for the short drive to Briarwoods, private road, no trespassing. He had been making this journey once, often twice a week for five years. Each time his father had something new to say, but his words came less confidently and there were long minutes when he did not speak at all. Alec had come to realize that his father was an erratic narrator of his own life. But that was mostly a consequence of the life he had led, a leader of the Senate ensemble. There were so many violins that it was sometimes hard to identify your own; the music was dissonant and naturally there were occasions you preferred to forget on grounds that one bad apple must never be allowed to spoil the barrel. Alec believed that life was, for the most part, involuntary.

From his wide bow window the old man could see the sixteenth hole of his old golf club, the long undulating fairway and the tiny green guarded by bunkers, one bunker so deep that when a player stepped into it he disappeared and when he struck the ball you saw only a great fan of sand, the ball rising from it as fragile-seeming as an eggshell, and it landed softly as cotton. The course was championship caliber and its members mostly scratch players, a different environment entirely from the years when the old man belonged and played on weekends. The course was easy then and only a few members played to a handicap of less than twenty. A scratch handicap meant that a man was not tending to business. He neglected his homework. He was not a serious man. Instead, he was a sport. With the exception of a few doctors the membership had always been political, members of Congress and their senior assistants, cabinet secretaries and their deputies, White House staff. Ambassadors were welcome if they called ahead. A quarter of the membership were lawyers or lobbyists. Kim Malone was puzzled by this new environment, so frivolous and so self-important at the same time. Where did they come from, these new members? Where did they find the time to hone their games to such perfection, booming drives and crisp iron play, twenty-five-foot putts rolled true. They worked out. They spent hours on the practice range, whole mornings with a five-iron. They played golf like professionals, even the women. And now and then when he looked from his second-floor window he saw a familiar face from the PGA Tour playing in a high-rolling foursome, hundred-dollar Nassaus and sometimes much more. Washington had always been a gambler's town, football, horseracing, backgammon, stud poker, golf.

My God, Alec, we wouldn't've been caught dead playing with Snead or Sarazen. They were too good for us. We'd've been embarrassed by our play. We were weekend duffers. And they would not have understood our conversation, always politics and government, the merits of a judicial nomination or the conference report on the minimum wage or the little river project the majority leader had tucked away in the supplemental appropriation for the army. Also, we spoke of confidential personal matters that even a golf professional could understand and take back to the locker room at Shinnecock or Medinah, and that talk was none of his business. When I played here years ago that bunker the size of a strip mine looked like a little kid's sandbox and even then it took us three, four shots to get up and down. The other day I looked out my window and saw the usual three lobby boys from AIPAC, guns, and motion pictures, with a newspaper reporter. Can you believe it? All four beautifully turned out, creases in their trousers, shoes shined, straw hats. They never spoke a word, those four, concentrating on their shots. Newsman laid one up three feet from the pin from two hundred yards out, beautiful shot, just superb. My day, no newsman played golf. They couldn't afford it and no club would have them if they could afford it. Eisenhower played golf. Newsmen bowled, like old Cactus Jack Garner. Or they played handball at the Y. Maybe one or two of them played tennis. Wasn't tennis Adlai's game?

They probably learned golf at Princeton, where they all go to school now because their daddies are rich.

Come to think of it, Adlai went to Princeton.

Newsmen go to Harvard.

It's the presidents who go to Yale.

Where did you go to school, Alec?

Two years at the university. And then I went to work.

What did you do?

You remember, Alec said. Snapshots.

I was always sorry you didn't go to work in politics.

I'm not good at politics.

You aren't?

No, Alec said.

I always thought you were.

Often in the past when Alec came to visit, the old man was watching the play with a friend who occupied the adjoining suite. Listening to them was like hearing one of Harold Pinter's wayward domestic dramas. Eliot Bergruen was a lawyer who had been in and out of government for fifty years but whose memory had stopped somewhere in the 1930s when he had been minority counsel to the Senate Finance Committee. He had gone on to become one of the capital's most successful lawyers, rarely the lawyer of record but essential at the table, saying little until called upon to sum up, which he did with scrupulous accuracy. Exactitude, he called it. Someone was in trouble with one of the federal agencies or commissions or the Justice Department itself; someone was on a hook and Eliot got them off the hook or made the hook disappear or turned the hook into a ladder. But of those years he had no memory at all. Neither did he remember his own name or the names of his children. He did not remember his wife, dead now many years. He did remember to address Alec's father as Senator, though for half of the previous century he had called him Kim. They had collaborated on numerous projects, reaching across the aisle, as it were. Collaboration was the essence of the legislative craft, half a loaf a kind of sacred grail or golden mean.

Eliot Bergruen and Kim Malone knew so much and had forgotten so much that younger men, seeing them years ago tête-à-tête at their downtown club, called their corner table the Graveyard. Eavesdropping was useless because their gossip was decades old and the names and situations were unfamiliar. Muscle Shoals, Trygve Lie, Warren Magnuson, Clayton Fritchey. Eliot had only a few tricks up his sleeve now and they were well thumbed, not always to the point. Occasionally he came up with a startling fact. Watching golf in the senator's room one afternoon Eliot remarked that Herbert Hoover was an eighth cousin once removed of Richard Nixon. Moreover, Lou Hoover was the greatest of all the first ladies, dignified and witty at the same time, well read, a radiant smile, nice legs, certainly a damn sight better than the harridan who followed her and the nonentities who followed the harridan, though he could not at this precise moment recall their names.

We've seen the best of it, he said.

What was the harridan's name?

Eleanor, Alec's father said.

That's the one, Eliot said. That voice! Those shoes!

She had a beautiful voice, Alec's father said. She was a beautiful woman.

No, Senator. She was not.

Bore a passing resemblance to Garbo.

Who's Garbo? Eliot asked.

Never mind, he added. I know. Senator from Mississippi.

That was Bilbo, Kim Malone said.

One of yours, Eliot said.

My side of the aisle, yes.

Dumb as a post.

That was the least of his failings, Kim Malone said.

They had been great friends and collaborators, though on the opposite side of things politically. With the advent of the Eisenhower administration — eight green years after twenty of drought — Eliot Bergruen prospered and continued to prosper until well into the second term of the Clintons, by which time both he and Kim Malone were museum pieces. They retired to the private hospital within weeks of each other in the summer of 2003. Eventually the old lawyer stopped speaking altogether. His family no longer visited him. His firm dropped his name from its letterhead. But Alec's father continued to insist that Eliot be brought in to watch the golf, the spray of sand that announced the shot, the derisory laughter that drifted up from the sixteenth green. Kim kept up a running commentary but Eliot did not notice. His gaze was fixed on the heavy clouds approaching from the west and the cherry trees that lined the fairway, their petals scattering in the breeze. Eliot did not speak and it was impossible to know what he gathered or if he gathered anything, the look on his face as faraway as witty Lou Hoover's. Still, Kim Malone enjoyed having him in and was always sorry when the nurse arrived to wheel Eliot back to his own room.

So long, see you tomorrow. Sleep well.

Yup.

When Eliot Bergruen died, Alec's father began to lose himself, concerned now only with his own unraveling condition. He insisted that he had ceased to see himself as a human being, hence his confusion, bad temper, idleness, and shabby appearance. He allowed himself to go to seed, allowed his hair and fingernails to grow like a corpse in the grave. He thought of himself now as a laboratory specimen confined to a bedlam-kennel supervised by indifferent technicians, careless vivisectionists. The vivisectionists wore half-glasses and cultivated an air of vulgar disdain. They were the sentinels of the modern world come to carry him off. They answered to no one. They were beyond the reach of any human authority. Alec's father stated that he was no longer in a situation of becoming. He was slipping backward, neither here nor there. He no longer had standing.

He said, I live in the calm of the horse latitudes. I am from the land of lost content.

Alec thought his father said "lost contentment."

No. Lost *content*. Nothing there.

Yes, Alec said. I understand.

No, you don't. But you will.

Do these vivisectionists have names?

I know who they are, the old man said.

Thin-faced? Long-nosed?

They are my enemies, he said.

But you've outlived your enemies. All your enemies are dead.

Not to me they're not. Wherever I'm going, they're waiting for me, each one with a score to settle. The residue of seventy years of public life. I'm outnumbered. They're crowding me. I've lost my immunity. Things were better when Eliot was alive. Eliot could back them off, did so on a number of occasions. Oh, he was good. He had no use for the law, you know. Didn't own a law book. Eliot knew human nature backwards and forwards and that was his great secret. The old man paused at that, frowning and moving his shoulders. I do so wish now I'd gone to his funeral.

Why didn't you?

I don't know, the old man said carelessly. Maybe I overslept. The vivisectionists were present. However, I was told it was a grand occasion, three members of the cabinet, the British ambassador, because the British have long memories and knew that Eliot had worked for Lend-Lease. Enough lawyers and lobbyists to fill San Quentin. The vice president gave the eulogy. All Eliot's women were there, or those who are still alive. They filled the rear pew of the church and all of them were smiling through tears, according to my informant.

His women?

Eliot had a rough-and-tumble love life. A fact that went unremarked by our I-don't-know-and-I-don't-care vice president, who preferred to concentrate on his services to the party. Eliot was quite a fine piece of work. And what I want to know is, where did he find the time?

Eliot?

Women loved him. That elfin look, his boutonniere, his habit of sending flowers, and inside the vase along with the flowers a little blue box from Tiffany's. He was a beautiful dancer, you know. The waltz, the tango. When he danced he was light on his feet. And he always had his hand up some woman's skirt. The old man made a gesture with his hands as if he were shooing away insects, and then he laughed. He said, Besides the elfin look and the dancing he had a cynical outlook on life that appealed to women. Eliot maintained that most Washington women were cynics. That was because they knew their men intimately. What was said at night in the darkness as opposed to what was said at the televised news conference or on the Senate floor. For God's sake be the man I married instead of the man I almost didn't marry. Words of that kind from the wife to the husband. Personally I never found that to be true, the cynicism of women. But that was what Eliot said, and he ought to know. I mostly spent my time in the company of men.

I'll be damned, Alec said.

You didn't know that? I thought everyone knew, common knowledge. He loved chasing women and he loved the Republican Party. I don't know in which order. Maybe they came in no particular order, merely situational. Republicans in the daylight, women after hours. The old man sighed and when he spoke again his voice was pale, losing timbre with each word. He said, Eliot got started with women during the Second World War when he was working for Lend-Lease. Washington, so gray during the Depression, was a wide-open town during the war, everyone working dawn to dusk and loving it. That was the first time in memory that we had a government that everyone looked to, even Republicans, much as they despised Franklin. Most of the men were away in the service. Their wives and girlfriends stayed home and went to work at places like OSS and the War Department and found that they liked it. They were women who were attracted to masculine atmospheres, high stress, sometimes profane, wisecracking, footloose. Also, the wages were good. I think it came as a surprise to women, how much they liked the work and how good they were at it. At any event, Eliot was Four-F owing to a bad heart. So he stayed home, too, dancing the nights away. And he lived to a hundred and three. My oldest friend.

I didn't go to the funeral because I didn't want to hear the eulogy, the old man added. I hate that p-prick.

Politics trumps friendship.

Eliot would have understood. Daylight rules.

The old man smiled wanly as the half-light of afternoon began to fail, the room growing dark. He mumbled something that Alec didn't hear, all the while scratching at his wrist. His skin was paper-thin and began to bleed. Alec took his father's hand but the old man was tremendously strong and continued to flay his wrist. At last this unexpected burst of energy began to ebb and he lay still. Alec felt in his pocket for the Leica, the beautiful machine he had owned for more than forty years, a birthday present from his father. It did not seem correct to turn it against him now, and Alec did not favor catching subjects unawares, their attention elsewhere. This seemed to him an invasion of privacy. The truth was, he preferred stationary objects, the Confederate infantryman or a garden at dusk.

I hope you don't hold it against me, that argument we had.

Alec smiled. Which one?

You know darn well which one.

Yes, of course.

I was out of bounds, the old man said. I admit it. But my God, son, you were a mystery to me. You were an enigma. Enigmas trouble me.

Alec had it now. That was the argument that had its origins at Arlington Cemetery — as it happened, the first time he had used the Leica professionally. A military funeral, a bright day in December, one of the World War Two generals laid to rest; a long shot of army brass standing stiff-backed in the cold, squinting into the sun. Alec had positioned himself well away from the gravesite and the other photographers. The morning sun was high in the southern sky. A sergeant major led the riderless horse, a black boot reversed in the right stirrup, the animal sleek as marble. From somewhere nearby an invisible bugler played taps, the notes distant and pure, vivid as primary colors, but unlike primary colors they did not photograph. One of the four-star pallbearers lifted his chin, in thrall to the moment. They gave the photograph four columns above the fold on page one of the newspaper, and the next day the managing editor called Alec in and asked if he'd like to do a tour in South Vietnam, six weeks only, and he'd replied no thank you, he had a wife and young daughter and for that reason did not belong in a war zone, the half-truth delivered with effortless aplomb; and all that time he was holding the Leica and imagining what a wonderful job it would do, so compact and durable, efficient in any light or in any weather. The lens was a miracle. Taking it to the war would be like taking a Maserati to a rodeo. Alec remembered the look of disappointment on the managing editor's face and realized that his days on the paper were numbered. Everyone was expected to take a turn in Vietnam. The other photographers had all put in for it, even the most senior man, a grandfather twice over who had nothing to prove to anyone, except he had been a combat photographer in World War Two, Pacific theater, and had won a prize and thought he was owed another. He looked up to Robert Capa as Kim Malone looked up to Henry Clay. All the photographers had Capa on their minds, his skill with movement in natural light, his merriment under fire. Also, Capa was attractive to women. The managing editor's disappointment was palpable because he thought Alec was a natural. Arlington proved it.

You told him no? Alec's father said when they met the next day.

Emphatically, Alec said. And he didn't like it.

I can see his point.

So can I, Alec said. He'll get over it.

You could do some good over there, you know. Your work is very powerful. You have the eye for it. Everyone says so.

No photograph ever ended a war, Alec said.

But we should all do our part. Whatever we can.

Photography glorifies, Alec said. It's not trustworthy.

Alec, the senator began.

Photography makes things worse, Alec said.

The senator rolled his eyes and sighed deeply. He did not understand how his own son could turn a blind eye to the war, fail to take a stand, the stand being an obligation of citizenship. Somewhere he had failed in his obligations as a father, as a United States senator if it came to that. But he had his own troubles. He was then in the middle stages of a difficult reelection campaign. The tide was running against him and the reason was his opposition to the war. His state was fundamentally conservative and in time of war a senator was expected to support the effort. Anything less was faint-hearted, almost a sin. His opponent was a retired army major who accused the senator of being yet another entrenched Washington bureaucrat with no knowledge of military affairs, a liberal meddler who had never himself "contributed." Not him, not his family, including his able-bodied son the newspaper photographer, all far from harm's way. This was the normal thing in Washington. Force the constituents to fight the battle. Don't you want a senator who's felt the sting of shot and shell? Alec, watching his father, said nothing further, but the look on the old man's face suggested to him that politics not only trumped friendship, it trumped blood.

Well, the senator said, it's your choice.

Sorry, Alec said.

No need to get sarcastic with me —

You'll win your race, Alec said.

Of course I will.

Push comes to shove, they'll want you back in the Senate.

It would have been quite an adventure for you, Vietnam.

Adventure? Not my sort of adventure.

Evidently, the senator said. I don't blame you for being scared. Anyone would be. I would be. I'm sure your wife's pleased.

That's what you think it is?

Sure. Part of it anyway. Why not?

I don't think it is, Alec said.

My only point is, I hope you've thought it through.

More than you have, Alec said. You didn't listen a minute ago. Photography is not trustworthy. Then, wondering how far he could push things with his father, Alec added one more thought. Photography doesn't belong in a war, he said, realizing as he said it that in six words he had swept away a hundred years of images, from Mathew Brady onward. But it was also true that Brady's photographs of the Union dead were beautiful and no less beautiful because they forced you to look and then look away before you looked once again. Robert Capa's falling Spanish militiaman was a masterpiece of arrested action, a true *nature morte*, as formally beautiful as Book 13 of the *Iliad*. The archive was full. Alec had no desire to add to it.

They were in his father's Senate office, its lofty ceilings, its walls lined with framed documents and photographs: the old man on an aircraft carrier wearing an officer's campaign hat à la Douglas MacArthur, in formal rooms with FDR and Harry Truman, Ike, JFK, LBJ, Adenauer, Ben-Gurion, Churchill. Kim Malone was an internationalist in a state that preferred its politics local. On a far wall, in shadows where they could be seen but dimly, were shots of the senator at the state fair behind the wheel of a vintage tractor, his blue serge suit spoiling the effect somewhat; a graduation ceremony at the university; at a Rotary Club dinner; on a park bench with Bernard Baruch. When the buzzer sounded a quorum call, the senator rose and put on his coat, ran a comb through his hair, glanced into the mirror. His legislative assistant looked in to brief him on the nature of the quorum. The senator listened carefully, then dismissed the assistant. He told Alec he would have to leave at once for the floor, an important procedural matter.

Always good to see you, son.

But by God you are a mystery to me.

In a moment Alec was alone in the historic office looking at the documents and photographs, the old man's public life. On his desk was a framed picture of his wife and son, pride of place it had to be said. Alec had been visiting this office for as long as he could remember. Before the photographs of Ike and JFK there had been Alben Barkley and Henry Wallace, Wallace removed sometime in the late 1940s, the errant farmer-commissar airbrushed from the American presidium. Cordell Hull, General Marshall. He remembered as a little boy sitting in his father's high-backed leather chair playing with an onyx pen set, and his father deftly removing the pens from his reach, not skipping a beat as he conferred with his legislative assistant. A grown-up's office, no question. Alec had the idea that dusty secrets hung in the air. His father's voice was always pitched low, the assistant's lower still. Even an eight-year-old boy was a risk. They talked in a side-of-the-mouth code, alluring and forbidding at the same time, the drama reaching its height when his father and the assistant burst into rough laughter, mirthless, the braying noise of the playground. The senator was getting even.

Alec wondered if he had made a mistake refusing the managing editor's offer. And did doubt lead him to his father's office seeking — what? Absolution? An argument? In the newspaper business war was the jewel in the crown. And his father was correct, he did have the eye for it and the agility. At the age of ten Alec was taking photographs for the old man's campaign, learning to blend into the scenery, though the trick was to make not yourself but your camera disappear. Your eyes did the work but in the excitement of the moment your eyes were filled with emotion. Probably the same was true for a war, perhaps more emotion than your eyes could accept, not that it mattered now. Whether his father was correct about fear was another question, one that could be answered only in the event. The truth was, Alec had no desire for the war, and desire always came first. Without desire you were not a craftsman but a careerist doing what they told you to do in hopes that something wonderful would happen, a prize or a shot such as Capa's of the falling militiaman. Like Verdi's *Requiem*, that one photograph would be sufficient for a life's work; yes, in the way that one glorious night of lovemaking would make it unnecessary ever to try again. So you would return often, one war after another, as the roué fell into and out of one bed after another, seeking perfection and finding it just often enough to keep your passport up to date with the relevant visas. You would never get enough of it, knowing there was always a prettier girl or a messier war on one continent or another, next month or next year. Your life would make a distinguished biography, most colorful, perhaps better read about than lived through unless you were named Capa or Casanova. Alec was satisfied with what he had done, saying no without hesitation. He knew at once he had spoken from the heart, as had the managing editor, who declared that he was making a colossal mistake passing up such a magnificent opportunity and never in his life could he have imagined that Alec Malone, of all people — and here the managing editor lapsed into French, as he had a way of doing when he was disappointed — was not after all *un homme engagé*. And asked what that meant, the managing editor thought a moment and said, "Not pledged," smiling briefly to take the edge off. What he really meant was, Not of the fraternity.

Alec took a last look around his father's office, the leather couch, the documents and photographs on the walls, the onyx pen set on the desk, the dust in the air, and felt like the angler who had hooked something very large. He felt the steady haul on the line but the fish would not break water. The line was taut. He had no idea what the fish looked like or whether it was a keeper or a throwaway, only that it was large.

Alec?

He turned around to face his father's private secretary.

The senator will be on the floor for some time, she said. Can I help you with anything? She stood to one side in the open doorway, an attractive woman in her fifties, a manila envelope in her hand. When Alec was a schoolboy she helped him with his homework. He looked at his watch and said he was leaving. No one was allowed in the senator's office when he was absent.

Alec moved closer to his father. The old man had the blank look of the Confederate infantryman. His hair, thin, yellowish, uncombed, fell carelessly over his forehead. His father's eyes closed, opened, and closed once again. Washington in twilight, Alec thought, its eyes shut, out of breath, quarrelsome, its spirit low, the long-nosed man drawing near. Alec placed his hand on his father's shoulder, feeling bone beneath the cloth. He left his hand in place a minute or more, then gave a gentle squeeze and turned away. His father muttered something but Alec did not hear what it was. Maybe the old man had been reading his mind. If Kim Malone had spoken French, he would have said to his son what the managing editor had said. Not *un homme engagé*, but he would not have smiled when he said it.

Alec rose heavily and stepped to the window, watching the day's last foursome motor up the sixteenth fairway amid long shadows from the setting sun, still visible through the trees. Cherry petals blew this way and that. The fairway looked like an aisle fit for a bride. High overhead Alec noticed the contrails of a passenger jet beginning its descent into Dulles and suddenly remembered his own plans for the following week, a job abroad shooting stills for a film company, a pleasant enough warm-weather job that paid well. He would be given the use of an apartment and a week to finish the shoot. He could stay on another week if he liked (uh, your own expense, Alec, but you can keep our discount), swim, play golf, drive to the sea. The company was agreeable; the director and the second lead were old friends. They were Hollywood people but unpretentious and hospitable, most professional in their approach to things. Really, it was a vacation masquerading as a shoot. He liked their Los Angeles stories and offhandedness, and he had not seen Annalise for months.

Alec watched the last foursome, now on the green lining up their putts. He recognized two of them, a political analyst often on Sunday morning television and a newspaper reporter. The floor nurse looked in and went away, her footsteps echoing in the corridor.

Who is that? the old man asked.

Man I know, Alec said. Newspaperman.

No. The person who was in my room.

The nurse, Alec said. She's gone now.

It didn't look like the nurse.

Who did it look like?

Someone else. The long-nosed man. He's been here all afternoon listening to us. He takes in every word but he never says anything. I've never heard his voice but I know he's foreign-born. He's not from around here. I don't know where he's from but I don't like him and I wish he'd go away. I'll sleep for a while, Alec. Wake me if there's a quorum call.

Alec nodded but did not reply. Of course he would have to postpone his trip and not make other plans. The old man slipped a little each day. Before too long, letting go, he would hear the voice of the long-nosed man and that would be it. The shoot was not important. They could get someone else to photograph. But he had been looking forward to it because of Annalise, a fair-haired friend of many years. Annalise was a burst of sunshine. At her insistence they usually gave him a bit part. Thanks to Annalise he had played various authority figures, an airline pilot, a doctor (twice), a lawyer, a sommelier. Alec had been looking forward to all of it, the shoot and the bit part and the promised rendezvous with Annalise, the actress playing the second lead, a middle-aged dancer whose life was in ruins. The part wasn't much but Annalise was glad for the work and looking forward to a week or more on the beach with Alec. Four or five times a year they got together at one place or another, usually abroad. Annalise had a careless attitude toward life and the farther she got from Los Angeles the more careless she was. The movie was being made in Morocco. Well, there was no help for it. He was all the old man had and no one should have to die among strangers. Alec watched the golfers motor off to the seventeenth tee, their laughter rising in the dusk. The political analyst was twirling her putter in her fingers, a gesture that reminded him somehow of Annalise.

When Alec turned back to the bed he saw the old man watching him.

Alec said, Are you cold? Do you want the extra blanket?

No blanket. He's dressed in white, you know. An ice cream suit. White coat, vest, trousers, shoes. He's standing in the doorway right now.

I'll tell him to go away.

He won't listen to you, Alec. He refuses to take instructions. He doesn't speak. He only listens. The old man took Alec's hand and smiled wolfishly, signaling a fresh thought. Did I tell you about Eliot's funeral? My goodness, the church was full. Full nave front to back. The p-prick was in the front pew with the children and grandchildren. Eliot's women were in the rear, all in a row like birds on a wire. One of them was a member of Congress when I knew her, a committee chairwoman. She had a most dubious voting record. Mrs. Danto. She was the one with the hat and the fur stole. She had the face of a gangster. What do you suppose Eliot saw in her? What was there about her except that she was for sale. Probably that excited him, negotiating the terms of the sale. Maybe it was a sale and lease-back arrangement such as's done with automobiles and real estate. Where *did* he find the time?

As you said, his evenings were free.

Did you go?

The funeral? No. I was out of town.

One of us should have been there.

I had a shoot, Alec said. Nantucket.

Is that where your movie star lives?

No. She lives in Los Angeles.

Pretty girl? his father asked.

Very pretty, Alec said. Not a girl.

What's her name?

Annalise, Alec said.

I never knew any movie stars when I started out. Or later on, except for the last few years, fund-raisers and the like. They're all over the place now. You can't go to a rally without seeing a movie star. Up close they look different. Personally, I always liked Gregory Peck. Sound fellow. Good Democrat. Is he still alive?

No, Alec said. He's gone.

Danto. Well, she's still alive, Mrs. Danto. And she was at the funeral.

Everyone says it was great.

Washington does very well with funerals, the old man said. The sense of occasion and so forth. Ceremony. Washington loves funerals and parades. He looked up suddenly and said, You make goddamned sure that p-prick doesn't come to my funeral, not that he would. His voice trailed away and when next he spoke it was barely a whisper. He said, I've forgotten your mother.

No, you haven't forgotten.

I've forgotten. She's disappeared. I can't remember what she looked like. I don't remember her name. She's gone, isn't she?

Yes, Alec said. Years ago.

She was a peach.

Yes, Alec said.

Wonderful company.

Yes, she was.

Wonderful campaigner, too.

Yes, Alec said.

But I've forgotten her name.

Margaret, Alec said.

That's right, Margaret. Everyone called her Mag. Her name was there all along. He paused a moment in deep thought. Remember that tough campaign, 1968? She must've made a hundred speeches. So damned nervous before the speeches that her hands shook. But she made them, sometimes two, three a day about what a wonderful state we lived in and how I could be counted on to keep it that way. She saved the Senate from that damned major, the alleged war hero. Got out the women's vote. Went all over the state in a bus. We did some things in that campaign that I'm not proud of.

I didn't know that, Alec said.

Not proud at all. But they had to be done. The son of a bitch was a menace.

No, I mean about mother and her nerves. You said her hands shook.

They did. She didn't like crowds. She never got over it. But she *pitched in*. Mag had grit. She did what had to be done, God bless her. Even so, we damn near lost.

Alec said, Tell me more about the '68 campaign.

I don't want to talk about it. I'm tired.

I can make you a drink. I think you could use one.

I'm boring you, am I?

Not yet, Alec said.

Is it dark yet?

Almost dark.

I'll have that drink, then. Make it a double.

Alec poured a thimble of Scotch into a glass, filled the glass with ice and soda water, and handed it to his father.

Alec said, Tell me about the campaign.

You were no damned help, his father said.

I wasn't running, Alec said.

Forget it, his father said. He rattled the ice in his glass. Your mother wasn't involved in what we had to do. She never knew about it. But the son of a bitch was a menace.

Yes, you said that.

He didn't know anything outside his own experience. Worse, he distrusted everything outside his own experience. With a trembling hand the old man brought the glass to his mouth and took a sip of whiskey. We tapped his telephone, for one thing. And for another —

Alec laughed. And they called you one of the consciences of the Senate. I forget who the others were.

Don't say that, his father said.

I was making a joke, Alec said.

It's not a joke. Not a *joke*. There were some ballot irregularities also.

He was an awful son of a bitch. I think you're forgiven.

You're good to say so, Alec. I didn't like doing it. The phone taps were indispensable. We learned our major was taking money from people he shouldn't've been taking money from. Out-of-state money. Chicago money. Mrs. Danto was the bag lady. That gets out, the damage is done, adieu Hero Major. All the Silver Stars in the army can't rescue you when you're down in the Chicago slime with Mrs. Danto.

But you had to do it, Alec said.

Yes, we did. Democracy. Sometimes you have to nudge it along.

I never heard that story, Alec said.

We leaked it to a friendly newspaper. Told them to chase the money. Told them where to look. Told them who to look for. Those were the days when newspaper publishers had some guts. Convictions. Publishers believed absolutely in the people's right to know what they thought and that was why they owned the paper, for crissakes. So they wrote two stories, short on fact, long on innuendo. The stories weren't meant for civilians. I mean the general public. They were meant for the two dozen guys who knew how to read between the lines. Later on, the story behind the story got around. It always does. Mrs. Danto told Eliot Ber-gruen during one of their pillow evenings. Caused quite a strain for a while, not forever. We were all grown-ups. But the word got out on the other side of the aisle and eventually on my side of the aisle and for a time I was in the doghouse. But nobody could prove anything. No witnesses came forward. And the major was fighting an indictment. The boys on the paper held up their end of the bargain, First Amendment blah blah blah, sanctity of secret sources, et cetera. So eventually the story went away. Always does. Deprive the plant of oxygen and the plant dies. Margaret never knew, though. I made sure. We try to keep these things in-house.

Jesus, Alec said.

There was a comic aftermath, the old man said. Mrs. Danto was in the House for thirty years. She's been in tough shape for a while. Dr. Alzheimer has paid her a visit. So a few years ago her grandchildren had the bright idea of commissioning a biography. They're proud of their granny, served in Congress all those years. They thought of her as a role model for ambitious young women and they thought also that a biography might, you know, help her out of the fog. So they found a historian who was happy to take on the task and then — he began to laugh, a kind of strangled cackle — made the mistake of sending a news release to the pa-pers. The piece wasn't read by everyone but it was read by some-one, because in due course a man came to see the grandchildren and offered to finance the project himself because he was such an admirer of Congresswoman Danto, but in order to do so he had to have access to the archive, all the private papers of granny. Every scrap of paper they had. Naturally the grandkids thought that was great. Told him where the papers were housed. And the very next day a fire-of-suspicious-origin incinerated everything. No paper, no biography. A few weeks later the kids received siz-able checks from an insurance company they never heard of. So sorry for your loss.

Jesus, Alec said.

Forget I said anything. I think about that campaign a lot. I must have a bad conscience. I can live with the bad conscience, though. What I couldn't live with was that son of a bitch in the Senate. You have to have loyalty to the institution or everything just goes to hell. That was the rule back then and we all lived by it. I don't know that conscience is negotiable currency in politics despite what you hear. Personally I don't think conscience stands a chance in the world as we know it. The world we live in. When you come down to it conscience is a utopian vision. It has no place in the Senate. Well, of course it has a place, but that place is not at the top table. The old man took a sip of whiskey, his eyes fastened on some distant object. He looked as if he were listening to an unremarkable speech on the Senate floor. He said at last, I'm tired, Alec. I've talked too much. I'm talked out. I'll rest awhile.

It's all right, Alec said. I've got to be going.

Going where?

Home, he said.

Are you still living in that little house?

I'm still there. It suits me.

Don't go just yet. Please stay. I want you to tell me a story. What do you remember most fondly? Something out of the ordinary. Not one of your damned shoots. Not the movie star. Something unexpected. Tell me something I can actually believe. Something about early days in Washington, when you were young. Something about private life. Something refreshing about the way we lived back then. Or the way you lived. I know the way I lived. Your life has always been a mystery to me, Alec. Not an unpleasant mystery but a mystery nonetheless. I've never cared for mysteries or riddles. They interfere with the legislative process. Isn't the point always to get things done? Have something to show for your day? I care even less for irony, the refuge of scoundrels who need an excuse for their refusal to act. To put a marker down. To bring things to a conclusion. So talk all you want. I'll be listening carefully even though I may close my eyes. Cheat on me and I'll know it from your tone of voice.

Speak up so I can hear, his father added, and with an unsteady hand he raised his glass, rattling the ice cubes.

More ice, please.

LUCIA

A LEC WAS SILENT a minute or more, allowing his memory
to drift backward to a vanished civilization as mysterious
as Phoenicia. His memories of it were scattered and not
entirely reliable. What did he remember most fondly? Alec supposed it was his rose garden. In that soft southern climate anything that germinated would grow but roses grew wonderfully.
They had no natural enemies except blight, old age, and insects.
When Lucia first arrived in the capital from Zurich she noticed
gardens full of roses and longed for a garden of her own. She believed, incorrectly, that Washington was a city of gardeners. She
did come to understand eventually that Washington was a city of
lookers at gardens, quite another thing surely.

Lucia found the people hospitable but their argot irritated
her. Washingtonians liked to refer to *this town*, often with a roll of
the eyeballs, as in, We do things a certain way in *this town*. *This
town*, the odds are always six to five against. Lucia thought the
city blanched, an overcooked vegetable. In high summer Wash-

ington was a metropolis of civic torpor, heavy velvety heat that clung to your skin like a cape. The tour buses moved in slow motion and when they halted at the Treasury or the Lincoln Memorial their passengers seemed to ooze from the interior, a slow-flowing damp-shirted civilian tide unaware that they were visiting a ghost town. Statecraft came to a standstill in the killing summer heat. The government evacuated to the Virginia horse country or the Eastern Shore or New England in the way that Madrid emptied into San Sebastian or the hill towns of Andalusia and Paris to Brittany or the Côte d'Azur. August was a lost month. Even the newspapers operated with skeleton staffs. Still, those workers who remained were careful to wear suits and ties and the women dresses. The government had its formal aspect.

After a furious courtship Alec and Lucia found a small row house on a quiet street in Georgetown, the historic district, well away from the commotion of the Federal Triangle. A family-owned dry cleaner occupied one corner, a one-room market the corner opposite. At any time of day a housekeeper could be seen carrying an armload of clothes to or from the dry cleaner. At two in the afternoon the brick sidewalks echoed from the high heels of well-dressed women returning from lunch or an appointment at the hairdresser, and a few hours later the faintly hilarious voices of the Bridge Bunch, a dozen women who had been gathering at Mrs. Wheatley's house since the early days of the Truman administration, second and third Tuesdays of every month except August, when Mrs. Wheatley and her staff motored to an oceanside cottage at Newport. Alec's mother was one of the regulars. There were not so many men on the street during the day, save for the esthete Ronald diAntonio who liked to walk his Afghan hound at four, and Admiral Honeycutt who took a brisk constitutional at five. They rarely met, and when they did the greeting was cool.

"Admiral."

"Ronald."

Alec thought the neighborhood had a European feel to it,

though precisely what that feel was he could not say, since he had been to Europe just once, as a child, accompanying his parents on a senatorial junket that featured American hotels and French museums; an embassy reception ended the day. Perhaps it was the lack of haste in the streets, and the regularity of the neighbors' habits, and the uniformity of the houses, many of them dating from the Federal period. The small shops, the dry cleaner, and a tiny grocery store down the street lent the neighborhood a mom-and-pop commercial aspect. Also, Alec found an appealing modesty to the cars that lined the streets — Volkswagens and Ford Falcons, the admiral's black Chevrolet, Ronald diAntonio's Dodge. Mrs. Wheatley had a Vuillard on the wall of her dining room but the car on the street outside was a 1955 Buick. European egalitarianism, Alec concluded, a disinclination to display wealth, at least out of doors. Lucia, who had grown up in Europe, agreed that the street was not the normal American street — whatever that was — but it did not remind her of Europe, either. It was true that many of their neighbors were elderly, Mrs. Wheatley near sixty and the admiral at least eighty years old, but there were couples their own age, too, with children. Tricycles and red wagons crowded the front stoops of three houses across the street, and that was not at all normal in a settled district in a European capital; young people could not afford the rent. More to the point, Lucia had the feeling that in Washington life was lived not in houses but in offices downtown, whereas in Europe it was the reverse. Alec was habitually late for dinner, and at parties the men seemed able to talk convincingly only of work, the projects they were involved in and office intrigue, meaning political intrigue. With the advent of the Kennedys, government had acquired a glamour entirely absent in Europe. Glamour would not be the word attached to Chancellor Erhard or Prime Minister Macmillan, though the Profumo mess suggested the presence of a demimonde, willing girls and their middle-aged suitors meeting at country houses for a weekend frolic while the wives looked on, and all of it spread across the front pages of national newspapers. There seemed to be no such demimonde in Washington, so buttoned up and serious-minded. Lucia's view was changed only marginally when one afternoon she encountered her father-in-law's great friend Eliot Bergruen emerging from Mrs. Wheatley's doorway. He was charming as always but a little distant and he did not linger. Eliot Bergruen had failed to ask after Alec.

Eliot? Alec said that evening. Impossible. You must have been mistaken.

No, it was Eliot. We spoke for a moment.

Huh. Well, Eliot handles wills and trusts among his other specialties, so probably that was it. A house call.

He looked so debonair with his boutonniere and his cane, Lucia replied.

Thick-waisted trees lined the street, at midmorning giving it the ambiance of a settled neighborhood in a small historic town. No one was about. In summer the trees provided welcome shade even in the back yard, the one that measured twelve by twenty feet, space enough for a round table and four chairs, bounded by a high wooden stake fence. The roses climbed the fence, white and yellow and five shades of red, large and small roses with gnarled stems that reminded Alec of the faces of old-timers in the city room of the newspaper, men (and a few women) with taut self-conscious faces, seen-everything faces, habit-of-service faces, world-weary and droll. They had unexpected answers to routine questions, as Alec explained to Lucia one night after she had asked about his colleagues at work, what sort of people they were. Alec rarely brought home anyone from the newspaper office. They were old, he said, with college-age children and, in a few cases, grandchildren. They have no interest in people like us.

But they did know things about the texture of life in the capital. Alec had overheard one of the young reporters complain about Washington's cab drivers, slow to the point of inertia, cabs habitually lagging behind general traffic. Negroes especially did not understand the concept of promptness, moving customers with dispatch from point A to point B. Time had no meaning for them because they were fundamentally lazy. Horseshit, one of the seen-everything faces said. They're slow because they're cautious, and they're cautious because they're scared. Cop pulls them over if they're doing one mile over the speed limit. That's a fifty-dollar fine and maybe a trip to the station house, where the paperwork is lost and they spend a night in the can, probably slapped around a little. Maybe you've noticed and if you haven't you should. In this town all the cops are white and the cabbies are black. And that's why they take their time motoring up Pennsylvania Avenue.

That's a terrible story, Lucia said. Can't something be done?

Not so far, Alec said.

Your father —

Alec laughed. No, no. He's involved in the Defense Department supplemental.

The garden had been allowed to decay, a matter of simple indifference on the part of the previous owners, but Alec and Lucia soon put it right. In the spring and summer the roses seemed to grow as they watched. In early evening, the garden in deep shadow, the rose petals seemed to Alec to assume fantastic shapes, harelips, cleft palates, divided faces, faces divided against themselves. Alec made shot after shot of the divided faces but was never able to capture on film what he saw with his own eyes. He liked to shoot at twilight, the buzz of the neighborhood all around him, the whir of air conditioners and the slippery sound of automobiles on the soft tarmac of the street, show tunes from Admiral Honeycutt's vintage phonograph. Then, round about six-thirty, they heard one voice and then another, a gathering chorus reminiscent of the chattering of songbirds at sunrise. Cocktail time had begun, latish because the upper bureaucracy worked late. Often the men didn't arrive home until well after seven, usually carrying a heavy briefcase. A briefcase and a frown, according to Lucia.

The brick house next to theirs, very grand, had a wide and deep back yard with a towering cedar at its center and benches and wrought-iron tables placed at intervals as in a park. A fountain splashed all day and all night, always the sound of falling water. Lucia called the neighbors' house the Alhambra. Each evening Charles, the Japanese butler, brought a tray to the garden. Alec and Lucia could hear the creak of his starched shirt and the clink of glasses and his murmured announcement that drinks were served, your excellency and madame — and in a moment the count and countess arrived and helped themselves to champagne, thank you Charles, no need to detain yourself. On his way out Charles lit the torchères that bathed the garden in yellow light. And not long after that, guests arrived speaking a variety of languages, settling into the events of the day, always so puzzling to foreigners, the interplay of the legislature, the courts, and the White House — called, not entirely with sarcasm, the Palace — all of it overseen by an amiable yet reckless press forever seeking accommodation when accommodation was the least desirable of the many, many opportunities open to democracies. The truth was, since the triumph of the Cuban missile crisis — a miracle of statecraft — America had lost its nerve. America had turned its back on victory. The Palace had settled for stalemate, and that was the true meaning of fear breeding fear, Munich turned on its head. Kennedy and his people had refused to go the last inch.

Alec was often late, so Lucia sat alone in their garden, shamelessly eavesdropping, listening to heavy accents that ranged from indignation to resignation and back again, hearing the voices of her youth, voices crowded into her mother's second-floor study in Zurich, words tumbling over themselves while her mother struggled to keep order. Lucia's mother, gone now five years, had been a professor of European history, an exile from Prague who settled comfortably — well, comfortably up to a point; Zurich was not Prague by any stretch of the imagination — in neutral Switzerland. Her mother's great fear was that the small languages of central Europe would disappear, Czech, Hungarian, Polish, Romanian, and all the dialects with them. These languages did not export; they were specific to the soil from which they sprang. Czech identity could be expressed only in that language, and the same was true for the others. In her mother's multilingual study all these languages were spoken except when making points of particular subtlety to the company at large — and a point was hardly worth making if it was not subtle — when second languages proved unequal to the task: the Hungarian listening to the Pole, or the Romanian listening to the Czech and striving to grasp precisely what was being said, at which time the company switched to the blunt instruments of German or French, admittedly with the utmost reluctance. Really, it was a kind of crime. The reluctance was most palpable when a German or a Frenchman was present. Fortunately, that was not often.

Well, her mother said with a decisive shrug, they took everything else so why not our language? Another of war's spoils.

They — an international they, Asians, Africans, Americans included — did not understand that Europe was not Europe without its central constituencies. Small nations, yes, but vigorous and fundamental to European culture. Was Asia Asian without Cambodia and Burma? Was America American without the upper Midwest and the cotton South? Lucia grew up with the idea of loss, things that were gone and irreplaceable. So she listened avidly to the voices of her youth magically transported to the garden next door, the voices of involuntary exile, echoes of the Caucasus, the Carpathians, the Masurian lakes, Galicia, the Andalusian plain. Most were in flight from the Soviets but there were also republican Spaniards who refused to return home so long as Franco was alive, and a few German Jews disillusioned with Zionism. Lucia listened and thought they were all displaced persons, voices in an existential state of emergency. There was a frontier and they were on the cusp, neither here nor there. The day-to-day life of the American government was of scant interest, merely an inescapable fact of life in Washington. Their obsession was with their own lands, occupied by criminals and usurpers whose specialty was subjugation and humiliation, the long totalitarian night. And as for the German Jews, they did not care for the desert sands or the desert sun or the desert food. They wanted only to return to their language, their music, and their communal life in Leipzig, Dresden, or Weimar, but their memories would not allow them to, and the East German authorities were unenthusiastic in any case. Lucia sat alone and listened to these voices as she would listen to music, Haydn perhaps, or Gustav Mahler. Fate had been unkind and no one had come to their rescue; and perhaps they, too, had been weak. And now they found themselves in America. One night Lucia heard two women discussing Washington. Apparently they were visiting and surprised at what they had found.

The city is very pleasant, one of them said. I expected vulgarity.

Certainly there is vulgarity, the other said.

Not the vulgarity I expected. They do not hate us. Instead, we are accepted.

Leisl, Washington is not Munich.

It is not Zurich, either. Or Paris. Or Warsaw.

Lucia's head snapped up at the mention of Zurich and for one moment she was tempted to say something in defense of her city. But what would she say? That in order to remain neutral, compromises were inevitable? Neutrality was a fundamentally unnatural performance, a cat doing a handstand. And now and again the cat was bound to lose concentration, look away, become distracted from the task at hand. The audience expected it.

They are too busy for vulgarity in its obvious forms.

I would be more generous than that, Leisl said.

You would, the other said. But wait. It's there below the surface.

I have not seen it, Leisl said.

It's there. It's always there.

But — Jews are everywhere in the government.

Tokens only, the other said. A cabinet secretary, one or two on the White House staff. Never, ever, let down your guard, Leisl. You should know better.

I think I might stay here, Leisl said. I like it. I think the president and his wife are *gemütlich*. I do wish the symphony orchestra was better. I wish the galleries were better. I miss our coffeehouses and the conversations with artists and writers. And I do so miss our language. But I feel safe.

Alec listened soberly when Lucia replayed the overheard conversation to him later. He said, Leisl was correct. We don't have that here. Washington has many faults, but anti-Semitism isn't one of them. They don't have time for it. The government absorbs all their energies and all their ambitions. Their loyalty is to their party and the government. People here speak warmly about the state they're from, follow the politics and the football teams and so forth. But religion or ethnic mumbo-jumbo doesn't play a serious part. They like the motto E Pluribus Unum.

But, she said, what about the cab drivers you were telling me about?

Alec laughed and said, Touché.

Lucia had the idea that the exiles would never become reconciled to America, nor would their children. America was their grandchildren's country, blue suede shoes and the senior prom, a job that promised advancement and no politics except briefly every four years, and if you didn't want to pay attention you didn't have to. That was the beauty of America; civics was an option. The Declaration of Independence promised a successful pursuit of happiness, not a pursuit of justice. Lucia's mother favored an engaged life of which the ballot box was but one feature.

She said, America is a barbarian country, whereas Prague is fraternal.

America is a fine place if you love capitalism.

But, she concluded, Prague would not be Prague again in her lifetime. And for that we have the Nazis and Soviets to blame. No one came to our aid.

Lucia herself had no memory of Prague, not the look of the streets or the sky, the castle, the bridge, the river, or the summer weather. She did not remember the house she was born in. She had no memory of the Nazis, and by the time the Soviets invaded she was living in Zurich. She hated the idea of Prague vanishing. She was appalled when she considered what the Eastern Europeans had endured at the hands of the Nazis and the Soviets, twenty-five years of misrule and the end not in sight. Lucia had a toehold in those times without having memory of them. She felt the shadow on her spirit. She was a part of that time whether she wanted to be or not. That was yet another legacy from her mother, an inheritance like blue eyes or left-handedness. And her own knowledge of the Czech language began to fade, had started to slip away when she left Prague, and but a trace remained by the time her mother lay dying in a Zurich clinic. Their last conversations were conducted in German. Lucia did not seem to belong in Prague or Zurich. She did not know where she belonged, only that the voices in the garden next door reminded her of home. She wished she had been kinder to her mother.

How strange, Lucia thought, sitting in her Washington garden and listening to anonymous voices that brought her so close to herself. She wanted to meet Leisl and Leisl's friend but she could not see through the stake fence, so the guests at the Alhambra parties remained a mystery, identified only by language. She imagined stout gray-haired women and small nervous men, wire-rimmed spectacles, scuffed shoes, clouds of cigarette smoke, and in the background the splash of a fountain. Lucia continued to sit quietly, listening to the party break up. She was still trying to fill Prague's blank page in her memory. She was just three years old when she left, by train according to her mother, on passports provided by a considerate friend at the Swiss embassy. They both wept when the train crossed the Austrian frontier at Salzburg, where a correspondence would take them to Zurich. Her mother remembered that Lucia cried and cried, inconsolable; her father had stayed behind but that was not the cause of her tears. Leaving Prague was the cause of her tears. Of that border crossing she had no memory either. Lucia was Czech by birth but did not feel Czech. Her mother and father were Czech but they were lost to her now.

Lucia adored Swiss life, flamboyantly healthy, hiking in the mountains in the summer and skiing the rest of the year. She believed herself a different person in the thin air of higher elevations. Her body would do anything she asked it to do. Life on the mountains was thrilling, as far from her mother's quarrelsome salon as it was possible for her to get. Lucia preferred nature's realm, climbing solo, nothing between her and the mountain, no one to rely on except herself. She skied competitively until she was sixteen and took a bad fall, shattering her leg badly enough so that on damp days her bones ached. The leg remained weak, so her racing days were ended and technical climbing was too difficult. She no longer had fluidity of movement, and she was the same person in the crystal air of higher elevations as she was on the flat.

All this time her mother dreamed of Prague, knowing they could never return. Her mother deemed the ski accident fortuitous since Lucia could now concentrate on her studies. Alas, she was an indifferent student, playful in the classroom, popular with boys. Her mother urged her to take music lessons, as there was a

Czech proverb that asserted that whoever was Czech was also a musician. But Lucia was unable to carry a tune; piano, then violin lessons were useless. As a further insult Lucia insisted she had no interest in politics, a distinctly Swiss attitude. Her mother smiled bravely and said not to worry, Lucia was Czech through and through whether she liked it or not. Her Czechness would assert itself at the proper time. Czechness was not a suit of clothes to be discarded on a whim. Czechness was bottomless and forever. Lucia had an adolescent's answer to that: her mother did not understand her.

Fifteen minutes later there was silence in the garden next door except for the sounds of Charles clearing away glasses. Lucia heard a noise and looked up to see her American husband at their back door. Alec looked so large, a giant almost. She said something to him and did not realize until the words were out that she had spoken in German. He seemed not to notice, late as usual, smiling apologetically. He had brought her a pretty bouquet of yellow tulips wrapped in cellophane. Upstairs the baby began to fuss. Alec laughed and said, Are you just sitting here in the dark? What's going on? Is anything wrong? She turned her head toward the stake fence but did not speak because suddenly her mouth was full of tears.

Lucia hoped that one day an invitation would arrive, and one day one did, hand-delivered by Charles. That afternoon she went to the dress shop on Wisconsin Avenue, the fashionable one everybody went to, and bought a black shift. She had her hair washed and cut and ordered up a manicure. She bought a new pair of shoes. Lucia stood in front of the mirror for many minutes trying to decide if her mother's Lalique gold choker would be suitable and decided that it was quite suitable. She asked Alec please, please not to be late that evening. Will you promise me? It means so much. You can tell them our baby's sick with grippe. Mathilde's running a fever. They were invited next door, six-thirty P.M. sharp, the Count and Countess d'An requested the pleasure of their company for cocktails.

Welcome to the Salon des Refusés, the count said with lifted eyebrows.

We are very happy you can be with us.

We are neighbors after all. It is time to be neighborly.

Most of the other guests had arrived — Alec had not been prompt after all; the president had decided to call a news conference and he had caught the assignment — and were visible in the garden through the French doors, open at the end of the long room. It was furnished like a country house in middle Europe. A stag's head dominated one wall, smaller heads of roebuck hung left and right. Here and there were landscapes, romantic vistas of mountains and forests, streams disappearing into valleys. The artworks were as mixed up as middle Europe itself, a Caspar David Friedrich next to a Kandinsky, Max Liebermann beside Klee, and a supple line drawing that could have been Matisse or Picasso, hard to tell which. Lucia was entranced by the look of the place, especially the preposterous stag's head. The interior was dark, light bulbs concealed behind heavy opaque lampshades. The stag was poised above an enormous fireplace, large enough for a man to stand upright with space left over for his top hat.

We are happy to meet you at last, Lucia said in French. The count's nationality was unknown to her. His accent gave no hint. He was of medium height and build, dressed in twill trousers, a blue blazer with silver buttons, and an ascot. The count had the assured manner of an aristocrat but Lucia suspected he was a bit of a roughneck. His hands were huge with knuckles the size of marbles, a gold signet ring on his right pinkie. His eyes were black as a Gypsy's. His age was somewhere between forty-five and sixty. She did not know why she had spoken French to him and then she noticed in his lapel the rosette of the Légion d'honneur. No doubt she had seen it subliminally. Of course the Légion d'honneur could be given to anyone for anything — successful winemaking, successful literary endeavors, or unspecified but surely successful services to the state.

My father shot it, the count said, pointing at the stag. It is hideous but I like it. The countess likes it not so much. But she puts up with it.

Where was it shot? Alec asked.

On one of our mountains, the count said. I forget which one.

My father was a beautiful shot, he added.

Beautiful shot, beautiful horseman. He died in the war.

Come, the count said, and guided them down the long room and through the French doors into the garden, bathed in soft light from the torchères. The night was warm with only a breath of a breeze. Alec and Lucia were introduced to Herr Doktor Professor Anwalt, Maître de La Goue, General Symjon, Ambassador Kryg, the linguist Madame Brun, and half a dozen others whose names flew by. Lucia counted two beards, one goatee, and four wire-rimmed eyeglasses. The women tended to be slender except for Madame Brun and her companion, both stout as tree stumps. One boxy jacket belonged to a thick-bellied Bulgarian, identified as a second secretary at the embassy, aggressively drinking a highball; he wore a little red star in his lapel and looked to be spoiling for an argument. Ronald diAntonio waved at them from his place beside the great cedar. Alec and Lucia took flutes of champagne from Charles's silver tray and followed the count and countess. The count explained that they liked to throw a wide net for their parties, including both the oppressors and the oppressed, the commissars, the refuseniks, and anyone in between.

They should get to know one another.

Unfamiliarity breeds contempt.

Somewhere about was one of Franco's henchmen, and nearby the woman they all called La Niña, a disciple of the venerated revolutionary La Pasionaria. All this was said with the barest hint of sarcasm. And then Ambassador Kryg was at their elbows and the count took Alec away to meet the Bulgarian. Bemused, Alec followed the count, met the Bulgarian, continued on, thinking all the while that Washington was his city, the city where he grew up and went to school. He knew the names of the Iowa congressional delegation and the woman who ran the brownstone brothel way out Sixteenth Street and the chairman of the English department at St. Albans School and the son of the D.C. police chief and Lyndon Johnson's daughters, but he did not know a person in this garden with the exception of Ronald diAntonio. He had never been in a place where the company was exclusively foreign-born. He thought to himself that if he listened carefully he might learn something. Alec took a fresh glass of champagne from Charles's tray and glanced back to see Lucia listening intently to Ambassador Kryg. Then the count was telling another droll story, this one about General Symjon and his collections of antique firearms and French postcards.

Dear lady, the ambassador said to Lucia, what a beautiful choker.

Thank you, Lucia said.

Is it Lalique?

It was my mother's, Lucia said.

Most rare, the ambassador said.

You are very kind, Ambassador.

Dear lady, it is a pleasure to meet you at last. We have a friend in common.

Lucia was startled. They had never met before and when she was introduced, her name was given only as Lucia.

Your father, the ambassador said. Andre Duran. But I have not seen him recently.

Lucia let a breath go by and did not reply.

I saw him in Trieste, the ambassador said.

He disappeared years ago, Lucia said.

Disappeared?

Vanished, Lucia said.

Dear lady, I am so sorry. I have distressed you. I had to speak, the ambassador said. Such a strange coincidence, seeing you here of all places.

Lucia said, How did you know?

Well, he said, and seemed to blush.

No, she said, tell me. I want to know.

Andre said he had a daughter called Lucia.

Lucia is a common name, she said. You must do better than that, Ambassador.

Well then, he said, and gave an embarrassed laugh. Ambassador Kryg was short, barely over five feet. He too wore the rosette of the Légion d'honneur in his lapel and also a heavy copper bangle on his left wrist of the sort that was said to combat arthritis. A neatly barbered goatee and heavy horn-rimmed glasses completed the ensemble. Ambassador Kryg laughed again and threw up his hands in mock defeat. Dear lady, you look exactly like him, the way you walk, your gestures, your smile, your dimples. I am bound to say, even the freckles.

Lucia was silent. She had no idea.

A quite remarkable resemblance. When I saw you I was in no doubt.

Lucia could not think what to say. She was suspicious of this Kryg, so ingratiating, so eager to meet her and share his information about her father. She stepped back, searching the garden for Alec, and discovered him deep in conversation with two men she had not met. She tried and failed to catch his eye. She said finally, Was my father in good health?

This was some years back, the ambassador said. I would say his health was normal.

Normal? What does that mean?

I think he had been through very much. He was tired. It is normal.

What had he been through, Ambassador? And why was he in Trieste?

I cannot say. The ambassador raised his shoulders and let them fall. I'm afraid I cannot remember. I believe he was in business.

What exactly did he say about me?

He said that you were most attractive. That you had been apart but that he planned to visit you very soon. I believe he said it was difficult for him to travel.

My father is dead, Lucia said.

I am sorry to hear it, the ambassador said.

He died many years ago.

Your father was much admired.

By whom? Who admired him?

The ambassador smiled thinly, his affability not what it had been. Andre Duran was admired by everyone who knew him, dear lady.

And which country do you represent, ambassador?

Czechoslovakia, he said. But that, too, was many years ago. I am retired.

At that, the countess swept Lucia away to join a nest of women gathered around General Symjon and Madame Brun. Lucia, stunning in her short-skirted shift and gold choker, was soon the center of attention. Alec had finished a third glass of champagne and was working on his fourth, utterly at sea in this company. He remembered reading somewhere that exiles by definition led interesting lives, had biographies worth knowing. But this group had proved elusive. He watched Lucia telling some story. He supposed it was a Swiss story but whatever it was everyone laughed at the end of it and Lucia beamed as if she were taking a curtain call. Alec found himself with Professor Anwalt and the writer Koch, both speaking English for his benefit. They were discussing another writer, Walta Bin-yameen, a formidable soul who had evidently met a tragic end seeking exile in Spain during the war. Had Alec read his work? No, Alec had not. Do so without delay, Professor Anwalt said as the writer Koch nodded solemnly and added that Bin-yameen's ambition was to be the greatest literary critic ever to write in the German language; and he succeeded. And then the champagne disappeared and, as if at the chime of a clock, everyone began to leave. The party was over.

We must do this again, the count said at the door.

I can't remember when I've had a better time, Lucia said. Your party reminded me so much of home.

I suspect we are a change of pace, the count said. Something different from what you're used to. Everyone was on good behavior tonight, even Madame Brun. She has a sharp tongue. Sometimes there are terrible arguments. People almost come to blows. Political differences, cultural differences, memories that are irreconcilable. They have grievances. You could call it a clash of civilizations except it's the same civilization, mostly.

Kryg was not on good behavior, the countess said.

Oh, no, Lucia said, it was nothing.

What did Kryg say? the count asked.

He made an uncalled-for remark about Lucia's father.

I didn't mind, really, Lucia said. It was innocent enough.

Kryg is never innocent, the count said.

What's all this about? Alec said.

It's nothing, Lucia said. The ambassador knew my father years ago. I was startled when he brought it up. I didn't expect it. My father was the furthest thing from my mind. I hardly think of him at all anymore. She turned to the count and countess and added, He left my mother when I was a small child. I never saw him again and I have no memory of him. He is dead many years.

I'm sorry, the count said. Kryg is often tactless.

He's a brute, the countess said.

Unreliable, the count agreed.

Kryg said I looked exactly like my father. Even the freckles. That was a surprise.

Poor darling, Alec said.

Nonsense, Lucia said. I thought your party was wonderful, even Kryg. I can't remember the last time I met so many — she laughed brightly — vivid personalities. Next time you must come to us.

Alas, the count said, I rarely leave my house.

He won't go anywhere! the countess cried. He's hopeless!

You only have to climb over the stake fence, Alec said.

Stop it, Alec. She knew he had taken too much champagne.

It's an ordinary fence.

Alec, Lucia said.

You could vault it if you wanted to, Alec said.

The count laughed at that and wished them good evening.

Later that night, Alec asleep, Lucia reprised her conversation with Ambassador Kryg. She had no idea she resembled her father. Her mother had but a single photograph, her father seated at a café table in Prague wearing a dark suit and a Borsalino, his head turned as if greeting someone. In profile he was hard-featured, a rough-cut young man with a low forehead, built like a bull, no freckles. He held an unlit cigarette in his right hand. Lucia had no personal memory of him. He had never been in her life. When she was fifteen her mother told her he was dead but did not say how or where he died. Her attitude was, Good riddance. Lucia did not press for explanations. It was then that her mother gave her the photograph. Your father looking his best, she said, and smiled, something she never did on the rare occasions when she spoke of him. God, she said. God, he was a good-looking man. All the girls wanted him.

Then Lucia remembered something Kryg had said. She was certain of very little in her father's life except for one thing: he had never been in business.

The Count d'An was a man around whom rumors collected. His money was said to come from tin mines in Bolivia or a ranch in the Transvaal or the diamond trade in Amsterdam. Alternatively he was penniless and kept afloat by his wife, who owned estates in the Balkans. He never talked about the sources of his wealth, the common trait — as Alec helpfully pointed out — of old money and criminals. The count and countess had only recently arrived in Washington, and no one knew from where. But they seemed to know everyone. Whatever he did and wherever he came from, the count had the gift of hospitality. He and his countess — she as refined as he was blunt — were the soul of courtesy, easy and at the same time aloof. Looking at him, his muscular build and his bright Gypsy eyes, Alec thought of the seen-everything faces at the newspaper. The count would be good at games, good at getting in and out of scrapes. Not easily fooled. Not good at distinguishing one mountain from another. Very good at aura. When Alec asked his father about the count, the senator shook his head and said the name meant nothing to him. Alec searched the newspaper's morgue but found only one reference. The Count and Countess d'An had been among the patrons of a fashionable equestrian event near Baltimore, proceeds to benefit the Girl Scouts. Beyond that, a blank slate.

Alec and Lucia went frequently to the garden next door. The count and countess were now Paul and Marie. Lucia believed she had found a parallel world in their company. She thought of it as an underworld — not Virgil's, not Al Capone's, perhaps something resembling the depths of the ocean explorer Cousteau. Evenings in the garden were fluid, slow-motion theater, a form of escape. There was a shifting cast of characters because the exiles often brought friends, a visiting parliamentarian or intellectual or anonymous someone who had crossed a border and shown up unannounced in Washington. Second-tier intellectuals from second-tier countries, according to Alec, but often interesting and attractive nonetheless. He meant exotic. They had spirit but were in no way lighthearted. In fact they were hard going. Difficult personalities, Alec said, and Lucia reluctantly agreed. Listening to them investigate the past, she did not always understand the references: names flew by and she did not know whether they were politicians or writers because they were usually described in the language of literary theory, the objective correlative, narrative line, sentimentalism, prolepsis. The names meant nothing to her, the Czechs Novotný and Slánský, the Hungarian Béla Kun, and the Italian Antonio Gramsci. Now and then a life jacket would fall at her feet: Arthur Koestler. But Lucia listened carefully all the same, finding something indomitable about them because they had lived through terrible times and had survived. Life had dealt them very bad cards and they were playing the cards with aplomb but without optimism. She thought they were damaged goods because they had seen so much and suffered greatly and were now ignored by the wider world, irrelevant and without standing, a nuisance. They were forever writing something, a critical article or manifesto, a novel or a cycle of poems or an allegorical play. At the slightest provocation they would quote passages from memory, well honed from nights in coffeehouses and private parlors. Lucia believed they were trying to reimagine their personal histories and what lay in store, if anything lay in store, and in that way they were sympathetic.

Also, Lucia said, the men had beautiful manners. Yet grief clung to them.

One of the men said to her, We were born on the wrong side of the tracks on the wrong side of the world. She thought the guests-of-many-languages had acknowledged defeat. They were yesterday's men, speaking in the rhymes and riddles of the disenfranchised. They were searching for some place to call home, and this search was doomed to disappointment because they already had a home but the door to it was closed and locked. Searching for another was like searching for a fresh set of genes. Meanwhile the exiles stayed on in Washington, the seat of what they called the American empire, as far-flung now as Alexander's or Caesar's. Since the assassination Washington had become tightly wound and bedeviled by theories of conspiracy — fertile ground, in other words, for the writing of a novel, a poem, or an allegorical comedy. These projects were begun but rarely completed. America was so large, so prodigious in its energies, so various, it was difficult for the exiles of small nations to grasp. The writers among them found themselves blocked, unable to move forward. Their material had vanished.

Among the exiles — and that was another difficulty, defining their status — refugee, exile, émigré, or displaced person — not from the point of view of American immigration law but their own sense of themselves. A few of them adopted (not without a sly smile) the German expression *gastarbeiter*, guest worker, except they were not guests and they did little work except for translations and the unfinished manuscript in the desk drawer. The Jews were the most reticent, as if what they had borne was unspeakable, a family calamity so private and distressing that it could be spoken of only among themselves, and no language they knew was equal to the task. At first Lucia thought that in their privacy and exclusivity the Jews were like the Swiss; she came to disown this opinion later. It was at one of the early soirees that she first heard the word "Holocaust" and was at once drawn in by unfamiliar place names, the hinterlands where the furnaces were located, Hitler's crimes set side by side with Stalin's and the accompanying argument over which were the more appalling, the signature crimes against humanity. Lucia was shocked into silence. The argument was tentative, the door to the awful room barely ajar; these were not stories for mixed company and certainly not with a glass of champagne in your hand, and in any case the need to forget and the responsibility to remember were in combat. Eichmann's trial had taken place only a few years back. Just once in Lucia's hearing did the argument spill over, reticence set aside in the passion of the moment. The linguist Madame

Brun and Ambassador Kryg put down their champagne flutes and attempted to settle the matter. Perhaps settle was too strong a word. A settlement would not be reached that night or any night.

Madame Brun, half a head taller than the ambassador, spoke first. The uniqueness of the Holocaust was its specificity. Gypsies and homosexuals and a few communists were not excluded but the target was Jews. To be so selected was appalling. Guilt was not established. What guilt? There was no guilt except the guilt of blood. The terrible burden was borne mostly by Jews. That was what made the Holocaust monstrous, uniquely monstrous; that, and the industrial efficiency and civic enthusiasm the Germans brought to their task. Whole communities vanished, men, women, and children. Medical experiments, work dawn to dusk, the ovens tomorrow or the day after.

Dear lady, the ambassador replied, the uniqueness of Stalin's labor camps was precisely the lack of specificity. Anyone could be imprisoned, bad communists, good communists, fascists, loyal Russians, disloyal Russians, intellectuals, brutes, Christians, Jews; the net was wide. The imprisonment came at the whim of Stalin and his clique. No one was exempt. No one in the Soviet Union was immune from the knock on the door, the cattle car east, the pistol shot to the back of the head, the anonymous body in the gutter or floating in the Neva. *That* is the modern world, dear lady. Utter randomness. You must read *One Day in the Life of Ivan Denisovich*. Solzhenitsyn calls it a novel but it is not fiction. I shall not mention the numbers, perhaps as many as thirty million souls, because as Stalin said, one death is a tragedy, a million deaths is a statistic. When Madame Brun replied, her voice was a kind of hiss, a voice of profound indignation shadowed by infinite melancholy.

Lucia turned away. She felt trapped on this corpse-strewn path into the past, and she was only twenty-seven years old, no scholar of history, no scholar of anything except the crystal air of the mountains. The Swiss were well known for keeping their noses out of other people's business, especially political business. Exiles in Switzerland were expected to conform or go away. The blind eye was a kind of national emblem, and if that meant peace at any price, well then, peace was the reward. When Lucia described the argument later to Alec, he listened with close attention and what seemed to be sympathy. When Lucia finished she was near tears. She could not remember having been so upset. Alec put his arm around her shoulder and said, We will never understand this. The Holocaust is outside our experience. The most we can do is look at the photograph and imagine ourselves inside the frame. It's a question of imagination. Of course there was sympathy. How could you fail to have sympathy. But sympathy never saved anyone from the hangman. The point was not to be complicit.

You're not, he said. I'm not.

I wonder sometimes if America is not a fool's paradise, Alec went on. But whether it is or it isn't, this is where we live. Our hats hang here. We are very far from Siberia or Auschwitz.

Alec, she said, that's so cold.

I can't pretend to an understanding I don't have, he said.

Mustn't we feel for them?

We can try, Alec said. It's insulting to them to think that we can succeed.

America was too large, she thought. There were too many people in it of too many tribes and languages; they would never understand one another. The definition of "understanding" seemed to be "success." And she, too, had turned away from the ambassador and Madame Brun as if their dispute were private, as perhaps on some level it was. She found it difficult to listen to them, their words so bitter and irreconcilable. Fate had placed them in opposition. It therefore came as a shock to Lucia when she concluded that, in some manner she was unable to account for, she belonged in the company of exiles. She was hearing a piece of music that was familiar but she had no idea where she had heard it before, unless it was her mother's European salon come alive once again.

One night she left the party late. She had turned her ankle on one of the flagstones near the fountain and had been caught and helped to a chair by one of the new arrivals. Alec had not accompanied her to the party, preferring instead to watch the baseball game on television. Nikolas was attentive, had brought her a glass of champagne and ice cubes wrapped in a towel. He expertly wound the towel around her ankle and insisted she sit a moment. Allow the ankle to rest. They chatted briefly about the company before Lucia said she had to go home, she only lived next door. Her husband would be waiting for her. Nikolas helped her down the front steps and into the empty street. Paul d'An had lent Lucia a cane, but she was unsteady all the same and hurting. The night was very warm, the street silent.

I have not seen you here before, Lucia said.

I've just arrived from Budapest, Nikolas said. They allowed me to come here and teach for a semester. My family remains in Hungary, my father and my sisters. My father is a Lutheran pastor, but of course he has no church so he has become a bricklayer instead, rebuilding someone else's church that will be used for another purpose, something not churchly.

Lucia smiled weakly. She was tired and her ankle hurt.

I am a linguist, he said. Also, I am a historian of Marxism. And a novelist.

She smiled again, seeing a joke there somewhere.

The disciplines are not incompatible.

Like bricklaying and the ministry? She looked at her watch.

Not a bit, he said. Nikolas lit a cigarette and said Madame Brun brought him. She said Paul and Marie were convivial and their parties the center of things. She was not wrong. Still, I don't know that I like it here. I think I would rather be in Europe. Not Hungary. Hungary's finished.

Do you know Zurich?

Not well, Nikolas said. I have not had much occasion to be there.

Poor Zurich. Nothing happens in Zurich.

Einstein happened in Zurich.

Yes, I'd forgotten.

And Max Frisch.

Who is Max Frisch?

Switzerland's greatest novelist. Also, he writes plays.

I don't know his work.

You have been away a long time.

Not too long. I suppose it's five years. She looked at her watch again, wondering if Max Frisch had been one of those who came to her mother's salon. The name was familiar. She remembered an elderly bald man with heavy round spectacles and an intimidating glare and wondered if that was Max Frisch.

The museum is good, he said.

Yes, she said.

Remember Café Voltaire? Where the Dadaists gathered, Jean Arp and the others. I always thought it funny that Zurich had a Dada scene. But maybe that was the place for it. The birthplace of Dada.

My mother liked to go there, Lucia said.

And I remember a restaurant outside of town. We had to drive. We had a wonderful meal —

She said, Chez George.

Yes, that's the one.

My mother and I often went there for Sunday lunch. Zollikon was the name of the town. The lake is nearby, in the summer filled with boats. Chez George served quail eggs.

You'll be glad to know it's still there. At least it was six months ago. I and a colleague were making a presentation at the university and the rector took us to lunch, three courses with wine. I have never eaten such food before. The dining room was quite formal and I'd neglected to bring a tie. It never occurred to me. The maitre d' lent me one so that I would be properly dressed and not stand out. Not feel like a — the Americans have a word for it.

Yokel, she said.

Yes, yokel.

Lucia said, Once a month we would go to Chez George by the lake, my mother and I. The Sunday treat, she called it. When I was young she always let me have a taste of her pilsner. The chocolate deserts were sublime.

I think you miss it, Nikolas said.

I do, she said. I hadn't realized I did. My mother is gone now.

I'm sorry, he said.

She had terrible cancer, Lucia said. She was very ill. Her death was a blessing to her. Perhaps not to me. I miss her.

My mother is gone also. But she died in the war. The Russians.

How terrible, Lucia said. You must have been very young.

I was three years old, he said.

Only three, she said, my goodness.

I hardly remember her.

Yes, she said. I can imagine.

You can imagine?

Yes. My father, when I was three.

Nazis or Russians?

He went away, and he was lost in the war. I don't know where. I have no idea how he died or where he is buried.

My father never recovered. I think he lost his faith.

My mother, Lucia began, but did not finish her thought. She did not know this boy well enough to speak of her mother's socialism, her salon, and the photograph of her father and the Borsalino hat.

So we have a European history, you and I.

I suppose we do, Lucia said.

Do you like it in America?

I suppose I do, Lucia said. My husband is American. I have a daughter, Mathilde. She is already speaking a little English and sometimes I talk German to her, nursery rhymes at bedtime. She looks Swiss, I think. My husband says she has a banker's face. Big cheeks and already jowls.

Lucia leaned against the iron railing that led to the sidewalk from the d'Ans' stoop. She realized suddenly that both she and Nikolas had been whispering. The street was so quiet, not even a passing car. She had no idea how long she had been there talking to the Hungarian boy, who was not loud as Hungarians often were but quiet and serious, most polite, a shy manner. Lucia tapped her cane on the railing and said it was time for her to go home.

Will we see each other again? he asked.

If you come to the d'Ans', of course.

I have enjoyed talking to you very much, Lucia.

Yes, it has been pleasant. But I forgot to ask. Did you like Zurich?

I did, he said. I like Swiss. I do not care for Austrians.

Nor I, Lucia said. They are very sure of themselves.

They're only Germans of another jurisdiction.

The Germans want everything, even Switzerland.

Well, Nikolas said, that's over now. The Germans are back in their cage.

Lucia smiled. I feel foolish forgetting Einstein.

Everyone forgets Einstein, Nikolas said, and blew her a kiss as he walked away.

As time went on, Alec and Lucia accepted only about one in three invitations to the garden next door. The ambiance had changed, many of the evenings marked by malaise owing to the stalemate in central Europe and the American preoccupation with Indochina. And there had been other unwelcome displacements. Ma-

60

dame Brun had died of a heart attack, the writer Koch of injuries suffered in a road accident. Ambassador Kryg had retired to Sardinia and General Symjon to Madagascar. There were new ambassadors and military men and a fresh parade of hopeful second-tier intellectuals. Nikolas was sometimes present, sometimes not. Everyone seemed to drink more, but the drinking did not bring hilarity. Even the arguments were muted, as if in recognition of their essential irrelevance. Frequently Lucia went without Alec, staying on for a nightcap with Paul and Marie after everyone else had left. It was there, one evening in the summer of 1967, that they told her they were leaving Washington and returning home. It was time. They felt they had outstayed their welcome. The assassination of the president had ruined everything and now there was a war growing more desperate each day. The war would surely end badly. How could America have gotten itself into such a mess? The French had warned them. The British and the Germans had warned them. But Lyndon Johnson and his cohort had refused to listen to anyone outside the charmed circle of advisers. They thought the war in Vietnam was a replica of the European war and it wasn't. There would never again be another war like the European war. Probably there was nostalgia for that war because so many of the senior American generals had fought in it. Hard to believe war nostalgia if you were a European, but that is what it is.

We have learned that Washington is a one-subject town, Paul said.

This war is not our subject, Marie added.

Next month it will still be the war, Paul said, but another facet of it. This war is like a diamond, many-faceted. It has the fascination of a diamond, too. The war will go on for years. That's what you have to look forward to, you and Alec. Even little Mathilde.

Alec's paper wanted him to go, Lucia said. He refused.

Good judgment, Paul said. I suppose they were disappointed in him.

He didn't say, Lucia said. I imagine they were.

She looked up then, above the stake fence to the second floor of her house. Mathilde's night light glowed dimly. In the sudden silence she thought she heard the crowd noise of a baseball game, Alec's evening television habit. She wondered if they were disappointed in him at the newspaper office. Alec said little about his daily routine except occasionally to point out one of his photographs in the newspaper, often complaining about how it had been cropped. He thought the photo editors had no sense of balance. The butchers, he called them, slicing up his photographs as they would slice up a side of beef. She did not believe he cared greatly for his work, yet he devoted long hours to it. Alec said he had respect for the craft.

So we are returning to our house in Kleinwalsertal, Marie said. No war in Kleinwalsertal. There will not be another European war in our lifetime unless the Americans and the Russians have one, in which case the field of battle will be central Europe, bad luck for us.

It's hard to stay apart in Washington, Paul said. You become complicit whether you want to be or not.

It was fun in the beginning, Marie said.

Washington was full of charm, Paul said. Gaiety, too, in the White House and the embassies. That was because everyone was so young.

We hope you will visit us, Marie said.

Yes, Lucia said. I will.

You have enjoyed our parties, Marie said.

Very much, Lucia said. I will miss you both.

You brought spark to our garden, Paul said. But now it's finished.

So many friends have passed on this year, Marie said. Died, moved away. It isn't the same as it was. Did you hear Ronald diAntonio was ill? I couldn't believe it. I always thought of Ronald as Peter Pan, never grew old, never grew up. But still, we were a part of things for a while. We couldn't have done it without our Charles. We asked him to come to Kleinwalsertal with us but he said he preferred Washington. He's going to work for the Argentines. We doubt he will fit in with the Argentines. Charles is very much fastidious.

You and Paul were the perfect hosts, Lucia said.

Paul refilled their glasses and turned to look directly at Lucia. He said, I know the things they used to say about us. Me. That I was a fugitive from somewhere, living on Marie's money, Nazi loot, a tin mine in Bolivia. Fantastic stories. They amused us so we did nothing to correct them — not that we could have. These stories have their own oxygen and are eternal, like Nosferatu. Washington prefers the speculation to the fact, is that not so? The facts are too prosaic for them. We came here because we thought Washington would be exciting. With Mr. Kennedy we thought, At last! Something of the modern world. A fresh start, as art had a fresh start in Vienna in 1910 and Berlin in 1921, a new generation in charge. We saw a kind of renaissance, not only in America but in the West, and we wanted to be part of it or at least in the vicinity because Washington would lead the way. That's why we came.

We were foolish, Marie said.

Not foolish, Paul said. Perhaps naive.

You have not one ounce of naiveté, Paul.

He laughed and gave a signature raised eyebrow. He waved in the direction of the long hall and said, We thought we were getting Kandinsky but instead we got Caspar David Friedrich. Perhaps naive is the wrong word. At any event, we were disappointed.

Lucia had been listening carefully, moving her eyes from Paul to Marie like a spectator at a tennis match. She said, Kennedy was only a politician, not an artist or a writer. He didn't want to build a new house, only to live prudently in the house he was given. Also, you didn't fit in. That's all. I don't either.

Paul smiled and gave a halfhearted shrug.

Marie said, Do you think you spent too much time with us?

Oh, no, Lucia said. This — she swept her hand in a wide arc — was my lifeline. From the beginning, I think. Something moved in Lucia's memory, elusive as a shadow. She couldn't grasp it and then she did and began to laugh. She said, Tell me one thing. Who was Leisl?

Paul said, Why are you asking about Leisl?

Yes, you never knew Leisl, Marie said.

I'm almost embarrassed to say, Lucia said. I was eavesdropping one night, before we even knew each other. Sitting in my garden and listening to the conversations and envious because I wanted to be there, too. And I heard two women talking about Washington. Washington's vulgarity. That was the word they used but what they meant was anti-Semitism. Leisl was the one who liked Washington and did not think it vulgar. Her friend disagreed.

That was her sister, Hana, Marie said.

You shouldn't eavesdrop, Lucia.

I know. But I did. It was hard not to. We are right next door after all.

Hana went back to Israel, a kibbutz near the Sea of Galilee. She said Israel was where she felt safe. Leisl remained in Washington. She was gifted in languages and I believe she worked for the Israeli embassy. Maybe one of the other embassies, I don't remember. We lost track of her. Paul took a cigarette from his pocket and lit it, the smoke curling into the night air. A year ago we heard some boys tried to hold her up. It was early evening, not far from here. One of the boys had a knife. Leisl handed them her purse, urging them to take it and not to hurt her. But the effort was too great for her. She dropped dead of a heart attack. The boys ran away and the purse was later found in a trash bin. All this was reported by a neighbor who saw it all from her living room window. The neighbor saw Leisl hand over the purse and drop to the ground. The boys never touched her. The neighbor believed she was frightened to death.

Leisl was a gentle soul, Marie said. She always wanted to believe the best.

I'm so sorry, Lucia said.

The sisters were very close, Marie said, but as different as chalk from cheese. If Hana saw an abyss she'd spit into it. Leisl would say a prayer as she balanced on the edge of it.

Paul said, Washington may not be vulgar but it is unspeakably violent. And not only on the streets.

They were silent then, Paul pensively smoking and Marie and Lucia looking into the darkness. At last Paul reached for the champagne and poured the last of it into their glasses. He had fetched a bottle of Dom Pérignon for their final evening together.

We had hoped to see Alec tonight, Paul said.

Working late, Lucia said.

He likes his newspaper, doesn't he?

He loves the office, Lucia said.

A Washington dilemma, Paul said, and they all smiled. Leisl was still with them.

I think he likes making photographs and the office is where they go to.

At least he isn't chasing women, Paul said.

No, he isn't chasing women.

I think Alec is a little bored with us, Paul said. I don't blame him. Our milieu is most particular, not for everyone. A milieu of misfits.

I hope everything is all right between you and Alec, Marie said.

Oh, yes, Lucia said offhandedly, as if she were replying to a question about the weather.

Good, Marie said. That's good.

Let's hope we meet again very soon, Paul said.

They walked her to the door, pausing to look again at the preposterous stag's head; it would fit in nicely at the ancestral *schloss* or whatever it was in Kleinwalsertal. They kissed goodbye at the door.

Take care of yourself, Lucia, Paul said.

She walked the few feet to her house, vaguely troubled by Paul's farewell. "Take care of yourself" was not an expression that came naturally to him. In her kitchen she found Alec watching the baseball game. He looked up in surprise when she told him that the d'Ans had sold their house and were returning to Europe. Alec said he was sorry to hear it. He knew how much their friendship had meant to Lucia. Your home away from home, he said, his eyes drifting back to the television set, an ugly argument on the field, catcalls from the bleachers. No more second-tier intellectuals, Alec added, and Lucia agreed with him: No more second-tier intellectuals. Alec was drinking a beer and she reached down for the glass and took a sip. She put her hand on his shoulder and kissed the top of his head, the place where the bald spot was. He didn't know it was there and she saw no reason to tell him. Premature, she thought, a premature bald spot, and there was nothing to be done about it. Wasn't prematurity always a lost cause? Alec was wearing his hair longer, sideburns that fell below his earlobes, a shaggy look she liked. He smelled of the darkroom and she liked that, too. Lucia stood quietly a moment, her hands on his shoulders and her chin touching his head, watching the argument on the field but thinking about her friends and how much she would miss them and their hospitality, the guests-of-many-languages, their worldly European flair even when they misunderstood things. Surely Paul knew better; Lucia had always taken care of herself.

Paul and Marie were gone in a week. The new owners of the house next door were lawyers and not especially sociable. Construction began almost at once. The fountain was removed. The great cedar was dismantled branch by branch and a tennis court installed, the work taking most of the summer and through Thanksgiving, and when it was finished the thump of tennis balls had definitively replaced the conversations of the guests-of-many-languages, though only on weekends. The lawyers were much too busy during the week for sport. On the rare occasions when they gave a party it was a muted affair, and judging from the fragments of conversation, the guests were lawyers, intimate with the deliberations of Congress. Now and again they heard a familiar voice from Sunday morning television.

By Easter, 1968, Alec and Lucia had decided their own house was too small. Mathilde needed a larger bedroom and Alec wanted space for a proper darkroom. Lucia wanted her own study, a private place for her books and her stereo where she could play Mahler and Haydn by the hour while she wrote in her diary. And the absence of the towering cedar was disturbing. When they looked skyward at night all they saw was the hazy reflection of the lights of downtown Washington. Also, the thump of tennis balls on the weekend drove them to distraction. The lawyers found it necessary to loudly dispute line calls. Out. It was in. No, it was out. My side, my call. Bullshit. Bullshit yourself, sore loser.

Alec and Lucia found a larger place down the street, across from Admiral Honeycutt's house. The new house had three large bedrooms and space in the basement for the darkroom. Lucia took the third bedroom for her study, installing bookcases floor to ceiling. She bought state-of-the-art stereo components. She bought the novels and plays of Max Frisch and the works of the Romansh poets, determined to become current with Swiss literature. She wrote furiously in her diary each morning, recording the ordinary events of the day along with her thoughts about what she was reading. Once a week she read the tarot, to no clear result. She also wrote intimate poems, many of those in a code of her own devising, and then she abandoned the code to write in Romansh. They were long-line poems of a romantic inclination.

From her third-floor window Lucia could see the summit of the Washington Monument and behind it aircraft drifting over the Potomac to National Airport — as in Zurich she had watched aircraft high above the Limmat approach Schaffhausen, reflecting sadly that the last time she had been on an airplane was the previous spring, two and a half hours to Bermuda, one week in the rain. She sat, feet up, composing her poems and watching the slow-moving aircraft and thinking of Zurich and the forgotten Café Voltaire and the waterside restaurant in Zollikon; like Leisl, she missed coffeehouses. On the wall behind her was the framed photograph Alec had taken so long ago, the day they met, Lucia in the doorway of the ambassador's office, his two children at her side, a mischievous smile present. Alec was not aware of it but she was looking at him and had been for a minute or more, wondering who he was and why he was photographing the ambassador. She thought he moved beautifully, like a dancer, the camera as much a part of him as his own two hands. She looked away, and when she looked back he was taking her picture. A single shot was all he needed. When he lowered his camera she saw his eyes, pale gray.

The new house had a large back yard with a garden at the far end, but the garden was not nearly so welcoming as the twelve-by-twenty space where the roses climbed the wooden stake fence and hung there in glorious profusion, white roses, yellow roses, five kinds of red roses, large and small roses that reminded Alec of the seen-it-all faces of his colleagues in the newsroom. This new garden was spacious as a prairie yet carefully manicured, fussed over, the dimensions all wrong. The garden was didactic, a schoolmarm's finger-in-the-face, violence at hand. It looked professionally laid out by a horticulturist who lacked humanity, an appreciation of asymmetry and chiaroscuro, the shock of the unexpected. The ensemble reminded Alec of anonymous passersby on any city street in America, banal as polka dots. He was profoundly disappointed and concluded that he and Lucia had made a terrible mistake buying this new house. Alec saw no way to re-make the unfortunate garden, owing to the dimensions and what had gone into it. The garden put him in mind of a nation governed by a tyrant, and it was too late to put things right. Surely it was wrong to tear out the roots of perfectly healthy plants. They would have to live with a mistake.

Alec regarded his old garden with the greatest affection for the rest of his life.

ALEC

LET ME TELL YOU a story, said Alec to Lucia.

My father was elected to the Senate when he was young, not yet thirty-five years old. He had the bearing, one might say the standing, of a much older man. He habitually wore three-piece suits, a gold watch chain strung across the vest, but the Phi Beta Kappa key that went with the chain he left at home. His hair was prematurely gray and his voice a confidential baritone, quite soft. He won in an upset against an unpopular Republican, sullen, unclubbable. That was what the political community was then, a club. Everyone knew each other. So word preceded my father: sound man, reliable, tended to business. A workhorse, not a show horse. Good poker player, knew when to hold and knew when to fold, and so forth. Everyone liked Kim Malone, he was in for the long haul, a serious man. I never knew him to listen to a baseball game or read a novel. His world was politics, specifically the Senate. He spent the ten weeks between the election and the inauguration reading the Senate rule book because he knew that the rules were the keys to the realm. The consequence was that from the beginning he was an inside man, drinks in the majority leader's office after hours, golf with committee chairmen on the weekends. After a year or so he became friendly with members of the White House staff and eventually the president himself. Kim Malone knew how to return a favor and keep his mouth shut. He never spoke to the newspapers until much later in his career, when it became unavoidable, and to his advantage.

This occurred when I was very small, seven years old, a Saturday afternoon in summer. My mother explained that she had a bridge tournament and my father would look after me. We drove to the Senate Office Building in her convertible, the top down. The day was very warm, heat rising in waves from the asphalt. The empty lobby was cool and our voices echoed in the great space. We mounted the marble staircase to my father's second-floor office. When we walked into his reception room there was no one about and the door to his private office was closed. My mother was not put off by closed doors so she knocked once and walked in to find my father with a visitor, the two of them in close conversation around his desk. He looked up with an expression of open alarm. Of course he had forgotten that I was his responsibility for the afternoon. I remember that he and my mother had a quick word sotto voce and that he gave her shoulder a squeeze before he kissed her and wished her good luck and asked her to telephone when she had news. They're better players than I am, my mother said. No they're not, he said. And call me, please. She left at once and I was directed to the leather couch and told to make myself comfortable and not make one sound.

You can take your jacket off, my father added with a wink to his visitor.

The visitor was staring at me with a baffled look. What was I doing there, a child in a senator's private office on a Saturday afternoon? Didn't I have anything better to do? The Senate wasn't even in session. It was as if the lion tamer had entered the cage to find not a lion but a white rabbit. To cover his confusion the visitor lit a cigarette, though he already had one burning in the ashtray.

Say hello to Mr. James, my father said.

Hello, Mr. James.

Mr. James works for the president.

Hello, Alec, Mr. James said, and blew a smoke ring that seemed to hang in the air forever, and a second to follow the first.

I took off my jacket. My mother had dressed me up in a blazer and short pants, white shirt, brown oxfords, because we were visiting the Senate Office Building. Both my father and Mr. James were in suits and ties. They had drinks in their hands. My father rose heavily and went to the sideboard to pour me a soda. He and Mr. James returned to their discussion, of which I understood very little except there was an absent party and this man was not a friend. There was a reservation somewhere and he had gone off it. He was not thinking of the national interest but of his own interest and it was urgent that he be brought to heel at once or there would be hell to pay and he would pay it. Mr. James was talking and my father was listening, not altogether comfortably. Mr. James was not a prepossessing man. He was painfully thin with a bony face and a gray complexion. He looked exhausted, as if he had not slept in weeks, whereas my father was heavy-set, pink-cheeked, the picture of good health. Yet the force in the room was Mr. James. The tension between my father and his visitor was palpable. Then suddenly Mr. James had a coughing fit and had to turn away, his hand to his mouth. He was so frail. He stopped the coughing fit by lighting another cigarette but there was no smoke ring this time.

We're counting on you, Kim.

It's difficult, my father said.

The Boss wants it.

I know he does, my father said.

If not, I intend to piss on the son of a bitch. And others'll get wet.

Timmy, my father said. But he was smiling now.

You know I'm right, Kim.

I'll speak to him, my father said.

It's going to have to be more than talk.

I can't put a gun to his head, Timmy.

The hell you can't. He's a goddamned traitor. Tell him I said that.

I'm not going to say that to him.

Tell him the Boss said it.

My father took a swallow of his drink and did not reply.

We'll be grateful.

I'm sure you will be, my father said. And then he cleared his throat and leaned close to Mr. James and said something I could not hear but whatever it was Mr. James smiled and lit another cigarette.

I was there for a long time and began to daydream. I always wondered if I acquired my taste for daydreams in my father's office that day, listening to him and his visitor talk about the senator who had gone away from his reservation and had to be brought back, forcibly if need be. On the mantel opposite me was an old pendulum clock. Each tick seemed to have the resonance of a pistol shot, and when the minute hand advanced it did so with a sharp click. I was hypnotized by the clock, sixty pistol shots punctuated by the click when the minute hand jumped forward. I believe in that way I came to conceive of time not as a smooth evolution but as a series of abrupt progressions, relentless and unsurprising so long as you anticipated the sharp click. I would say that was my introduction to the modern world, except really I was just a little boy sitting on a leather couch listening to two men of government trying to settle a score. Then Mr. James raised his voice and said one last thing that I do remember word for word. He said, Of course I'm playing politics. What else would I do? I play politics the way Caruso sings Puccini. With a damn sight more at stake.

What were they talking about? Lucia asked.

I have no idea, Alec said.

Did you ever ask your father?

Never did. I like mysteries.

Really?

Yes. Definitely.

I like your story, Lucia said.

I told you so that you could know me better.

I know you pretty well. We're to be married after all.

I want you to know how I grew up. Sitting in my father's office watching Timmy James blow smoke rings and threaten to piss on a United States senator. But that's my father's world, not mine. I was never attracted to Washington the way my parents were and perhaps that's because they were from someplace else. They were immigrants. Union Station was their Ellis Island, the Lincoln Memorial their Statue of Liberty. Most everyone in Washington is from someplace else but soon enough they switch allegiance. And they do not acknowledge this allegiance shift when they visit their former home because the residents there are outsiders. They are civilians and they wouldn't understand the reinvention of self. More to the point, they would not understand the mystery of government. How it works actually, the rules and regs, the greater arcana. My father called it "the privilege" of public service. Washingtonians, at least the Washingtonians I'm talking about, feel closer to the pulse of things than other people do. Election returns come in and your neighbor across the street finds himself without a job and the next day or the day after you drop by for a drink and the talk is subdued because of the corpse in the parlor. He's still your friend but he isn't the same friend because he's an ex. Ex-senator. Ex-congressman. And when you're out, you're out. There are no second acts in American politics unless your name is Nixon. So you say goodbye to the cloakroom and become a lobbyist or of counsel to a law firm and they're the same thing in most cases. Washington is a present-tense city, zero-sum. You can forget almost anything but you shouldn't forget where you're from. Don't you agree?

Yes, Lucia said.

They met while Alec was on assignment for the Sunday magazine, portraits to accompany an article on ambassadors — the Iranian, the Brazilian, the Saudi, the Australian, and the Swiss. Ambassadors at home on the weekends, watching American television, playing with their children, examining their stamp collections, building a ship in a bottle, reading Pascal. The Swiss ambassador, not quite understanding what the project was about, was dressed in a dark suit and foulard tie as if headed for his office — which, in fact, he was. Alec was placing his lights and wondering how to persuade his subject to relax when he saw a slender, beautifully built young woman in the doorway, two small children at her side. She was unsuccessfully suppressing laughter at the scene before her, and then she bent down and whispered something to the children, giving them a little push in the direction of their father. Alec took two quick shots of the children hanging on the ambassador's blue serge trousers, his startled expression — as if, Alec remarked later to the photo editor, the brats had demanded passwords to the numbered accounts. Quickly Alec turned back and shot the beauty in the doorway, her arms crossed, her hair falling over her right eye, an expression of the utmost amusement. Three cheers for the ambassador, the old goat; she was much too young for him, a freckle-face who looked to be barely out of college. When she moved away from the doorway Alec saw that she had a slight limp, an imperfection that only increased her allure. He took a dozen correct poses of the ambassador for form's sake. The shot that would make the paper was the one of his small children hanging on his trousers.

May I have the name of your wife? Alec asked the ambassador when they were alone.

My wife?

Yes, in the doorway with the children.

She is the au pair, the ambassador said curtly. Her name is Lucia Duran.

How do you spell that? Alec said.

He sent Lucia the photograph of herself in the doorway — it was a fine candid, and he wondered yet again if he were not in the wrong business, his taste ran more to beautiful forms than the grit of the news — and asked if she would have dinner with him. She replied that of course she would and he named a place, a date, and a time. When Alec arrived at the restaurant, a little late, not much, she was seated and drinking a glass of wine. She asked him if he was always late, and he said sometimes he was, not always. Unfortunately his work was governed by deadlines. In that case, she said, why aren't you on time? Because the deadlines keep changing, he said, noticing again the spray of freckles on her cheeks and aware that she was irritated with him. He remembered hearing somewhere that the Swiss had a fetish about punctuality, obsessed as they were by timepieces. The waiter was at his elbow so he ordered a glass of Chianti.

He said, I made a bit of a mess of things at the embassy with your ambassador. I thought you were his wife.

She stared at him a long moment. How could I possibly be his wife? His wife is fifty and quite stout.

Well, I didn't know that. Ambassadors often have wives younger than themselves. Most of the time, in fact. Why — he sought an ambassador from a country she would not know — the Laotian has a wife young enough to be his granddaughter. And I thought that was the situation with the Swiss.

We have nothing to do with the Laotians, she said. They are in Asia, whereas we are in Europe.

They are exceptionally randy in Laos. It's the damp tropical weather. Also the Buddhist spirits.

I don't understand, Lucia said. What means "randy"? But she was smiling when she said it so Alec guessed he had gotten over that hurdle. He was charmed by her accent and the way she sat up straight in her chair as if she had taken lessons in good posture. He complimented her on her dress and the little gold pin she wore. She said the pin had been her mother's, though it was an ordinary gold pin, nothing special. He thought she was blushing but with the freckles it was hard to tell.

He said, Where did you get the limp?

She brought her legs under her chair and shrugged off the question.

I'm sorry, he began.

Skiing, she said. A bad fall.

It's hardly noticeable, he said.

Yet you noticed it, she said.

They sat in silence a moment and she began to tell him about her work at the embassy, looking after the children, seeing that they took their baths and did their homework. The ambassador and his wife had taken the children to Williamsburg for the weekend. The ambassador wanted to know more about the nation's colonial beginnings and he thought he might find out from the blacksmith's shop and the chandlery. Also, such an experience was educational for the children. She did not get out much herself. She was invited to all the embassy parties — ghastly, boring parties, but it was something to do in the evenings. However, her wages were good and she had a room of her own.

She asked Alec about his work and he told her, somehow making it sound both more and less interesting than it was. Mostly his assignments were on the Hill, covering committee hearings.

78

The Hill?

Capitol Hill, he said. Congress. Men in front of microphones. You try to get them chewing on the bows of their eyeglasses or taking a drink of water. Pointing a finger at a witness, that's good. And the witness pointing back, even better. It's an unwritten rule that you don't take a picture of them when they fall asleep. Professional courtesy. That's still life. The paper doesn't like still life.

Nature morte, she said.

The paper likes action, he said.

And that's what you like?

Not particularly. Probably I'm miscast as a newspaper photographer. I'm not much interested in the news. I prefer things in repose.

You do?

Yes, he said. Tell me about the accident.

What accident?

Your skiing accident.

I was competing at St. Moritz, leading the trials. And then late in the afternoon I went off on my own, alone as I loved to be, off piste. Where was the harm? A tune-up for the race the next morning. I misjudged a mogul and flew into a tree. Left leg broken below the knee. No more ski competitions for Lucia. I was heartbroken. I thought my life was over. I loved competitive skiing, it meant the world to me. It still does, except now I watch it instead of doing it.

That's a sad story, Alec said.

Don't you like competing in the news?

I never think about it.

But it must be competitive.

I suppose it is. But you either get the shot or you don't. I don't think of the news as competitive. It's grass growing on a lawn. Who cares if one blade grows higher than the others, unless of course you care like hell about what a pretty lawn you have.

Lucia smiled broadly and took a swallow of wine. She said, I was going out for a while with a boy at the State Department. He lived in a house with four other boys. What a place. They acted as if they were still at university. So much filth. An icebox full of beer. It was disgusting. He wanted me to cook for all of them and then he wanted me to sleep with him but I said no thanks and that was the end of that. I think I will go home soon.

All they talked about was the news, she added.

How long have you been here? Alec asked.

Not even a year, she said.

I hope you don't go home.

Of course I will go home. But not just yet.

Good, he said. I'd like you to stay.

And you? she said. Do you involve yourself with disgusting girls with beer in their iceboxes who offer to sleep with you as a reward?

Not yet, he said.

I think this country isn't grown up.

They were sitting outside on the terrace of the Italian restaurant on New York Avenue, a favorite of young staff assistants on the Hill and journalists. Each table had a candle in a Chianti bottle. The waiters wore white aprons and seemed almost to dance as they moved among the tables, trays of food nicely balanced on the tips of their fingers. The night was balmy, spoiled only marginally by car exhaust from New York Avenue. Conversation was spirited because everyone was talking serious politics, the bill that was stalled in committee, Republican obstructionism, Democratic timidity, cynical newspaper reporters. "Everyone's trying to screw Jack. That's what it's about."

Their food arrived with two more glasses of wine. Lucia began to talk about Switzerland, hiking in the Engadine in the summer, skiing the rest of the year, a healthy outdoor life except for the foehn, the dangerous summer wind. Washington's climate was not healthy owing to the tropical heat, so damp everything went limp. Thoughts went limp. Thank God the embassy was air-conditioned, but air conditioning was unhealthy also because it was unnatural. As she spoke she moved her head left and right, not looking at Alec but prospecting far away, the Engadine perhaps or some other idealized grown-up non-Washington milieu.

I am talking too much, she said.

Alec scarcely understood what she was saying. He heard her voice but listened to it as he would listen to unfamiliar music, gradually gathering the tempo and the melody but baffled nonetheless. He was in a state of enchantment listening to her voice. She had paused and now was talking about friendship, how difficult it was to become close to people. Probably that was her fault. Swiss were reserved. Mountain people were reserved generally. Still, she was alone much of the time.

He understood that. He thought Lucia's admission startling and now she sat in a glum little zone of silence while voices rose around them. He had the idea that unless he said something equally startling the evening would be ruined. He would never see her again. Alec hardly knew where to begin. He touched her hand.

I want to tell you something about myself, he said.

You do?

I do. Will you listen?

Of course, she said.

I just broke up with the girl I've been seeing, Alec said. She's married, her husband is overseas, posted to the American embassy in Moscow. He doesn't want her with him because of the hardship, no amenities, constant surveillance. But he doesn't want to come home either so he's staying on for a second tour because his work is so challenging and important. He's fluent in Russian. He's certain to be promoted very soon and that will mean a larger apartment and a more generous allowance and at that time she can join him and they can have a normal life together. He knows how difficult it is for her, alone in Washington, but things are difficult for him, too, similarly alone and without amenities and under constant surveillance. He works twelve-hour days, seven days a week, because there isn't much else to do in dreary Moscow. His work has become his life and he's working to good effect because of his skill with the Russian language and his affection for the Russian people. He understands the Russians. He believes they are soul mates. The ambassador personally asked him to stay on. In two months he would have leave. How did Italy sound? A holiday in one of the hill towns in Tuscany or farther south, Capri or Rimini, one of the places we've always talked about going to. The trouble was, they had never talked about visiting the hill towns of Tuscany or farther south either. She had no idea where Rimini was located on the landmass of Italy. She was from Minnesota. So was he.

He told her he was dreaming in Russian. Thinking in Russian.

He told her that when they had a child, and if the child was a girl, they would name her Nadezhda, meaning hope. If it was a boy, Vladimir, Lenin's nom de guerre.

She thought he was losing his mind. His mind had disappeared into Russia.

Alec paused there because he did not know how to put the next part into words that Lucia would understand and sympathize with. She was bent forward, her chin cupped in her hand, staring at him intently, her wine and food forgotten. She was silent while he grappled with his next thought. At the table beside theirs one of the loud young men was saying that the problem in Congress was that bastard Johnson, wouldn't give the president the help and support he needed. It had been a terrible mistake putting Johnson on the ticket, just terrible. Bobby was against it.

So she took up with me, Alec said. She was lonely. She didn't know Washington well. She said she distrusted it, its glare, its rootlessness, its self-regard. She had no children and few friends. There was no anchor to her life, only her cat and her apartment way out Connecticut Avenue and the grace-and-favor job someone had found for her at one of the foreign policy associations — they call it a think tank. We met at the think tank when I was doing a shoot, Alec said, watching Lucia's mouth edge into a small smile. And we were mightily attracted to each other, although it took us a while to connect because of the distrust she had of Washington, a distrust that specifically included the press, even photographers.

She told me the story in bits and pieces.

He bought a little dog and called it Katya or Strelya, a name like that, Russian in origin. The dog kept him company at night. That caused her to wonder how Katya or Strelya would get on with her cat, called Fluffy.

At any event, the two months came and went and there was no Tuscany or any other part of Italy because of the Cuban missile crisis and its aftermath, when all of us were working our nuts off, as he said, and all leaves were canceled indefinitely. Gosh, I'm so sorry. But this is important. Do you realize we almost went to war? I can tell you that there were some pretty tough moments here at Embassy Moscow and it's only a question of time before they try again. The telephone communications were always bad, lapses and static. They had to shout to make themselves understood. Normal conversation was impossible. Once or twice she heard the dog barking. Alec paused once more.

Lucia said, What was her name?

Alec said, Olivia. His name was Robert. Robert Sorrensen.

Lucia said, How much of that was true?

I don't know, he said.

Did she believe it?

Some of it. Most of it. She didn't know what to believe. She was suspicious of the hill towns of Tuscany.

I would be, too, Lucia said.

And the dreaming in Russian.

So she took up with you, Lucia said.

She did. Eventually.

And was that a happy time for her?

It was an improvement on what she'd had.

Was it an improvement on what you'd had?

It was, Alec said.

Were you in love with her?

I would have done anything for her.

That means you weren't, Lucia said, the words harsher than she intended and so she smiled, making a joke of it.

Olivia used to tell me wonderful stories about the Iron Range. Her parents were radicals, born in Norway. She couldn't take their politics seriously. They were forever plotting the overthrow of the government in Minneapolis in order to set up a rump state in Ely or Babbitt. Olivia was very close to her parents. Politics to her was a sideshow. That was one other reason we got on so well. What she wanted really was a family of her own, a real house in a real neighborhood, the school down the street. That was the life she wanted.

Lucia was silent a moment, wondering how to frame the next question. She said, Was Olivia in love with you?

I think she was, Alec said. Not for keeps, though. Not for marriage. We never talked about that.

A family of her own, a house in a neighborhood. Is that enough?

It is for many people, quite a number of people, really. Anyhow it's what she wanted.

But not what you wanted.

I hadn't given marriage much thought.

This does not sound like a love match, Lucia said.

Oh, it was. It was in its own way. We had good times together. We looked out for each other. And when all else fails you can't beat lust.

Lucia smiled broadly. What happened then?

She went back to Minnesota.

No regrets?

She didn't like cheating on her husband even though by that time she was certain he was cheating on her. Whether he was or he wasn't, he made it clear that he preferred life in important Moscow rather than life with unimportant her. That seemed to be the end of her dreams of a family, a real home in a real neighborhood, the school down the street, and all the rest. There was something boastful about him now and somewhere in Moscow he had acquired a new accent. When he wasn't dropping Russian words and phrases he was talking about the State De-pot-ment and the ambassa-duh. The transatlantic static on the line concealed much but it couldn't conceal that. That was the way with him, the job and the climb up the ladder. The farther from her the better. Still, he was her husband and she didn't like cheating on him.

And you. What did you think?

I didn't like it either. But not enough to stop it.

That sounds like an honest answer.

It is an honest answer, Alec said. You see, they were childhood sweethearts, students together at UMinn–Edina. He was a wonderful student. His attention to studies was one of the things she found attractive about him. His ambition was to see the wide world and for a time that was her ambition, too. Ambition was an attractive thing in boys, she said, until suddenly it wasn't. Olivia thought their story was a Washington story and one other reason why she distrusted Washington. Why, he was just a boy from Hibbing. His parents and grandparents were Iron Range people. And now their boy was in Embassy Moscow, a rising star at the State De-pot-ment. Unless that, too, was a fiction.

Is he still there?

I don't know. Olivia went back to Edina. I got a postcard from her the other day, a picture of the open pits of the Iron Range. No message. Love, Olivia.

And the mighty attraction?

It was a mighty attraction, Alec said. Over now.

Lucia sipped her wine, her eyes fastened on his. That was what you wanted to tell me?

Not just that. The whole story.

Didn't you tell me the whole story?

Ninety-nine percent, he said.

And that one percent?

I've forgotten, he said. You always forget one percent.

She smiled at that and speared a last forkful of lasagna, chewing it without enthusiasm. The restaurant was emptying but not the table next to theirs, embroiled in an argument about the Democratic nominee in 1968, six years hence.

Lucia said, Are you ambitious like Robert?

No, I'm not ambitious.

Maybe that's the one percent, she said.

Oh, horseshit! the loud young man at the nearby table roared and then fell silent, abashed. Diners rising in their chairs sat down again. The restaurant itself came to a sudden halt as if a heavy hand had pulled on its reins. The secretary of defense and two younger men took seats at a table near the hedge that ringed the terrace. At once they began to confer, their heads close together. They gave no indication they knew they were in a public place. They might have been in an office, for instantly documents were produced from a briefcase and each began to read. When a waiter approached he was waved away. The surrounding silence gave way to murmurs of conversation, including the loud young man, much subdued now, commenting only that Lyndon Johnson had about as much chance of being nominated as the man in the moon. It was Bobby's turn. As he spoke his eyes drifted off in the direction of the table near the hedge. At last he shook his head in admiration. He's so brilliant. He's the most brilliant SecDef this country has ever seen. And do you know why? He's in command of the facts, that's why.

86

I like making pictures, Alec said. I suppose ambition comes into it somewhere.

But you don't think about it.

Not much, he said.

Lucia nodded her head at the table near the hedge. Who is that?

That is the secretary of defense. A local hero.

Alec wondered what had brought the secretary of defense to this restaurant, not on anyone's list of highly recommended. What it had was an agreeable terrace, so long as you didn't mind the exhaust fumes from the street. The prices were in line and the waiters were friendly. Alec watched the owner walk to the secretary's table and place a hand on the shoulder of one of the younger men, who rose to his feet to introduce the secretary. So the owner was a friend of the secretary's friend who, from the look of him, was more likely an aide. The owner produced a bottle of wine, opened it, placed menus on the table, and departed. The secretary and the two others continued to read documents. The wine was poured but not tasted.

I had an affair such as yours, Lucia said. Except he was not married.

Did it end well?

He was not a suitable man, she said. He was older. He was fifteen years older than me. I think he was a professional bachelor. That was the way he saw himself and I didn't mind. We had good times together. He was a keen skier. Lucia paused, smiling at the thought, her eyes far away. Beautiful skier, really. It was a pleasure watching him. We often raced and he only beat me once. He didn't like losing, not at all, especially to a girl with a bad leg. Stefan was a competitive personality. Every time he lost he'd go into a funk and I'd think about losing the next time, but I never did except that once.

Most men are competitive, Alec said.

But not you, Lucia said.

Not particularly, said Alec. Also, I don't ski.

I think my affair was very much like your affair with the exception of the marriage.

A mighty attraction?

Lucia smiled. Fun, isn't it?

Assuredly, Alec said. Then, Does it bother you that Olivia was married?

No. She was lonely. Her husband was far away and inattentive. Probably she thought she had lost him for good. Lucia laughed suddenly, moving her head from side to side. This is a strange conversation for me, she said. We hardly know each other.

We know each other, Alec said.

Not so well, Lucia said.

What did he do? His work.

Stefan was a banker. Also, he wrote literary articles for one of the Zurich papers. His articles were highly regarded. They were very difficult. Stefan wrote in High German. And then I left for America.

Because of the literary articles?

They were not connected, she said. You never ski?

I never learned.

I think you would be good at it. You have the body for it. Lucia took another sip of wine, making a face. Since we have come to know each other so well, I do not mind telling you that this wine is filthy.

As bad as that?

It tastes like ink, she said. So, she went on, I left Switzerland because I wanted to visit America. I thought I should see it. Stefan was against it. He warned me that America was not anything like Switzerland and that the differences were not agreeable. But I thought that was the reason I should go. Everyone talks about America, what they like about it and what they don't, so I thought

I should see for myself. Stefan had never been to America except once, at a conference where no one spoke German. Also, I was a convenience for him and he didn't want to lose the convenience. Someone told me of the ambassador's need for an au pair. So I took the job at the embassy and I have to say that Stefan was not entirely incorrect in what he said. America lacks density. It lacks . . . Lucia sought the word and came up with "thrift." Alec listened hard, wondering why the United States should be reduced to a single word or phrase. They would never reduce their own countries to a word. He hoped she would not complain about American innocence. Lucia thought a moment and added, But I am enjoying very much my dinner with you.

It's thrifty, Alec said. Especially the wine.

Lucia ignored his remark, gesturing instead at the secretary of defense and his aides, still huddled over their documents, not speaking. She said, Are you a part of that?

No. I only take photographs for the newspaper.

You're not involved in the other?

Not really. Alec did not know how far to take this thought. He said, I like the craft of photography, the details you have to pay attention to. The feel of the camera. I'm like the man building a ship in a bottle and at the end of it that's what you have, a ship in a bottle. It's honest work. I don't know that it's anything more than that.

You made a wonderful shot of me, Lucia said.

It was good, wasn't it? Five seconds. It took me five seconds.

What's wrong with that?

Nothing's wrong with it. Best shot I've made in months. Five seconds.

I don't understand —

It was you, Lucia. You were the shot. I just happened to point the camera in the right direction.

That is foolish, she said.

Not foolish, Alec said.

I think you are a utopian, Lucia said.

She took a sip of wine and looked at the table by the hedge. She said, Your secretary of defense looks tired. He looks as if he could use a good meal and something better than this filthy Chianti. Lucia put her chin in the palm of her hand and continued to scrutinize the secretary of defense. She said, I'm used to it. There was always politics in my mother's house. Politics and books, more books than politics, I think. But they were the same thing. Books were politics, especially novels and poetry. If they didn't have politics they weren't worth reading. My mother said I would marry a political man, a reformer. We would reform the world, this man and I. She was quite sure of that, although I never believed it. She was sure of herself, my mother. She believed in socialism the way religious believe in the church. She thought of the Soviets as the antichrist, corrupting socialism, luring it into a nasty orthodoxy. In the end all the Soviets believed in was themselves. Brutes. My mother called them brutes. Still, she never lost her faith. She had a love affair with socialism. After my father left us she went to bed with socialism. I think she was a utopian. Our apartment was filled with utopians, all of them speaking secondary languages and failing to understand one another when the points were subtle. Also, they were gnomic. They were in love with theory, even my mother. Of course she is gone now, dead three years next month.

Through the candlelight Alec saw Lucia's eyes fill with tears.

I miss my mother, she said. Even her socialism.

Alec nodded without knowing exactly what he was agreeing to. His own political house had to do with campaigns and elections won and lost, legislative programs, the number of congressional districts in Iowa, the supplemental appropriation for the army. Belief didn't come into it since disbelief was unthinkable, along with UFOs and atheism. Alec supposed his father believed in elections. Certainly he believed in the apparatus of American democracy, two political parties, conventions every four years, the Electoral College. Elections certified democracy. In that way democracy was part of the furniture, and if your party lost this year's election you'd get it back next time or the time after. The pie was large, slices enough to go around. Socialism was not on the table, at least the table Senator Malone dined at. Socialism was not an election issue and hadn't been since Joe McCarthy, and socialism to McCarthy was a slogan, the commonist conspiracy, the commonist menace, commonism in the State Department. Joe McCarthy couldn't pronounce the word correctly even when he was sober. Alec tried to imagine his father explaining McCarthy to Lucia's mother — his bogus war record, his mastery of the televised image and the trumped-up charge, and the peculiarities of the state of Wisconsin where all rivers ran north. None of the arguments that had enraptured Europeans for two generations had resonance chez Malone. Alec was tempted to tell Lucia of his own political house but guessed that now was not the time, their meal almost finished but the night with a ways to go. Lucia was silent now, her expression taut. Alec knew she was thinking again of her mother's death. Her still face was lovely in the light of candles.

Tell me more about your mother.

Lucia shook her head.

Your house sounds more interesting than mine, Alec said. Was Stefan a political man?

Oh, no, she said. Not Stefan. Stefan was a banker. His literary articles were a sideline, weekend work. When he was not skiing. He would not have approved of the house I grew up in so I never mentioned it. With us it was a physical thing. He never talked about his banking and I never asked, and I never talked about my mother and he never asked. That was how we got on in the world day to day, more or less. Lucia saw no need to add that Stefan was often rough. She liked his roughness for a while and then she didn't like it. She felt manhandled. She said with a smile, That's enough said. Ours was a Swiss story. Untranslatable.

Lucia looked closely at Alec, trying to judge his reaction. She wondered if he could read between the lines. Stefan never could. Really, she was judging his sincerity. This Alec was certainly not Stefan, who prized silence above all else. Silence and discretion, she amended. Alec was more attractive than Stefan, she thought, with his pale gray eyes and disarming manner; he knew how to tell a story, too. Alec looked at her straight on whereas Stefan was a personality in profile, a one-eyed jack. When Alec spoke his voice was soft. She did not think he would be rough.

Alec said, How is it a Swiss story?

Lucia paused fractionally. It's dense, she said.

I think I want to go home now, she added.

All right, he said.

With you, she said.

On their way out she gave a little mischievous wave to the secretary of defense, who smiled and waved back. In the car Alec kissed her, their lips barely touching. He took a roundabout route once they were under way, to the Mall and around the Lincoln Memorial, the Capitol behind them. There were pleasure boats on the Potomac, their running lights slithering on the gray surface of the water. The opposite shore was a thin dark line. One very large yacht motored slowly in the direction of National Airport, two smaller boats ahead and two behind like pilot fish. A full moon rose in the eastern sky. Alec wondered aloud if the large yacht was Kennedy's, the *Honey Fitz*. It was large enough, one hundred feet long at least, displaying only a few running lights. Inside, a rosy glow came from the saloon. Alec turned to Lucia and explained about presidential yachts, a perquisite like Air Force One and Camp David. He thought he saw people on the fantail, guests for the evening cruise. They could be any-body — the shah of Iran, Charles de Gaulle, Che Guevara, the ghost of T. E. Lawrence, or a movie star like Lauren Bacall or David Niven. Who knew who they were? Picasso? John Stein-beck? Maybe even his father if there was something Kennedy wanted badly enough and thought that a night on the *Honey Fitz* might get it for him. They were drinking and having a fine time on the Potomac. De Gaulle had decided to lecture the shah. Picasso was playing gin rummy with David Niven. George Jessel was telling jokes. A president could call anyone to his table, refusals not accepted. Not that anyone would want to refuse. What would be the point? Alec imagined shooting them wide-angle, focusing on Lucia telling them about her mother's political house, her devotion to socialism, Kennedy listening intently while he smoked a cigar, Che nodding in approval.

And then they were around the curve and entering sedate Rock Creek Park. Alec was trying to slow things down. He returned to his yacht reverie, speculating to Lucia that even now Kennedy was enjoying a bullshot on the fantail of the *Honey Fitz* while his secretary of defense was scrutinizing documents and ignoring his meal at the so-so restaurant on New York Avenue. Lucia was laughing, her head nestled into his shoulder, her hand warm against his chest. She murmured something he couldn't hear. Her scent filled the car. He was dizzy with it.

What did you say?

Drive faster, she said.

Five hours later they were still entangled in his bed, windows thrown open to the balmy night. Alec had the idea they were one body. In the darkness he saw an ankle and did not know whose it was. He didn't move, liking the mystery. They had been lying together in silence, not quite dozing but not awake either. He asked her if there was anything she wanted — every phrase was now a double entendre — and she answered yes, she wanted a cup of tea. When he came back with the tea she was sitting up, the sheets gathered around her, staring into an abstract distance. She blew on the tea to cool it, then balanced the cup and saucer on her belly. She began in the middle of her thought, no preamble. She had some sympathy for the husband. What was his name? Robert. She understood Robert, his contrived accent, his excuses, his delusions of importance, his evident weightlessness. She thought probably he was losing himself in Russia. He wouldn't be the first to do so. Even Russians were nervous, Turgenev for example, who seemed to find tranquillity only in France. She understood this because Robert reminded her of herself. Often she felt she was slipping away, losing touch. Her American thoughts were different, looser, without context. Probably she didn't know how to express herself properly. There were times when she felt she could not breathe and yet unlike Robert she was unable to enter fully into American life. She recognized this as fear and believed it common among displaced Europeans. Turgenev became an itinerant, Baden and Paris and provincial France his preferred locations. Always he was drawn back to Russia, though he refused to die there. He would give the motherland his heart but he wouldn't give her his soul. His great subject was the landmass of Russia and how its citizens accommodated themselves or not. At the end he too was weightless. Russia was mightier than he was, a tempest that swept all before it. Lucia spoke slowly. Her voice was drowsy. She said, Turgenev had his idea of Russia as my mother had her idea of socialism.

But I don't know what I have, she said.

You have me, he said.

Right now I feel happy with you, yes.

My American, she added.

We have found each other, he said. It's unusual. You had to come all the way from Switzerland.

To find you, she said.

And if I hadn't been assigned the shoot at the embassy . . . He did not finish the thought. Life did hang by threads, enigma its core. Her arms were around him now. She whispered into his ear.

He said, I don't want you to lose yourself or slip away.

It's difficult for me, she said.

94

In America there's something for everyone.
There is?
Definitely. It's a promise.
I'm trying, Lucia said.

Lucia gave notice at the embassy, something that was not done but she was determined to do it. In the event, the ambassador and his wife were understanding. Lucia had been very good with their children and they wished her the best. You and your photographer, the ambassador's wife said. And he is the son of a United States senator! You have done well for yourself, Lucia. He looks to be a fine young man with a promising career. And you seem much happier now than you have been. We were worried about you. America is an unforgiving country. Americans are quick to forget when it suits their purposes. And quick to remember for the same reason.

Lucia moved in with Alec and got a job at the National Zoo. She had always loved animals, bears especially. She was a guide for groups of foreign tourists owing to her fluency in French and German. After hours she helped with the cages. Lucia found the zoo workers entertaining, many of them young and at loose ends; they constituted a kind of family, animals included. In due course she met Alec's parents and found them welcoming. Alec's mother was a chain smoker and in that, if in no other way, she reminded Lucia of her own mother. The senator was more reserved. He reminded her of a music teacher she'd had in Zurich, a better talker than he was a musician or a teacher. Senator Malone spoke in a heavy baritone that rose and fell as if he were reading from a script. Alec called it his toga-talk. The senator did not treat his son with respect so her relations with him were guarded. He invited her to call him Kim, but she could not bring herself to do it so continued to address him as Senator. When they told his parents that they planned to marry, Alec's mother was delighted and full of ideas, the wedding to be held at the Episcopal church in Chevy Chase, the reception at one of the downtown clubs. A champagne reception with an orchestra, toasts to finish things off. The chaplain of the Senate can do the honors.

Would you like that, dear?

We have other plans, Alec said.

Let Lucia speak for herself, Alec. It's her wedding. It's the bride who decides. It's her day. But we are so happy you decided to have the wedding here as opposed to Switzerland, so far away.

We'd planned to elope, Lucia said hesitantly.

Elkton, Maryland, Alec said.

Alec's mother lit a contemplative cigarette, her lipstick bright against the white paper. We could have such a nice wedding reception at the club, all our friends, all your friends, a day to remember always.

The Johnsons will come, the senator said. Maybe even the president. Jackie, too.

Lucia looked at him, startled. They will?

Of course they will, the senator said. Jack and I go way back. We've known the Johnsons for many, many years. Last year we were at the ranch. The senator went on to speak of other Washington personalities, men and their wives. Lucia did not recognize the names but understood they were important. The names flew past. Humphrey. Dirksen. Udall. Acheson. Krock. She had the picture of a theatrical troupe, introduced and then hustled offstage. Lucia was tongue-tied. She did not know what to think; the idea of the vice president at her wedding, perhaps even proposing a toast, asking her to dance, was alarming. The president and Jackie likewise was unthinkable. She wondered what her mother would say. Surely she would approve of the president, who with his charm and mordant humor was seen almost as an honorary European. But her mother would be suspicious all the same, of Kennedy's robber baron father and the vice president's oil connections. The vice president had once shown up at a reception at the embassy, moving briskly around the room, the ambassador at his side; and then he was gone, vanished through the double doors, one of his assistants explaining that he was obliged to return to the White House for a meeting with the president. The ambassador did not believe him. He had done his duty and now wanted to go home or to his office on the Hill, drink a double Scotch, make some calls. Lucia felt her chest tighten and for a moment she thought she would faint. She turned to Alec and was unsettled to see his stony expression.

We've made our plans, Alec said.

Let Lucia have her say, the senator said.

I want what Alec wants, Lucia said.

They were standing in the living room of the Malone house in Chevy Chase, cocktail time. Alec and his father and mother were drinking highballs, Lucia a glass of champagne. Alec had brought a bottle for the occasion. The room was brightly lit and filled with photographs of Washington personalities, some of the most recent shot by Alec. Many of the photographs were quite old. Lucia's mother's study was similarly decorated — perhaps decorated was not the exact word for it, more a statement of principles. Her photographs were grainy and formal. The subjects wore hats. Turgenev, Adorno, James Joyce, Walter Benjamin, and a lithograph of Robespierre. Lucia looked at the Malone collection and wondered if any of them were of Swiss ancestry. Doubtless not. The Swiss did not figure in the American experience. In that way, the Washington personalities were no different from Turgenev, Adorno, James Joyce, Walter Benjamin, and Robespierre. Where was the Swiss imprint on the world? But it was the simple truth that the Swiss had never been colonizers. They were content in their mountain fortress, occasionally venturing abroad when business required it. All the men in the Malone photographs looked well fed and wore blue suits, except for one very well fed adventurer who was dressed in riding boots, jodhpurs, and floppy hat, an exceptionally toothy grin below a bushy mustache, robust to the point of caricature.

A reception would mean so much to your mother, the senator said to Alec. And to me, too. I have an idea! Perhaps a smaller affair, the wedding and reception right here in this living room. I can get the chaplain of the Senate —

That should be Lucia's choice, Kim. Alec's mother looked anxiously at her daughter-in-law-to-be. She did not know her well and they had never had a private conversation. Lucia appeared pale, her eyes downcast. She had finished one glass of champagne, Alec had poured her another, and now that was gone. Mag thought they had pushed Lucia too hard. The poor girl was out of her depth, totally dependent on Alec. She hoped her son knew what he was doing but had no great confidence on that score. Alec had always gone his own way, bullheaded like his father. His bullheadedness sat side by side with an alarming indifference to the world around him, as if what happened there was no concern of his. He did not seem connected to anything, not his work, not his country; perhaps this girl, now on her third glass of champagne, was the solution. Also, Alec had not a clue as to what his wedding day meant to his father and mother. An only child was always a burden.

The senator said, Whoever does the service, we could still have a restricted reception of twenty people, perhaps a few more.

Too many hurt feelings, Mag said sharply. It's the best way in the world to make enemies, especially in Washington.

You have a point there, the senator said.

The Johnsons, for example.

But they would head the list!

And the Dirksens and the Humphreys. What about them?

The senator fell silent and Lucia had a sudden sense of futility, a vertigo. She was unable to see the way ahead. Her list would have included only a few names: the ambassador and his wife; and Andrea and Jeanette, au pair girls she saw often in the park; two or three others from the zoo. The bear girl and her husband. Lucia had friends in Switzerland but she had been out of touch with

98

them and they could not afford a trip to America in any case. Lucia had thought of herself and Alec as a nation of two, subject to their own laws and customs, but now she wasn't so sure. Alec's parents had their own claim. She realized that she would be surrounded by strangers at her own wedding if the Malones had their way. The thought of being introduced to people she did not know at such an intimate occasion appalled her. She would not know what to say — and then she imagined her father arriving, risen from the dead wearing his Borsalino and smoking a cigarette, introduced to the vice president and all the other notables, astonished that his daughter moved in such elevated circles. He was not himself disconcerted, appearing perfectly at ease in a fine suit and polished shoes. Yet it was apparent from his looks and his manner that he was an outdoor man among indoor men. Women were drawn to him and it was a moment before he and Lucia embraced. Hello, Papa. Hello, Lucia, you look lovely today. Where have you been, Papa? I have been away, he said, living in Czechoslovakia. I live in the country, a beautiful house on a mountaintop . . . Lucia's thought vanished there and she was back in the Malones' living room.

When are you going to have this elopement? the senator asked. I'm going to have to get out a news release. They'll be interested back home.

Lucia looked at Alec, but he only smiled, and took her hand. He said to his father, Next week.

And then what?

Ten days on the Eastern Shore, Chestertown. I've rented a sailboat.

Lucia looked at him again. This was the first she had heard about a sailboat.

We'll go cruising, Alec said.

You seem to have thought of everything, the senator said.

Alec has been wonderful, Lucia said.

And where will you live?

We've bought a place in Georgetown, Alec said. Small. But it has a back yard with a rose garden. You'll love it when you see it. He turned to his mother and added, It's just down the street from Mrs. Wheatley's.

A pretty house, Lucia said. Wonderful shade trees all around. The street reminds me of a street I knew well in Zurich.

That's nice, dear. I myself have never been to Zurich.

We'd like to be at the wedding, the senator said.

It's all arranged, Alec said.

Does that mean yes or no? the senator asked.

I know you will be very happy, Alec's mother said.

That evening, out of Alec's hearing, Margaret Malone invited Lucia for tea, just the two of them, so that they might come to know each other better. Friday afternoon, she said, and when Lucia responded that she was working at the zoo until four, Mrs. Malone said that was perfectly all right. Come when you can, come as you are. They sat on the screened-in porch facing a wide lawn with shade trees; the sprinklers were working because of the dry spell. The family cat was asleep in the big wing chair — Kim's chair, Alec's mother explained, but the cat appropriated it when the senator was absent. Did you have cats when you were a child?

Dogs, Lucia said. Spaniels.

This cat is sixteen years old.

Alec and I have never discussed pets, Lucia said.

Pets are not at the top of Alec's list.

They're not?

Not in my hearing, Mrs. Malone said, smiling briefly, pouring tea and offering the accessories, sugar, milk, lemon slices, little cakes on a flowered plate. She lit a cigarette and looked hopefully at her daughter-in-law-to-be.

Mrs. Malone, Lucia began.

Call me Mag, please. Everyone does.

I know you're disappointed about our wedding plans. Lucia paused, gathering her thoughts. She said, Alec wants something for us alone, only us, for us to remember. I have no family so of course I agree with him. Whatever he wants, I want. I think he does not want a commotion.

Commotion, Mag said.

Too many people, Lucia said. Then it becomes something for them and not for us.

But — his father and me?

And the others, Lucia said, believing already that she had said both too much and not enough and was putting the case badly. She wished she could have spoken in French, the language of diplomacy. Even German. Mag Malone was tapping her cigarette on the edge of a glass ashtray. She looked out the window when the sprinklers abruptly ceased but her exasperated expression did not go away. Lucia said, The Johnsons and the . . . others. She could not remember the names of the senators and statesmen they knew so well, so well they were like family and would be insulted if they were left off the guest list.

But if your parents were alive —

They aren't, Lucia said. They are both gone.

— you would want them there.

Lucia shrugged, a slight movement of her shoulders. The subject was impossible.

I see, Mag said. She had never met a girl so literal and wondered if that was a specific trait of the Swiss, like French cynicism or German anxiety. Lucia was a wonderful-looking girl and appeared devoted to Alec but there was something elusive about her, a strange trait in one so literal. Mag did not know how far to go with this Swiss, soon to be a member of her family, the mother of her grandchildren. She wanted grandchildren more than anything. All her friends had grandchildren. She did not want to make an enemy of her daughter-in-law-to-be, but Mag had always been direct and saw no reason not to be direct now.

Mag said, It's hard for me to admit that I never understood Alec, even as a little boy. I never understood what made him tick and I still don't. But that isn't the point actually. The point is that he never understood us, his father and me. I am bound to say that he didn't make much effort. He never asked us the usual questions — how did you meet, where did you go on dates, how did you know you were right for each other, and if there were doubts, what were they? I think Alec made his own world but what that world is I cannot say. I don't know if he has a destination. I think he has an ad hoc sort of life, but of course I may be mistaken. His father and I live in a public world, not every hour of every day but often enough, and it's a glass house, too, not always but sometimes. Not to everyone's taste, glass houses. I imagine it can be difficult for a child, a father in the public eye. But politics is Kim's life and it is my life also, has been from the beginning. What you would call the rhythm of our life is governed by election cycles and by whatever important matter is before the Senate. There's always something, on the floor or in one of Kim's committees. That's public business. I can hardly remember the time when our life was not public. Alec has never understood or if he has understood he has never appreciated that his father does serious work, essential work, the people's business. He is frequently away and so am I. Our dinner hour is interrupted. Weekends, too. Our schedule fits into the political calendar, not the other way around. In that sense our time is not our own and that's the bargain you make. I should say the bargain you choose because no one forces you. No one holds a gun to your head. Kim doesn't regret it and I don't either except we seem to be estranged from our only son. We have friends who are in the same boat. We all knew there would be a price for the life we chose. We none of us thought the price would be our children's affection.

Lucia waited for Mag to say more but evidently she had said all she was going to.

Lucia said, Things look different to a child than to a parent.

Yes, they do. And unfortunately they are the ones who must adapt.

And if they don't?

They will be disappointed.

I don't think Alec is disappointed.

I hope not, Mag said.

Definitely, Lucia replied.

Have you spoken to him of this — estrangement?

Never, Lucia said.

Alec hasn't brought it up?

No. Not once.

Mag took a cigarette from the box on the table but did not light it. She said, Kim thinks the sun rises and sets by Alec. He wanted very much for Alec to follow him into politics. It was not a stupid dynasty thing. Kim thinks of public service as an honorable way to spend your time, making a life of the public's business. Politics can get nasty. Your hands get dirty. You lose things you thought you could never lose. You compromise again and again. Kim did things he wasn't proud of and I wasn't proud of, either. But we got through it. And the business got done. And every six years you go back home to see if the public has approved. And if they have not, you're out the door. Kim thought Alec had the temperament for politics but Kim was wrong. If I were a sentimentalist I would say Kim's heart was broken. But it wasn't broken, only hardened. I hope you and Alec have many children and that they bring you great joy. Mag moved her cigarette back and forth in her fingers, her expression drawn. Then she asked Lucia if she had been close to her mother.

Yes, Lucia said, I was.

Did she work?

She taught European history.

And your father?

I barely knew him, Lucia said. He went away one day and did not come back.

I'm sorry, Lucia.

He is *disparu*, Lucia said, using the French word without realizing she had.

What did he do, dear?

My father?

Yes, his business.

He — And Lucia paused there. Her mother had never spoken of her father's work. She said he was a political man, that they were political together. Lucia said, He was killed in the war. The Germans killed him.

Mag nodded slowly and lit her cigarette. She stared through the screen to the lawn, darkening now at dusk. The grass was still damp from the sprinklers. She remembered the day years ago when they bought the house, fearing that the price was beyond their means. Her mother lent them money for the down payment, an embarrassment for Kim. He didn't want to take it but Mag insisted, forcing his hand. She wanted the house. She wanted to begin life in Washington on a correct footing. She was pregnant and wanted a decent bedroom for the baby and room for the other babies that were sure to follow, and those were arguments that Kim could not challenge. They both understood they would be in Washington for many years. Now Alec had gone and bought a house without telling them, not that he needed permission but simply to share the news. Eleanora Wheatley, daughter of a suffragette and a merchant prince, had a word for men like Alec. She called them egoists.

Mag said, I mentioned a moment ago that Alec had made his own world and that I didn't know what that world was. Well, we all make our own worlds and those worlds tend to be mysterious to outsiders. Even a spouse sometimes, if she is unlucky. I do fear that Alec is forever searching for the thing that is just beyond his reach. But the point is, Lucia, I don't know what my son believes in and I wonder if he does.

DAMASCUS

ALEC AND LUCIA were married by a justice of the peace in Elkton, Alec's parents in attendance. The bride wore white. After a glass of champagne at an inn nearby, Alec and Lucia motored to Chestertown to pick up the boat for what turned out to be ten days of perfect weather on Chesapeake Bay. At the sports shop Lucia bought a black bikini and Alec a long-billed fisherman's hat. Lucia took up sailing as if she were born to it, having an instinct both for wind and for tide. On a broad reach, mainsail and jib bellied in the breeze, the vessel heeled over, Lucia was reminded of a thrilling downhill run, snow flying all around her, the destination out of sight but not in doubt. In the evenings they put in at one or another of the port towns, anchoring and taking the dinghy ashore for a dinner of soft-shell crabs or grilled fish. They talked constantly about the life they would have together, and whatever qualms were present disappeared in the Maryland twilight. Back on the boat by nine, asleep by ten, sometimes twelve, depending on how athletic their inclinations.

They were excited at all hours, at noon when becalmed and in the early morning not becalmed, the anchor dragging. Alec poked his head above the gunwale in time to see the sandbar and hit the tiller with his bare foot, the sudden movement causing Lucia to cry out, a sound somewhere between an ambulance siren and an animal's howl. At the end of the week they decided to buy a sailboat as soon as finances allowed.

Bliss, she said.

Mathilde was born one year later. They had always led a quiet private life and now that they were a nation of three became even closer, Mathilde the center of attention. Lucia sang Swiss lullabies to her while Alec took pictures, hundreds of them. He enjoyed making shots of a subject who refused to obey commands; all responsibility rested with the photographer. Lucia settled happily into motherhood and after a short time returned to her work at the zoo one day a week. The sailboat was put on hold. Instead, Alec bought a Ford station wagon.

Alec's mother offered to look after Mathilde, which she did with almost comical enthusiasm. The first day she arrived with boxes of English tea and the silver tea set that had belonged to her mother. It's yours and Mathilde's now, she said; so when Lucia arrived home from work at the zoo she and her mother-in-law enjoyed a cup of tea together while Mathilde made noises from her crib. Mag Malone was always eager for news of Alec, how he was taking to fatherhood and particularly how things were going at the newspaper. Fine, Lucia said, though truthfully Alec did not speak much of the newspaper, only if there had been an interesting shoot, and those did seem to be few and far between. I think he will move on someday, Lucia said. When, I don't know. What will he do? Mag asked, alarmed because the sons of many of their friends seemed rootless, itinerant almost. I don't know that either, Lucia said. I think he is somewhat bored by news. I think that since he has become a father Alec is an indoor man. Did I tell you he bought a new car?

Alec's work had settled into an undemanding routine. He wondered if this work was too routine and too undemanding for a man just shy of thirty years old. He did feel at odds with the advent of the Count and Countess d'An and their menagerie next door. Suddenly he and Lucia were part of the émigré community, visiting two or three nights a week in the big garden with the towering cedar and the fountain that splashed all day and all night. The community seemed to Alec to look backward, concerned with old wounds, grievances that went back generations, and these were irreconcilable so they stayed on in America as if on the platform of a railway station, waiting for a train that never arrived. Someone somewhere should have come to their rescue. Taken an interest. Given assistance. Stood up to the Nazis, the Soviets, and their collaborators. Probably large nations always manhandled small ones, though that was not the way Lucia spoke of diminutive landlocked mountainous prosperous Switzerland, charting its own harmless course for centuries without civil unrest or war, unless you counted the unpleasantness caused by the megalomaniacal Bonaparte, author of the bloody battles of Zurich. One night Alec mentioned cuckoo clocks, making a joke. But his remark was not taken as a joke. Lucia was offended. After a moment of cold silence she said, An old complaint. I have heard it before. The truth was, Switzerland was the envy of its neighbors.

Mag had warned her. Alec sometimes caused offense without meaning to.

A gentleman never offends someone unintentionally, Lucia said, quoting the Count d'An.

So true, Mag said, feeling disloyal but sympathetic to her daughter-in-law. She was reminded of certain senators who were mindlessly partial to their states. The more obscure the state, the more partial they were to it. All in all, a harmless bias, though tiresome.

We are proud of our country, Lucia said.

And with good reason, Mag said, believing that at any moment Lucia would break down. She had not touched her tea. Her voice was unnaturally low. Mag said, I am sure if Alec knew you were upset he would apologize.

He did apologize, Lucia said. But he was not sincere.

Men, Mag said, in the absence of anything else to say.

Yes, Lucia said.

You must speak to Alec about it. This must not come between you.

I intend to, Lucia said.

I'm sure Alec meant no harm, Mag said, but Lucia did not look convinced.

Alec's work routine had been disturbed by the return of the chief photographer from the war. Ed Weekes was subdued as he gave a briefing on what the photographers could expect in Vietnam, the blood and the filth, killing heat and close combat in the rain forests and rice fields. No shortage of material, he said. There was material everywhere you looked, even up at the sky. You had only to decide where to aim your camera, which, by the way, had to be kept immaculate at all times owing to the frequent thunderstorms and the filth. The army was superb, would take you anywhere you wanted to go in comfort and relative safety. The army wanted the story of their heroic troopers in the papers and the division commanders saw their units as career-builders, publicity always welcome. You had to be careful, though, deciding where to aim the camera. The troopers didn't like you taking shots of their dead. Hated it, in fact, and it was easy getting into very bad trouble.

Someone asked Ed if there was an army escort with him in the field, monitoring what he did and how he did it. Did you have a babysitter, Ed? Oh, no, he said, they don't give a shit. It's the grunts who give a shit. They don't like you taking pictures of their dead friends. As a matter of privacy. Taste, we would say. They don't like interference of that kind. You couldn't explain to them that you were just trying to do your job. They didn't give a rat's ass about your job. I tried to make it clear that my shots were framed in such a way that no one could see the dead man's face. He would not be recognized by friends or family. I was making a simple shot of an infantryman on a pallet, his weapon across his chest. His face was out of the frame. He was covered by a poncho anyway. But that seemed to enrage them even more. I didn't know what to make of it so I put my camera down. To tell the truth it was a kind of no-win-type situation.

I didn't like it, Ed said.

Things were sort of out of control.

The company commander, a captain about the age of my son, came to take me by the arm and lead me away. For Christ's sake shut up, the captain said. You're making things worse. Their blood's high. We had a God-awful morning. You're a stranger here. You're not one of them. So back off.

So, Ed said, you have to watch where you point your camera. There are some things off limits. You have to find out for yourself. It's not like here, a ceremony in the Rose Garden or a congressional hearing. He fell silent then, having said all he felt he could say. After a moment one of the other photographers asked if Ed had found the war a worthwhile assignment. His work there was widely admired. Ed, did you have any fun? Ed waited a full minute before replying.

I'd call it a civic duty to go, he said.

Would you go back, Ed?

If they asked me to, he said, I would.

Alec had listened to all this with incredulity. Ed Weekes had lost his bearings. Who could believe in photography as a civic duty? Now and then a picture brought enlightenment or delight.

Sometimes one brought grief, the sharp pain of recognition or remorse. That was all you could ask for. Most of the time a photograph was merely illustrative, a witness being sworn in at a congressional hearing, a woman's umbrella bending against the wind on a city street. Of course going to the war was a wise career move but that was something else entirely. That night, sitting in their garden waiting for the babysitter so they could go next door for cocktails, Alec related the conversation to Lucia. He described Ed Weekes, a tough, no-nonsense character, three decades on the job. He lived to photograph the news. Now, after Vietnam, he was — diminished. He'd lost his swagger. Probably he was too old for war duty. Everyone knew that combat was a young man's game, a young man's legs and restlessness and lust, a desire to get the shot at all costs. Lucia misunderstood. She said, You're not going over there, are you, Alec? I'd hate it if you were. No, Alec said. I have you and Mathilde. Why would I go to Vietnam? I don't know, she said. Maybe you'd think it was your civic duty. I don't think that, he said. That isn't the way I think.

She wanted to make certain, so she asked him, Why not?

Alec said, I'm just a photographer, Lucia. I don't make any great claims for what I do. I'm good at it. But it's not worth a life, mine or anyone else's. I don't like war and I don't intend to contribute to it.

I'd never forgive you if you went.

Drop it, he said, suddenly angry.

I don't like it when you speak to me like that.

Then drop it, he said, more gently now.

Thirty minutes later Alec was standing near the d'Ans' fountain, drinking champagne. Lucia had retreated to the back of the garden, she and two of the second-tier intellectuals deep in conversation, leaving Alec with Ronald diAntonio and General Symjon. They were talking about the assassination, the latest report, more questions. The killing was almost four years back but its shadow was still present, a stain on democracy's honor. Ronald thought Washington was disoriented, no longer the hospitable place it had been. The city had lost confidence. Its sense of itself was rattled and it seemed suddenly old and enfeebled, yet at the same time truculent as a schoolyard bully. The war went on and on, Johnson's war, which he could neither win nor end. General Symjon remarked that Washington reminded him of his own capital after the Anschluss. No one could believe it, yet there it was, a beautiful grande dame transformed overnight into a witch. Do you think the CIA was behind Dallas, Alec? What does your father say? Alec mumbled something noncommittal. His father refused to discuss the assassination and even now, facing a difficult election, was vague and unconvincing in his campaign speeches and the audience Q and A that followed. Oswald . . . acting alone . . . the country must move on . . . put this behind us. The general said that the important thing was to draw the correct lessons. This will happen again, he said. Once begun, there is no end of it. Assassination is a hereditary disease. Ronald and the general began to speak of cities, the character of the metropolis, how one capital differed from another. Paris, the seat of government, was only nominally a political city; Washington was nothing but. Alec was only half listening, preoccupied as he was with Vietnam as a civic duty. Then the general said something so odd that Alec touched his arm and asked him to repeat what he had said.

I was telling Ronald about Damascus, the general said. I see it as a dark, sullen city without any particular charm. Routine architecture, much of it of recent construction. As it happens, there is great beauty in Damascus but the beauty lies in the interior spaces. You must get inside the walls, into the courtyards. Once inside the courtyards you must open the doors that lead to the great rooms. Then it is fabulous. Beyond description. You find yourself in another world, centuries past. Mosaics of the most extraordinary complexity, mesmerizing in their intricacy. I dare-say — the general smiled in recollection — you find yourself in the skin of another.

Every so often Alec arrived home late to find the party next door still in full throat. He could hear the general's parade-ground voice and Lucia's laughter. Alec would dismiss the babysitter, old Mrs. Bazaroff, who lived around the corner and loved Mathilde, and take his daughter into the garden where they would sit quietly together and look at the roses. Alec was teaching her their proper names: 'Betty Prior', Rosa 'Eureka', Rosa 'François Rabelais', and the grim-faced one he called Rosa 'Photographera'. That was the one without character and the one Mathilde took to. She was such a sweet child, grave of manner but with an impish smile when she chose to use it. After the rose reverie Alec would read to her and put her to bed and return to the garden, this time with a drink in hand to wait for Lucia, who always arrived slightly breathless with startling stories from the émigrés because there were always new arrivals with fresh anecdotes from their troubled homelands, eyewitness accounts of indignities and dissension. She would ask him about his day, and as he told her of his assignments he knew how banal he sounded, recounting the shoot on Capitol Hill or the White House, a portrait of some new cabinet member or senior Pentagon general. She had no more interest in this work than he did.

But there was something new today, he said.

The entertainment editor had assigned him — a temporary thing, she had said, but see what you can make of it — to a shoot at a small theater off Connecticut Avenue, a rehearsal of a contemporary drama. Alec liked the way the actors used their bodies, how they stood, and how they gestured. A tilt of the head or a sudden shift of weight had meaning no less assured than the lines they spoke. He was accustomed to shooting men at microphones, often reading from a script. Prepared text, they liked to say. These actors, especially the women, were lithe and composed assembling disparate parts into a harmonious whole. Alec found himself shooting from unfamiliar angles to get in the skin of the actors. Later, he joined the company for a beer backstage, curious to see how their off-job manner differed from their on-job manner. They were exceedingly affable, interested in his work for the newspaper and attentive when he described shoots in the Oval Office or on Capitol Hill, the staginess of them and the symbols — the microphone at the hearing, the gesture with the furled document, an American flag always somewhere nearby. While the actors talked among themselves Alec squeezed off a dozen shots — not for the newspaper but for them. Alec decided that their on-job manner and their off-job manner differed pretty much as his own did. You had a working face and a nonworking face. Same face, different focus. An audience made the difference.

Alec told Lucia that he had produced a unique portfolio; at any event, he had never done anything quite like it. The editor of the entertainment pages agreed but not for the same reason. We'll use one of them, she said, but forget the others. These are not what we expected. Why the odd angles? The way you photographed this troupe, they look like anybody you'd see on the street. We wanted the sort of shot you make on the Hill or in the Rose Garden. Something with some glamour to it.

They aren't glamorous people, Alec said.

Wrong, the editor replied. They're actors. My readers want to see actors. Actors mean glamour.

Driving home, Alec had the idea he was not meant to work for other people. He had lived in Washington his entire life but could no longer recognize himself in it. Perhaps he knew it too well. He knew suddenly that he was an artisan in search of material, the block of wood that became a refectory table, the iron slag that became a cemetery fence, or the lump of gold that became Lucia's choker. He was in search of a subject and wondered if he had found it on the stage of the theater off Connecticut Avenue. He felt an affinity with the actors in a way that seemed impossible with political figures — and that was the trouble, they were "figures." Nor was it a matter of age. One of the actors was older than his father. He was loose in his skin, that one, with a natural merriment. Photographing the rehearsal, Alec felt a part of it even while he was trying to make his camera disappear. He saw himself growing old before his own eyes with nothing much to show for it except a White House press pass and a portfolio of staged glossies.

Then something very strange happened, Alec said.

The night was chilly. He stopped at the traffic light just beyond Washington Circle. A man and a woman, lovers from the look of them, were talking earnestly on the sidewalk in front of a Greek restaurant. The man wore a red scarf and a black short-billed cap of the sort favored by V. I. Lenin in his revolutionary youth. He held his cigarette ash end up, between his thumb and forefingers, gesticulating as he spoke, unmistakably a European. Alec watched them with his photographer's eyes, and when the woman turned toward him his breath caught in his throat. Olivia Sorrensen stared at him as she listened to the man in Lenin's cap whose voice rose in a sour inventory of complaint, the internal contradictions of the State De-pot-ment, filled with idiots who failed to appreciate his genius — and then his words were lost, run together in frustration. The accent was pure Hibbing via Foggy Bottom. Olivia's face was pale in the wan glow of the streetlights. Her eyes grew wide and she made a little gesture with her hand that said to Alec, Don't interfere. Alec was in the process of rolling down his window. Robert Sorrensen looked at him sternly, evidently the look he liked to use at embassy gatherings.

Alec said, Excuse me. Which way to M Street?

You're on M Street, Robert said.

Yes, of course. I mean Wisconsin Avenue.

Well, make up your mind.

Alec couldn't help smiling at this sorry imitation of an out-of-patience ambassador. Olivia's hand went to her forehead as she looked away.

Wisconsin Avenue, Alec said.

Robert ground his cigarette beneath the heel of his shoe. He said, Straight ahead.

Thanks, Alec said pleasantly. Good night to you. Good night, miss.

Good night, Olivia said.

Have a pleasant evening, Alec said.

The light turned green and he put the car in gear, accelerating slowly. In the rear-view mirror he saw them watching him and then Robert turned to her, his shoulders rising, saying something more. Olivia shook her head but continued to watch Alec's car slowly drift up M Street. And then they turned and walked the other way. Two feet of distance separated them but it might as well have been a continent. Olivia did not seem much changed except the look in her eyes when she made the defeated gesture that said to him, Don't interfere. Don't come close. Drive away. Alec continued to watch them in the rear-view mirror. Robert was wiry of build, thin-faced, narrow-shouldered. He seemed to have a prisoner's pallor but that could have been the glare of the streetlight. Robert put a cigarette in his mouth. His lighter flared and in a sudden movement he tore the cap off his head and tried to stuff it in his pocket — Lenin no more, merely another disappointed apparatchik. The cap fell to the ground and they both reached for it, bowing, holding the pose. And in that moment, Alec said to Lucia, they both seemed like actors lit by stage lights.

Why did you stop? Lucia said.

I don't know, he said. Impulse.

A strange impulse, Alec.

Not so strange. I felt sorry for her. She was a nice girl. She deserved better than Robert.

Why did you tell me that story? When she first heard the story of the Sorrensens she was charmed. She remembered the Italian restaurant and the filthy Chianti and Alec's soft voice as he described his affair with Olivia, lonely because her husband was bewitched by Russia. He told the story without one ounce of bravado and she liked that, too. Lucia believed she was listening to a romantic and she felt in safe hands. But she was not charmed now, believing that Alec was leaving something unsaid. She waited for the answer to her question.

Because it had life, Alec said. Because it was genuine. Like the actors were genuine.

Then the count and countess moved to Kleinwalsertal, the lawyers arrived, and Alec and Lucia bought the larger house down the street. Like Damascus, the exterior was commonplace, whitewashed brick. The brickwork needed repair and the window frames a fresh coat of paint. But the interior was very fine, a living room and separate dining room and large kitchen. Alec's plans were on hold, and he himself was gripped by a stubborn inertia, unable to find a clear way forward. He and Lucia saw the émigrés but not so frequently. Once a month they would be invited to someone's house in Falls Church or Bethesda and once a month they would have them back. Often Lucia went alone, Alec delayed with a shoot. Ambassador Kryg died, his funeral held in a tiny church in far northwest Washington, the body flown from Sardinia for the occasion, the casket draped with the Czech flag. His many decorations were displayed in a row atop the flag. Sitting with strangers in the second pew, Lucia found herself in tears, the ambassador buried so far from home; his family was long gone and he was attended only by the exiles. She had no idea whether Sardinia had been a success or only another anteroom. She had never forgotten their conversation concerning her father, a subject to which they never returned. No doubt Kryg was a brute and unreliable but she felt a kinship with him, his funda-mental Czechness, his displacement.

After the ambassador's funeral, invitations from the émigrés slowed and then ceased and now when Alec arrived home from work Lucia was waiting for him. When he asked her what she had done with her day, she'd reply that she'd gone to the Na-tional Gallery or the Corcoran. Lunch with someone. Often she went to the zoo to see her friend the bear girl. Now when they went out in the evenings it was to the houses of Alec's friends, some from the office, some whom he had met on the job, others from his school days in Washington. They were pleasant, occa-sionally hilarious evenings; they called themselves the govern-ment in exile, plotting Nixon's overthrow in 1972. The war went on and on, water rushing downhill. At the center of events was the enigmatic Nixon, a closed personality, an actor in the national drama for three decades, a dark figure neither liked nor trusted; yet the American people trusted him. No one at the table had a line into the White House so their various theories about what the administration was up to were the purest conjecture. The journalists among them were the most frustrated. They had al-ways had friends in the administration, whichever administration it happened to be, but this one was different. What did Nixon do in his spare time? Did he drink? He was said to drink but no one had seen him drinking. Drink was the key to Nixon but the facts awaited verification. Nixon's drinks were like Kennedy's girls — no leaks. They worried the moral equivalent of a double Scotch as opposed to a willing debutante but could come to no satisfactory means of laying out the story in a newspaper article. The secrets were there to be flushed, like a covey of stubborn quail. But they refused to show themselves.

Lucia was unable to comprehend the allure of Nixon, so awk-ward physically, so humorless. She had formed a friendship with the wife of one of Alec's oldest friends, a foreign correspondent for one of the newsmagazines. Gretta was new to Washington — she had met her husband in London — and not au courant with American politics, especially Nixon politics. At dinners, as fragments of Nixon's biography flew by, Lucia was able to supply context for the various shards: Hannah, the dog Checkers, the Republican cloth coat, and the Fund. Gretta and Lucia were usually seated close to each other by the thoughtful hostess, who assumed they would have much in common, immigrant girls from Sweden and Switzerland, prosperous neutral nations content to remain on the margins of events. But now and again a name would surface that would mean nothing to Lucia and she would look down the table to Alec.

Explain to Gretta. Who was Irving Peress?

And Alec would bring the table to a full stop with a laborious explanation of the army dentist suspected of communist tendencies as Gretta's eyes grew wide with astonishment. She and Lucia would laugh gaily as the impatient table returned to its reprise of the Hiss case, Whittaker Chambers, the Maryland farm, the microfilm, the pumpkin, and where Nixon fit in.

At the end of the meal the men stayed at the table. A bottle of cognac appeared together with cigars as the conversation continued, everyone talking at once, frequent laughter and cursing. The life of Richard Nixon was inexhaustible, as various as a Balzac novel, with ever so much yet to come.

Lucia and Gretta retreated to the couch. They talked about their children and their husbands and the houses they lived in and where they went on vacations. Gretta confided that she returned to Sweden for a month each summer to see her family and friends. She liked speaking her language again, liked catching up with everyone, liked hiking in the woods, adored herring in oil. Her family had a cabin north of Stockholm, near Sundsvall on the Gulf of Bothnia. Do you know it, Lucia?

No, Lucia had never been to Scandinavia.

It's beautiful, Gretta said. So wild. So quiet.

Every summer for a month?

Yes, Gretta said. I insisted before Charlie and I were married.

It's been years since I was home, Lucia said.

You must go, Gretta said. It's important for us not to lose touch with our countries. Would Alec object?

I don't know, Lucia said. I don't think so.

Insist, Gretta said. We are not slaves after all.

Gretta went on to talk of her family and extended family and friends whom she had known since childhood, friends from grammar school and university. Her parents were no longer young but they were vigorous, great walkers. Her father owned a small sailboat. They had a rough-made tennis court at the cabin, and she and her father would take on her two brothers, family games that would last for hours, evenly matched games. All the time they were playing tennis her mother would be at her easel on the bluff overlooking the water, painting landscapes. And at the end of the afternoon we gather in the kitchen and cook dinner, a family feast. Of course there are disagreements. We are a normal family and Swedish and everyone has his own opinion, especially my brothers. But it is a wonderful month for me . . .

Oh, Lucia. I'm sorry. Did I say something wrong?

Lucia was near tears. I'm envious, that's all.

Do you hate Washington?

Lucia shook her head.

Well, then —

Things are so complicated, Lucia said.

Gretta gave her a close look, understanding at once. She said, You need a month away.

Perhaps I do.

Insist on it, Gretta said. Washington is very foreign to us. Dentists with communist tendencies. Pumpkins with microfilm. Washington is difficult in other ways. It is very provincial. It is a provincial town concerned with itself alone. They are always so preoccupied.

The men, Lucia said.

Yes. Charlie is different here than he was in London. We often went to the opera. The symphony. Three or four times a month to the theater. In London we knew different kinds of people, actors and artists. We knew layabouts also. There are no layabouts in Washington. Maybe you've met some. I never have. Our London layabouts, goodness they enjoyed themselves. Doing nothing, having a wonderful time. Charlie was exciting to be with, so — she lowered her voice — ardent. Ready for anything. Sometimes I go to New York just to get away. I miss Europe.

So do I, Lucia said.

We could go together sometime, Gretta said.

A weekend in New York.

Yes, a weekend. Girls' night out.

Lucia glanced over at the table, Alec and Charles and the two other men and their wives. The men were looking at Gretta, her almost-black hair and her fine features, her blue eyes. In Sweden and later in London she had been a model, much in demand. They were looking at Lucia, no doubt wondering what it was that engaged them so, their heads close together, their voices low. They were telling secrets, that much was obvious. Theirs was a zone of closed intimacy.

Washington was different when Kennedy was president, Lucia said.

It was?

Yes. At times almost lighthearted.

It makes a difference to them? Who's president.

Yes, it does.

Gretta broke into a wide smile. It makes no difference in Sweden. One is like another.

Of course we have our king.

Nor in Switzerland. Except we don't have a king.

Everyone everywhere mourned Kennedy. Was he as good-looking as his photographs?

Better, Lucia said.

You met him?

At a reception, Lucia said. I was working as an au pair for our ambassador. I went with the ambassador and his wife and we talked, the president and I. I had no idea what to say to him but he put me at ease right away. He had beautiful eyes. And mischief. I would say he was up to mischief.

The world is more amusing when there is mischief, Gretta said. Mischief and layabouts.

Gretta, Lucia said, there's something else. She looked at her friend, already beginning to smile, and decided not to go on with something else. She said instead, I think Alec is unhappy at work.

That's a very bad sign, Gretta said. Was that what you wanted to tell me?

He doesn't talk about it much, Lucia said.

Strange, Gretta said. The office is topic A in our house. Even so, I always thought Alec was a little different in his approach to things. He never seemed quite as invested as Charlie and the others. Maybe it's because he grew up here.

I can't imagine growing up here, Lucia said.

If he wants to move on, you should encourage him.

I should?

Something else might be more interesting, Gretta said, with a two-way smile.

Lucia did not reply. Both women glanced at the dinner table. Charlie was saying something about the war, a fresh offensive with more casualties than expected. When he finished, no one said anything.

Lucia? Alec said. Time to get home, don't you think?

I'm going to New York on Friday, Gretta murmured. Do you want to come?

I can't, Lucia said. Someone's invited us to dinner Saturday.

Okay, Gretta said. But one last thing, and please listen to me. When you take your month in Switzerland, go alone. Let Alec take care of your daughter. Every so often it's good to get away by yourself, see friends, be on your own. A change of pace for you without responsibilities. Europe is lovely in the autumn. Send me a postcard.

One night a week later, Lucia said to Alec, Perhaps I am a little homesick.

I thought you might be, Alec said. It's been quite a while.

Does it show? My homesickness?

A little, Alec said. It's natural.

Only a visit, she said.

I have to cover the campaign, Alec said. The midterm elections. You can't imagine how excited they are at the office. I wish I could be. He hesitated, thinking of one airplane flight after another, with a Holiday Inn at the end of the day. He said, I'll be gone most of next month, on the road with the candidates. Perhaps then, if you like.

I think I would, she said.

It's the perfect time.

October in Switzerland, Lucia said. Zurich in the fall.

It's settled, then. Mathilde will love the mountains. She can practice her German.

I'll get Mrs. Bazaroff to stay with her while we're away.

Alec was startled at this unexpected turn. You're not taking her?

Not this time. She'll be fine with Mrs. Bazaroff.

Poor Mathilde. She'll be disappointed.

Mathilde will be fine, Alec.

I didn't realize you wanted to go alone. I assumed it would be you and Mathilde.

Is there anything wrong with me going alone?

No, he said. It's fine. I assumed —

Okay, she said, and when she spoke she heard Gretta's voice.

Will you have a place to stay?

I'll find one. I still have friends in Zurich.

Alec said, Just so long as his name's not Stefan.

Oh, Alec, she said, don't be silly.

By now he's probably fat and rich, Alec said.

And married, Lucia said, though she did not believe he was married.

Good, Alec said. I'll call the travel agent.

She leaned across the table and kissed him.

This will be my last campaign, he said suddenly. I'm leaving the newspaper, finding something new. I don't know what. Maybe another city.

When did this happen?

I've been thinking about it forever, Alec said. Lately he had been photographing antiwar demonstrators and found he had little sympathy or compassion for them. He did not photograph them sympathetically. They seemed to blame the troops for the war and Alec believed the troops deserved compassion. They were the ones who were dying, three hundred in the past week, one bloody offensive after another.

What city? Lucia said, alarm in her voice. Where?

New York, he said. Los Angeles. I don't know. I haven't thought it through. It's something for us to think about, though. We can make some decisions after you get back from Zurich. Think of it as an adventure. Do you know my assignment tomorrow and the day after tomorrow? The Sunday magazine has decided to run a photo essay on ambassadors. How they spend their time away from the job. The sports they favor. What they do. Where they go. The Colombian, the Irish, the Moroccan, the Japanese, and the Nigerian. Sound familiar?

Lucia smiled but did not reply.

Alec was surprised at her lack of enthusiasm. Fear was in her voice. He said, Would you mind leaving Washington?

But our house —

We'd sell it. The way prices are now, we'd make a fortune. He began an explanation of the Washington housing market, un-precedented inflation, but Lucia shook her head.

I hadn't thought about it, she said. I don't know. Lucia turned from him, a bothered expression on her face. They were sitting in their garden after dinner. A warm night, and from the open window next door they heard faint laughter and applause, a television program. She smiled, remembering a remark she'd heard that afternoon. Television is to America what the drum is to Africa, a sacred instrument.

I think you have more of a life here than I do, Alec said. And I grew up in Washington. Either it changed or I did.

Perhaps if you made more of an effort . . .

That's what I used to say to you.

Yes, you did.

And look what happened.

And your mother, Lucia said hurriedly. I think she couldn't stand it, being separated from Mathilde. She comes over here all the time. She loves being with her granddaughter. And Mathilde loves her gran.

True enough, Alec said. But is that a reason to stay? Then a fresh thought came to him, an entirely unexpected idea. He said, Maybe we should go to Europe.

Oh, Alec. She started to laugh.

What's so funny?

Europe's not your place. That's silly.

How do you know Europe's not my place?

Don't be crazy, she said. I can't see you there, is all.

I can fit in anywhere, he said. And we're not getting any younger.

Europe, she said, and forced another laugh. Is not the fountain of youth it's cracked up to be.

Lucia picked up phrases of American slang all the time but this one was new to him, at least from her. He wondered where she heard it. Probably at Mathilde's school, or from the bear girl, the friend she visited so often at the zoo. At the moment Lucia spoke, Alec began to smile, attracted by the idea of Europe, a change of venue, something novel, a voyage of discovery. Who knew what Europe was cracked up to be? Alec wondered if he could find a fresh subject abroad, something remote from the news, from deadlines and thoughts about civic duty. The image before him was Ed Weekes, itching to return to the war zone in Vietnam, Ed as worn out as Washington itself, settled now into a long twilit afternoon, the Nixon gang in charge. No matter who was in charge he felt himself a stranger in the city, almost a stranger to himself. There were days when he believed he was sleepwalking. Last week, riding home on the bus, he looked up to find himself at Massachusetts Avenue Heights, eight blocks past his stop. Alec had commenced a reverie about sailing on the Chesapeake Bay, the weather warm, dead calm. His was the only vessel in sight, and his thoughts turned to Europe. He longed for something unfamiliar and wondered if Europe was his subject. Of course he was surprised at Lucia's lack of enthusiasm. Perhaps she was becoming a good American after all, suspicious of foreign entanglements. She had ceased to slip away as he feared she was when in the company of the exiles, awash in resentment and nostalgia. Switzerland would be good for her, and when she returned they could think about a place to live. And meanwhile he could think about job prospects, something exciting.

Maybe it's not a good time, Lucia said. My trip home.

You'll be fine, Alec said. He had no idea how to begin prospecting for a job in Europe. He had no European contacts. The only Europeans he knew lived in Washington.

It's been so long, she said.

That's a good reason to go now, Alec said. He had one friend who worked for Agence France-Presse, an older man, Henri somebody. He could take Henri for lunch, pick his brains. It would be wonderful not working for a newspaper or agency, just setting up as a freelance, picking and choosing. Somehow you had to establish yourself. You needed to do more than show up at Orly with a Leica and a bag full of film.

Not always, Alec, Lucia said.

What? Alec said, lost in his reverie.

On a Wednesday afternoon two weeks later they were waiting at the gate for the short flight from National to JFK, where Lucia would board the Swissair overnight to Zurich. Alec and Mathilde were inspecting the bears at the gift shop, Alec waiting patiently for his daughter to make up her mind. Lucia watched them, Mathilde inspecting each bear before putting it back in its place, Alec standing, his hands clasped behind his back, watching as if the decision would decide the fate of the world. His face was unreadable. She thought of it as his Chinese mask, nothing given, nothing accepted; and yet he was instantly recognizable as an American, loose-limbed in his khaki trousers and polo shirt. Nothing could be further from a Chinese than Alec Malone and still she thought of his look as Chinese. Lucia wondered if he unnerved his subjects, his face as blank as a camera's lens. Now Mathilde turned toward him with a brown bear in her hand and he nodded as he handed her a banknote. The cashier was watching this pantomime with an amused expression. When Mathilde handed up the money the cashier took it and carefully counted out the change, placing each coin in the little girl's hand. Alec said something and Mathilde smiled and put the coins in her child's purse.

Lucia heard Mathilde say, *Danke, Papa.*

Alec said, You're welcome, sweetheart.

They stood a moment more looking at the goods on offer.

The flight was announced. Lucia called to them but her words stuck in her throat. She had an instant of irresolution as she watched them turn and come toward her hand in hand, Mathilde clutching her bear, Alec so tall. At that moment she wondered how she could love anyone but him, them. But it seemed she had reinvented herself in America as everyone was supposed to do, and some of these reinventions came without notice or fore-thought. Sometimes you made the choice, sometimes it was made for you. A land of opportunity certainly, pushed along by hap-penstance — take one turn and not another, open this door and not that, remain at the party longer than you intended, and your life changes utterly. You find you are in harm's way and the harm comes willy-nilly, out of left field as her husband liked to say. Per-haps "harm" was not the correct word because you were borne aloft, weightless; harm was the last thing in your mind. Still, when she thought about it — connecting the dots, as it were — the events of that evening could be traced to a ski slope in the Enga-dine, a beautiful run on virgin powder and her downhill ski sud-denly out of control. She heard her bones snap when she fell. The shock was so great she felt no pain, at least not right away. Pain came later, and later still the souvenir, a limp that became more pronounced in night air. Had she not broken her leg she would never have gone to America as an au pair. Au pair work was not her interest. Her interest was competing in Europe, the downhill, the giant slalom. The downhill was her specialty. Also, she loved the company of skiers, their physicalness, their daring, their love of the cold. And if she had stayed healthy and contin-ued to improve her technique, surely she would have been a can-didate for the Winter Olympics. She believed something precious had been taken from her in the Engadine. She was diminished, her life's dream forfeit.

Call me when you get in, Alec said.

If the pension has a phone, Lucia said.

Safe trip, Alec said. He kissed her deeply.

Probably there won't be a phone, Lucia said. I'll cable.

Mathilde began to sniffle but stopped when Alec swept her into the air and held her suspended like an acrobat. Alec let her down slowly into her mother's arms.

Lucia said, See you very soon, darling. Be a good girl.

Mathilde clung to Lucia, her arms tight around her mother's

neck. For a long moment they did not move. Mathilde was sniffling again.

I'll be back before you know it, Lucia said.

Tell mama what you call your bear, Alec said.

The little girl was breathless. Swissbear, she said. I'm calling her Swissbear.

Then Lucia was in the cabin searching for her seat. The aircraft was not crowded. She fastened her seat belt as the plane eased away from the gate and began its slow progress to the far end of the field. All Lucia's irresolution returned as she stared out the window. She saw the lights of the Capitol dome but did not pay attention. She sat motionless as the plane took off to the west, banking sharply over Georgetown University. She searched for her house but could not locate it. She saw the spires of the National Cathedral and then they were in cloud and as suddenly above it, into the blue; dusk was coming on. Lucia opened the newspaper and read it listlessly. Toward the back of the front section she saw a photograph of a demonstration on the sidewalk in front of the White House, an antiwar affair, beards for the men, sandals for the women. It seemed that every day or so protesters showed up on the White House sidewalk. Her own thoughts were far away, memory snowflakes that seemed to dissolve upon arrival. Lucia put the newspaper away, then picked it up again to look at the credit line. Photo by Alec Malone. She dropped the paper on the seat next to hers. Lucia closed her eyes.

She was back in the Engadine, the brilliant blue sky and the snow as clean and soft as down. She was alone, the time late afternoon. She was meeting friends for drinks, *glühwein* and fondue at the second station. A boy she was interested in had joined the crowd. Oh, she was flying, skiing as fast as she had ever skied, and then she was turning cartwheels, the sky and the snow and the snow and the sky turning above her, out of control absolutely. Her goggles were filled with snow. She had lost her gloves and a fingernail. Her leg was under her at an unnatural angle. Lucia wept not from pain but from grief. Her grief was of the sort reserved for the death of a loved one or the end of a precious dream, a dream she had held her entire life. When she heard her bones snap she lost consciousness, but grief stayed with her. She remained in the hospital one month, eating little, speaking not at all. She tried to adapt herself to her new circumstances as everyone said she must do. But she was not good at adapting. She was determined to find again what she had lost. But soon enough she understood that nothing could be done, not with money, not with love, not with friendship or God. She was kaput. When the stewardess touched her arm and said they would be landing shortly at JFK, Lucia gave a start and cried out.

She was over the Atlantic now. She ordered a split of champagne, thinking of the Count and Countess d'An and the night she was leaving the party at their house and stumbled on the loose flagstone, her leg buckling, and she felt a strong hand on her elbow and another around her waist. Nikolas had come to her rescue and so she stayed on for another glass of champagne. She did not know him well, in fact they had only been introduced earlier that evening. She had forgotten his name and had to ask. Nikolas was one of the second-tier intellectuals who naturally was not second-tier in his own country but a prodigy, a full professor of literature, a fixture in the lecture halls and at the many discreet protest meetings in Prague and Budapest and beyond. His aim was to sweep away the arthritic hand of the Soviet occupation and install true socialism, socialism with a human face, practical socialism whose salient feature would be freedom of speech. Lucia did not truly understand his politics, though many of his phrases were reminiscent of her mother's salon. She was drawn to his conviction, his voice and manner, his wit. Nikolas was very clever. He had long, wavy brown hair and wore a six-foot white scarf whatever the season. The scarf was his signature. He had the rough looks of a mountain peasant, a heavy jaw and a bulbous nose and permanent stubble; no one would call him handsome.

Instead, Nikolas had vitality and a beautiful smile. Lucia looked into his black eyes and saw a thousand years of dissent from authority — any authority, parental, the state, the church, the sciences. There was nothing the least dutiful about him. She remembered thinking that he would be a handful for anyone who came to love him. His voice was gruff but his eyes sparkled. When he spoke, she smiled without quite knowing why, except the experience was like tapping your foot to an infectious rhythm. Nikolas had written one successful book, an allegorical novel whose subversive meaning had somehow eluded the authorities, who readily granted him permission to visit America. They thought he might be useful. Keep your eyes open. Tell us what you hear and see. Report back.

Nikolas said, They thought I would make a fine advertisement for the Hungarian way of life. Because I was so reliable.

He had a year's appointment as a visiting professor at one of the Washington universities, and when the year was up he arranged to stay on. He was extremely popular with his students, his classes always oversubscribed. His female students called him Professor Nik. He disappeared for a time, and when next seen had been granted political asylum. Professor Nik was now an official émigré, much in demand at conferences and symposia.

Nikolas was too young to be unconditionally accepted by the older émigrés — and perhaps his novel was a bit facile, a bit too quick with its ironies, and quite a bit too caustic in its treatment of the aging European diaspora. Nostalgia was the enemy of progress. Madame Brun believed he was not serious. He was charming in his own way, a sensuous boy, but he wrote with a curled lip. Yet he was popular among the Americans he had come to know, fellow academics and State Department analysts and those few journalists who covered foreign affairs. Nikolas was always good for a droll quote. He did have a biting wit — the drum analogy was his — and if he had read half the books he claimed to have read, he was a very well educated man indeed. Nikolas confessed to Lucia that he had a photographic memory and a talent for speed-reading and mimicry — gifts, he said disarmingly, like wavy brown hair and a big nose. He and Lucia were drawn to each other over the glass of champagne. It turned out that Nikolas was a distant cousin of a friend of the Countess d'An, so they were certain to meet again.

The next week they had coffee at one of the Georgetown cafés, then graduated to afternoon movies in out-of-the-way locations. One afternoon they drove to Baltimore to see *Catch-22*, a work of genius according to Nikolas, though Lucia thought it violent. They conversed in German. Lucia told him of her mother's salon in Zurich, making it sound *gemütlich* and clandestine at the same time. In his company she found that she remembered the smallest details, the brand of tea her mother served and the name of the shop the little cakes came from. Now that she was speaking German again she recalled whole conversations in her mother's salon. Nikolas seemed to unlock her memory.

Lucia said, Do you know the work of Walter Benjamin?

Nikolas said, Of course.

They talked about Benjamin all the time, his monomania, his paranoia, his obsession with commerce, his difficult sentences, more difficult even in German than in English translation. Walter Benjamin was a displaced person of the most radical sort, in Lucia's mother's opinion, and Nikolas readily agreed. Lucia was about to say that her husband had never read Walter Benjamin. Had no idea who he was. But in the end she said nothing. She never brought Alec into their conversations.

Nikolas was eager to speak of his family, his mother an illustrator, his father an artisan in the building trades. Nikolas had an older brother but the brother had disappeared, walked out the door one day and never returned; they had no idea where he was, but he had always been a wild lad. Wasn't it strange the way people could disappear, here today and gone tomorrow, without explanation? Yes it was, Lucia said; one more thing that bound her and Nikolas together. Very soon the afternoon movies led to afternoons at Nikolas's studio apartment in Arlington, Mrs. Bazaroff engaged two or three times a week now to look after Mathilde when she returned from school. Relations between Mrs. Bazaroff and Lucia grew chilly and Lucia knew that her trusted neighbor would soon leave them, much as she loved their little girl. But that was a bridge that could be crossed only when arrived at. Even so, Lucia was put off by the older woman's not so subtle expressions of disapproval. She no longer inquired into Lucia's whereabouts nor when she intended to return home, as if neither answer would be the truth. Mrs. Bazaroff was almost a member of the family, having looked after Mathilde since she was an infant. But she had always been partial to Alec.

Lucia was in a vortex she could not control. Not that control was uppermost in her mind; Nikolas was uppermost in her mind. She both did and didn't want to control the vortex. Desire and conscience were at war within her, though war was surely the wrong word because the struggle was undisclosed and unacknowledged, a behind-the-scenes business. As for the covert nature of her affair — what else was she to do? She was a married woman. She had a young daughter. She had to take precautions.

They came in very high, the aircraft throttled back. The Bernese and the Glarus Alps were visible to the south, their summits glittering in the dawn. Lucia thought she had never seen a sight so beautiful. The Zurichsee was below her, blue as a robin's egg. The aircraft made a wide turn, shuddering, and settled at last into its glide path. The city looked no different to her. She identified the Rudolf Brun Bridge and the Landesmuseum. Everything was as she had left it. She turned from the window and silently prayed that Providence would be kind; things would work out.

Lucia and Nikolas were trying to arrange a weekend rendezvous when Alec proposed she make the visit to Zurich. Nikolas quickly secured an invitation to lecture at the university, and he and Lucia met there, at a café they both knew well, on the first of October 1970. They spent two hours in the café, drinking coffee, drawing things out, then walked to the pension where Nikolas had booked a room. He asked her right away if there had been any trouble about Mathilde. No, Lucia said, no trouble. And you? Nikolas asked. I am where I want to be, Lucia replied. In Zurich with you. No place else? he asked, teasing her. He had found she teased easily, a temperament thing with the Swiss. But she only laughed and pulled down the sheets of the bed, where they spent the remainder of the morning and most of the afternoon.

Alec was glad his wife was taking a holiday. She had seemed so down in the dumps, snappish with Mathilde, distant with him. She appeared to have cut off all contact with her émigré friends. The truth was, Lucia was tired and needed a break. Mrs. Bazaroff, with feelings of high foreboding, agreed to stay in the house while Lucia was in Switzerland and Alec on the road with the campaign. She knew what Lucia was up to — Mrs. Bazaroff was not Russian for nothing — and had known for months but had kept her mouth shut. She had never approved of Lucia's friendships with the émigrés, some of whom she knew from her church and the musical evenings she attended. They were a conspiratorial lot, brooding and sly, volatile, great talkers, bone idle. They always knew what was good for you, boulevardier commissars. They also knew, or suspected, that Lucia was involved with Nikolas Janos and so there was talk; rumor piled upon conjecture, the bread and wine of expatriate life. Mrs. Bazaroff grieved for little Mathilde but did not consider it her place to intervene. Mr. Alec would not have believed her anyhow, being fully as credulous as most men. God, what dolts they were, unable to see what was in front of their own eyes. In fact the closer it was, the blinder they were. Mrs. Bazaroff knew things would end badly. How else could they end? Lucia and her layabout paramour were living inside a novel by the hysteric Dostoyevsky where the ending was always predictable. In any case, Alec was destined to be the last to know.

Lucia emptied her bank account — she had been careful over the years and had amassed a sizable nest egg — prudently leaving behind a thousand dollars to keep the account active in the event things didn't work out. She had been taught to leave a little something in reserve for emergencies. But as it happened, things worked out better than she could have imagined. Nikolas was loving and enthusiastic, full of plans, eager to explore Lucia's bohemian Zurich of memory — though he did joke with her that bohemia was difficult to imagine in a city whose devotion to the secret accumulation of great wealth was spiritual in its intensity.

They took a trip to the Engadine and hiked for a week, putting up at modest rest houses en route. It was at one of the rest houses that Lucia discovered Nikolas's work routine. She was awakened at five A.M. by a murmur, Nikolas talking to himself. She saw him hunched over the small table near the window writing furiously and knew soon enough that the murmur was not speech but the sound of Nikolas's pen racing across the pages, one page after another, and when he finished one he dropped it on the floor. The writer's heavy shoulders strained with the effort, his head bent like a bull preparing its charge. She imagined steam coming from his ears as if his brain was a mighty turbine. Fascinated, she watched him for a quarter-hour. Watched the pages accumulate at his feet. Watched the rhythmic motion of his head. Only once did he pause, his pen raised one foot above the page, and in an instant he was writing again. She closed her eyes, listening to the sound of his pen, the sheet dropping to the floor, a hiss as he drew a fresh sheet from the ream placed to his right at the edge of the table.

At breakfast the next morning Lucia told him what she had seen.

I disturbed your sleep! he said.

I didn't mind, she said. I was fascinated.

It's the way I go about things, he said.

I've never seen anything like it, she said. The concentration.

It's the way Balzac worked, he said. How else do you write eighty novels in thirty years? Plus journalism, sketches, short stories, reviews, personal letters. He was a titan! Nikolas said, loud enough that the people at the next table looked up in alarm. He wrote at night, slept during the day. Wasted eternities in fashionable salons. But even so, the greatest novelist of the nineteenth century. He never wrote a bad book.

And his love life? Lucia asked.

He loved women and women loved him.

He had many women, then.

Many, many women. There was something preposterous about Balzac, his taste for highborn women, his absurd get-rich-quick schemes. He wanted to import Russian oak for the making of French railway carriages, projects of that kind. None of them panned out, not one. He wanted so to be rich, surrounded by liveried servants and valuable paintings and costly garments and countesses. But at the end he had but one woman, Madame de Hanska, to whom he was completely faithful. She was filthy rich and not good to Balzac. She mocked him. She allowed him to die unattended.

This is not encouraging, Lucia said.

Read Zweig's biography, Nikolas said. It's all there.

Stefan Zweig figured in my mother's salon, Lucia said. Not personally. But they were always talking about him.

And well they might. Another titan. Nikolas signaled for another plate of eggs and a biscuit with jam. More coffee.

Balzac drank an ocean of coffee each day, Nikolas said. His doctors believed that was one reason he died so young, age fifty-one. Coffee ruined his stomach, and his work habits ruined his heart and mind. Eighty books in just over thirty years. Victor Hugo gave the eulogy.

I have to tell you, Nikolas went on, that Madame de Hanska was lovely whereas Balzac looked like me. Ate like me, too. Nikolas accepted his second helping of eggs with the biscuit on the side. Breakfast concluded, they took a long walk in the mountains. Nikolas was agile for a man of his size. After an hour, Lucia took the lead. They walked along paths and through meadows. As they climbed the air grew chillier. They were often in shade, looking down the valley with its chalets spread out before them. They did not talk much, content with the view and the exertion of the climb. Lucia's leg bothered her, unaccustomed as she was to mountain walking. She realized suddenly that Mathilde had never seen a mountain. She was growing up a flatlander and that was impermissible. A child should know snow-covered summits, the world beyond the tree line. Lucia paused, waiting for Nikolas to catch up. When at last she decreed that they head back to the rest house, he agreed readily. They took the road back down walking arm in arm. Lucia had never been happier. She chose not to wonder where all this was leading. She didn't care where it was leading. It seemed to her that she was at the threshold of the European life she had always desired.

That night at dinner they celebrated with a bottle of sekt, and when they returned to Zurich Lucia began a long letter to Alec explaining the facts of the matter, believing he would understand and wish her well once she told him what was in her heart. If he refused to understand — well, that would be shortsighted of him. People had to accept what they were given.

THE RED THREAD

THEIR PENSION was situated on a quiet square bordered by shade trees. There were tables and chairs under the trees and a dour concessionaire who sold coffee and croissants from a cart. Traffic was light. Lucia bought stationery at the shop on the corner and settled herself at one of the tables with her coffee and croissant, a sheet of blank white paper before her. She wrote nothing for the longest time, watching pedestrians in the square while she organized her thoughts. The day was overcast but warm for October. Lucia was lulled by the quiet and the orderliness of the square. She smiled as an elderly couple passed in front of her, the man thickset from what appeared to be a lifetime of good living, the woman slender with an athletic spring to her step. Lucia tried to think of herself and Nikolas in forty years, living comfortably in Zurich or some other European city, still companionable, still in love. She found herself unable to peer far into the future. She could not imagine what they would look like, gray hair, a slower step certainly. She had seen an artist's projection of John F. Kennedy at seventy years old, jowls and thinning hair, eyeglasses; he looked like his father. Probably Nikolas would be a famous writer, a spokesman for his generation — *their* generation. That was what he wanted for himself but she was not sure she wanted it for him. People would stake claims. She thought about the various claims, invitations to conferences, speaking engagements. He would be expected to have an opinion about everything under the sun, so there would be no time for repose.

Lucia watched the elderly couple stop at the concessionaire's for coffee, taking their time making a selection. She imagined the apartment they would have when Nikolas was famous, five or six rooms at least with a bedroom big enough for a desk so he could write at night. The desk would be long and deep to accommodate the manuscripts and reams of blank paper. The window would look out onto a city square, empty at night but in daytime filled with trees and flowers that would change with the seasons. They would have the apartment and a country place somewhere near a good piste for skiing in the winter — she wanted to watch the racers flying hell-bent top to bottom, success or failure measured in tenths of seconds — and for hiking the rest of the time. She wondered if Nikolas wanted children. They had not spoken of a family. There was plenty of time for that. Lucia knew that she was bourgeois to the core but she knew also that their apartment would become a salon, a gathering place for intellectuals. She looked at the blank sheet of paper before her and thought that it was much easier thinking about the future than the task at hand. She watched the elderly couple take their coffee to a table and sit, laughing about something; the woman was telling some story, her husband looking at her with an attitude of the utmost anticipation. They looked as if they had been together forever with the entire afternoon yet to come. They looked invulnerable. Lucia tasted her coffee and found it had grown cold. She drew the sheet of stationery close to her and after what seemed a long time began to write.

Lucia wrote that she was unable to help herself. She had found the man she had desired her whole life and had come to assume did not exist. She thought he was an illusion, someone who inhabited her imagination. But that was not true. He was real. Nikolas Janos was real, he was heaven-sent to her and now he was inside her and all around her and it was the same with him. Do you remember Madame Brun? One night she described to me — us, but I think you were not listening carefully — the apparatus of the communist state. She called it a tapestry of many colors. A bright red thread ran through it. The thread ran both vertically and horizontally, described circles, arcs. Madame Brun said when you lived in such a state you could not move without running into the red thread; your personal life, your professional life, your work, your recreation, all of it circumscribed by the red thread. Didn't it sound ghastly? Worse than ghastly. But if you apply that picture to a lover — unable to move without finding him and happy that he is there — then it becomes not ghastly at all but sublime. That is the way it is with us. I feel as if I have been reborn, Lucia wrote. From the very beginning in America she had felt out of her depth, homesick one moment, clinging to Alec the next. She was so very young and without experience. She was lonely. Their first years together had been a dream, their little house with its rose garden, her work at the zoo. Alec was so attentive. Mathilde arrived. But then the dream began to come apart. She saw herself imprisoned in a glass cage; things were visible but she was unable to grasp them. Had he experienced that? She was displaced, her heart out of joint. She looked forward so to her evenings at the Count and Countess d'An's and almost at once she felt her world turn. The way I felt was lawless, she wrote. I was searching for excitement of the sort I knew as a young girl, not a piste this time but a soiree in the open air. I knew they were dangerous company, rootless unsettled people, not dangerous to themselves but definitely dangerous to others because they had so little to lose. I knew the house next door was unwholesome for me and for us and yet there was nothing I could do about it. I knew you hated the evenings at the d'Ans'. You cannot deny this. This was not a world you knew about or cared for. That is why I was so surprised when you suggested we live in Europe. I don't believe Europe is your place. I saw you arrive at our house — the back light went on, and I knew you were home — and sit alone in the garden until the party ended. You and your evenings of baseball and reverie and I was unable to share either one. And that drove us apart. And one night I tripped on a loose flagstone and my life changed and I knew nothing I could do would put it right. I was overwhelmed and without resources. Perhaps that is not entirely true: I had resources but they were put to selfish purposes. I tell you that the glass of my cage suddenly shattered and shattered glass cannot be made whole. Nikolas and I seduced each other, that's the truth of it. It did not begin that way but that was how it came to be. I have no regrets of it. I went to Zurich to see if I had lost my mind or found it. You must not blame yourself.

Alec read her letter in the garden late one afternoon. He had not bothered to unsling his camera bag and it hung heavily from his shoulder, unnoticed. When he got to the part about Nikolas and Lucia seducing each other he tried to recall him, what he looked like and how he spoke, his bearing. And he remembered Nikolas quite well, a burly young man with a mop of dirty hair, a beaked nose and a heavy belly, a white scarf, a man easy to pick out in a crowd. He knew it, too. He was Hungarian or Polish, a youthful spirit despite his bulk, younger in age than heedless, overwhelmed Lucia. If there was danger, Alec had not seen it. He stared at the letter in his hand trying to recollect this Nikolas. He did not remember whether they had ever spoken. He thought not, though there were so many of them — Czechs, Bulgarians, Hungarians, Poles, Russians — in and out of the garden next door he could not be sure. They were all damaged goods, a second-rate theatrical troupe giving nightly performances of the heartbreak of central Europe. Alec had listened to them for hours at a time, achieving sympathy but not understanding. They did not seem to mind. Probably to understand them fully you had to have been there at the beginning, whenever the beginning was — Xerxes, Martin Luther, 1848, 1917, Munich in 1938. This Nikolas was too young to care about it. No, he wasn't. Heartbreak would be wired into his genes. Alec remembered that he had written a scandalous novel.

The light began to fail. From inside the house Mrs. Bazaroff called to him but he did not answer. Then he said, Just a moment, please, in a voice he knew was not his own. Alec continued reading but could not get the sense of what Lucia was writing. Something about Mathilde, something more about arrangements for custody and child support and the things she had left behind. It seemed to him she was writing in a foreign language, verbs and subjects in violent disagreement. One thought led to another without transition. Her handwriting was sloppy, the words aslant on the page in blue ink; the letters resembled sloops bearing into a brisk wind. They had had such a good time on Chesapeake Bay, perfect weather, the boat all you could ask for. Lucia thought that the motion of the sea and the smell of salt water was sexy. She said it again and again. She was right, too. They had sailed Chesapeake Bay for ten days and not had a conversation with another human being; instead, Lucia talked to the crabs. Something childlike about it but wondrous also. He had taught her how to sail, explained the difference between the main and the jib, compass bearings, the tides. She was a natural. He remembered that they were going to buy a boat but never got around to it. Out of the corner of his eye he saw Mrs. Bazaroff in the doorway, and then she turned her back and moved silently into the house. Alec came to the end of Lucia's letter understanding no more of what he was reading except that she was gone and would not return. Zurich was her home. Her life she would share with Nikolas. Alec could not imagine what had gone wrong so suddenly except of course he was not to blame himself, whatever it was. Alec realized that she had not given his last name, as if Nikolas was all her husband needed for a positive identification. Then he returned to the beginning of the letter and saw that she had. But her handwriting was so bad that he could not read it exactly. His name was Janos or Junot, something like that.

Inside the house the telephone rang but Mrs. Bazaroff did not answer and the caller gave up. Alec folded the letter and stood tapping it against his thumbnail. That morning he had been in Des Moines, at a rally for a Democratic House candidate; Hubert Humphrey was the featured speaker. Humphrey and Kim Malone were close friends and allies, so the former vice president invited Alec into his hotel suite to photograph him with the candidate and his advisers, an important strategy meeting, one last push to save the Senate and the House for the Democrats. Humphrey looked exhausted, his face drained of color. He and the candidate and the advisers had been talking about the war, a discussion that had left them dispirited. Alec sent the photograph by wire to the newspaper and his editor was delighted, an exclusive shot, Humphrey jowls-to-the-floor. Take a week off, Alec. Spend some time with your family. Alec caught a midday flight to O'Hare and two hours later a nonstop to Washington, all in all an easy day. He had not heard from Lucia in weeks but he had the idea she would be waiting for him when he returned, a surprise; and Mathilde had been out of sorts, wondering where her mother was.

He had bought something for Mathilde in Iowa but now couldn't remember what it was. The letter still in his hand, Alec walked to the rear of the garden to look at the yellow roses, dim in the half-light. He thought they needed water. Washington was in a state of autumn drought. Roses never grew as nicely in this garden as they had in the small garden that measured twelve by twenty feet. Probably it was the soil. Perhaps the light was wrong. Roses needed beaucoup sunshine to thrive. But drought was the real enemy. Of course the garden was too crowded, too many varieties of plant life. The nasturtiums and hollyhocks were especially frumpish. He wondered if he should try to buy back his old house. This one was too large for him now. Interior spaces weren't all they were cracked up to be. Alec turned on the sprinkler and listened to the hiss of the spray.

He returned to Lucia's letter in order to read the last sentence once more. He held the paper close to his eyes, the light was so poor. Really, it was only ambient light reflected from the clouds that hung low over Washington.

I tried so hard, she wrote.

Mrs. Bazaroff called again from the interior but Alec did not reply. He was testing the sincerity of Lucia's last sentence. He read it again and again, a heartbreaking four-word sentence. He wondered if it had come to her naturally or if she had to think about it, her pen between her teeth, trying one line after another until she found the one that struck a clear note. He supposed she was sincere. There would be no reason why she would want to lie at such a time. Lying was not in her nature. Lucia had always been straightforward. Forthright would be the word, a quality the Swiss were meant to have in abundance, along with a tremendous capacity for affection. Well, probably the Swiss were no more affectionate than anyone else — Americans, say, or Hungarians. Affection came hard in a cold climate, witness the Germans. Alec thought back over her letter, her attempts at explanation (if that was the word), and concluded she had help writing it. The phrases seemed to come from another culture or, more pointedly, another decade, a decade in the future, perhaps the 1980s. No one knew what the eighties would bring. Each decade had its signature. The Silent Generation of postwar conformity; the Me Generation; in the twenties it was dancing barefoot in the fountain of the Plaza Hotel; in the sixties stoned at Woodstock. Alec thought Lucia's letter was prophetic in some way he could not explain. *The way I felt was lawless.* Assisted or not, he believed she was writing from some future time. In a decade or two her letter would achieve coherence. *I tried so hard*, and perhaps she had. All the same, Alec felt she had clubbed him in the stomach.

He turned away, his mind filled with static, harsh and unintelligible. Darkness gathered. When Alec looked up he saw only the thin layer of clouds that shrouded the Washington sky. No stars were visible. Alec stared at the blank slate above and concluded he had put faith in the wrong system, the one that was misleading, well out of date. He had misunderstood the cosmos. He had held with the Ptolemaic system in which the sun eternally revolved around the earth when there was much evidence to the contrary. In order to keep faith he had done what the medieval people had done, proposed that the sun moved around the earth while at the same time the planets moved around the sun. The dance floor revolved as the dancers waltzed, everything in motion. There were no fixed points in the universe. This seemed to give them comfort, and in due course they tried Galileo for heresy. Alec smiled at this thought as he continued to gaze at the concealed heavens. After a moment he turned to walk back into his house.

Lucia will not return, Alec said to Mrs. Bazaroff. She is remaining in Europe.

It had taken Alec twenty minutes to tell the story but his father had drifted away after five, barely into the hors d'oeuvres. He heard nothing about the count and countess, Ambassador Kryg, Nikolas Janos, or Lucia's father. Nothing about sailing on the Chesapeake Bay or the ordeal of Ed Weekes. Alec continued anyhow to give an account of those early days which had apparently been so mysterious to his father. When he finished talking his voice was barely a whisper. The old man was sleeping soundly now, his face waxen but his breathing regular as a metronome. He looked older when he was asleep than awake. Looking at him, Alec had a feeling not of consanguinity but of longevity; they had been in the way of each other for a very long time. Rarely did a day pass without his father entering his thoughts in one guise or another. When the nurse looked in, Alec asked her how long the old man had. She said it was hard to know, and in any case she did not do predictions. Alec said, Take a guess, I won't hold you to it. The nurse thought a moment and said, More than a week but less than a month. He was failing obviously, each day a trial, but his heart was strong.

He likes it when you come, she said.

I know he does, Alec said.

He looks forward to it. He asks me to read the headlines in the paper so he's up on things. The war, the election.

He has most of his marbles, Alec said.

Was he really a senator?

Really was, Alec said. A good one, too.

Sometimes, you know, they make things up. We have the king of Sweden down the hall. Every few days he calls one of us in to announce a Nobel Prize. Harmless old man, sweet-tempered. She smiled briefly and said, Stay as long as you like, I'll be back to check on him in an hour.

Alec stepped to the window and looked out. The hour was late and it was nearly dark except for the lights on the lawn of the hospital. He saw activity on the sixteenth green and cupped his eyes to the glass so he could see better. It took him a moment to focus. A boy stood in the sand trap lofting ball after ball to the green. He would hit one shot and drop a fresh ball and hit another. After each shot he carefully raked the sand, as any professional caddie would do. The boy looked to be no more than ten or twelve years old, tall for his age and skinny, probably one of the weekend caddies or the son of a member who lived nearby.

Then Alec noticed an older man standing off to one side, his arms folded across his chest, watching the play with fatherly pride. There were a dozen or more golf balls on the green, some of them only inches from the cup. The boy was a prodigy. Finally he gave a last sweep of the rake, collected the balls on the green, and walked off down the fairway with his father. Through the open window Alec heard their companionable laughter.

Then he was in his car and driving back to Washington, thinking about the boy practicing sand shots. Doubtless he saw himself one day as a member of the PGA Tour, making a Sunday run at the Masters or the British Open, knocking a sand shot two inches from the pin, applause filling his ears and trying not to notice because applause was a distraction, a concentration breaker. The point wasn't the applause, the point was the ball in the cup. Alec had caddied occasionally for his father on weekend afternoons, the men talking politics as they lined up putts. Alec would drift off into one of his reveries and forget to remove the flag or follow the line of his father's drive as it sliced right into the rough. He would be thinking about the blond-haired girl in geometry class or what he had planned for the weekend. His father would yell at him, *Watch the goddamned ball*, and Alec would come to just soon enough to follow the ball's flight, bending right into the rough and bouncing into the woods, out of bounds. His father barely noticed. Ball flight was Alec's assignment. By then the senator was engrossed in a discussion of the supplemental appropriation, completely screwed up by the idiots in the House. When he reached the ball and found it unplayable he picked it up and lofted it back onto the fairway, still talking about the House and what was to be done. Alec decided he was not made to be someone's caddie, especially his father's caddie.

Alec turned on the radio, German music from the classical station.

Traffic was light in early evening but he was driving slowly, troubled by the lights of oncoming cars. His eyes were getting worse each day. He had difficulty reading the newspaper in the morning, though by noontime he was focusing all right. Alec plodded past the Pentagon and over the Fourteenth Street Bridge to the Jefferson Memorial, reflected unsteadily on the corrugated surface of the Tidal Basin. The reflection looked like one of Pollock's expressionist canvases.

Alec was trying not to think about the story he had told the old man — early days in Washington, something out of the ordinary, something unexpected, his mysterious life — but that proved difficult. He had never spoken the whole story — beginning, middle, and end — to anyone. When he was younger he had ruminated on it often, measuring the what-ifs. He had long since decided that the events of those years were fated. He believed he had the story correct in its essentials: the house next door, the exiles in the garden, Lucia's fascination with the Count and Countess d'An, and his own strange brooding on the Ptolemaic system of fathoming the cosmos, a reverie sure enough. They really had called the White House "the Palace" and Walta Binyameen was a frequent reference. And Alec truly was the last to know, and from that he concluded that he was incapable of grasping how people actually behaved; he had never counted himself a prophet. He supposed that all the guests-of-many-languages were gone now. If the Count and Countess d'An were alive they would be of very great age, early nineties at least. A year or so after Lucia left him, Alec had a letter from the d'Ans in Kleinwalsertal. Nikolas and Lucia had come for a visit while they were touring southern Germany. Mathilde was with them. Such a charming child, Alec. You must be very proud. Lucia looked well. No mention was made of Nikolas. Tactful silence, Alec thought at the time, though simple negligence may have been closer to the mark. Alec had not answered the letter.

It did not occur to him to try to win her back. That door was closed and locked, no light visible from her side or his. She was gone and that was the end of it. The next day he gave notice at the newspaper. They were not pleased that he had quit in the midst of an election campaign, for God's sake. But Alec sensed relief also; he had always been miscast, never part of the team. That afternoon he walked to K Street for a conversation with Eliot Bergruen, who promised to do what was best for him and for Mathilde once he heard what Lucia wanted and whom she had hired as her lawyer. Was Lucia a fit mother? Yes, Alec said, she was. Leave this in my hands, Eliot said. When I know more I will call you and we can decide what to do. That is to say, how far we can go. You must provide me with a list of your assets, beginning with the house.

I'm sorry, Alec.

So am I, Alec said.

Was she ever happy here?

In the beginning, Alec said. And toward the end.

The lawyer gave a fleeting smile. I understand.

Can I ask you a question, Eliot?

The smile vanished. Go ahead.

Did you ever feel you might have taken a different path? Run for the Senate like my father. Gone into the government.

I was in the government, Alec. I worked in Lend-Lease.

Stayed in the government, then.

The lawyer leaned back in his chair, hands locked behind his head, staring at the ceiling. He said, Naturally you're upset. Take a month off, get away from things. I have learned in my life that clear thinking arises from repose, intervals of noninterference. Recreation, if you will. One returns to one's task refreshed. I have learned also that nine out of ten problems solve themselves if you leave them alone. Let nature do its work. By nature I mean fate.

And the tenth?

You take the tenth by the throat.

And that's why you didn't remain in the government?

I was not speaking of the government, Alec.

Or choose one path instead of another.

You have suffered a shock. Your task is to get the shock out of your system. Never look back, that's the key. The backward glance is the guarantor of an unhappy life. Strangely enough, I learned that in the government. What was a waste of time and what wasn't. Good luck to you, Alec. I'll be in touch.

The next day Alec took his clothes to the dry cleaner, then continued down the street to the park. He sat on a bench under a shade tree and watched a group of Georgetown students, all with open books, listening to their instructor. Then they took their places and began to read, evidently a rehearsal in the open air. They seemed to be concentrating intensely, reading, he now understood, Shakespeare. When they took a break Alec asked the instructor if he could make photographs, he was from the newspaper. The instructor gave his permission and the students gave theirs and Alec began to shoot, remembering the afternoon at the theater off Connecticut Avenue. He shot with mounting excitement, staying out of their lines of sight, making his camera disappear, attempting to intercept the awkwardness and innocence of amateurs. He returned the next day and the day after, and when he finished with the actors he photographed playgrounds and parks, an empty swing, an empty bench, a tennis court at dusk, a beech tree with initials laboriously carved in its trunk. Mostly the photographs were without people, but now and again he made a long shot of a solitary figure on a park bench or looking into a store window. Of course he understood that the shots reflected his closed-down state of mind, the unconscious orbit of the sleepwalker.

Something had been lost that could never be regained. Some doors, once locked, never opened again. No one had the will. The eventual show, at one of the M Street galleries, was a success, especially the shots of the student actors. That winter Alec took his camera to Annapolis, photographing boats at anchor, under sail, in dry dock. He concentrated on dry dock. Wrapped in canvas tarpaulins, the vessels looked like sleeping beasts. Alec rented a sloop and sailed alone in Chesapeake Bay, freezing cold. But the deserted coves and harbors made wonderful material.

One night he put in at St. Michaels, moored the sloop, and went ashore for dinner. After dinner the bar was crowded. Alec looked in for a nightcap and at once found himself in conversation with a cameraman — he called himself a cinematographer — on the job in picturesque St. Michaels. They were shooting a movie, second-unit stuff, two scenes only on the harbor. A low-budget affair, Tommy confided, but the dailies looked very good. They talked shop for an hour. Alec explained that he was now freelance but had worked for a newspaper in Washington for ten years. At last he was free of that.

Tommy said, I thought Washington was exciting. A good gig.

It's only the government, Alec said.

Then a woman was at Alec's elbow. Who's your friend, Tommy?

Annalise, meet Alec. Alec, meet Annalise Amiral. She's the actress I was telling you about. A pro. Beautiful to work with.

Tommy wandered off and Alec bought Annalise one drink, then another. She described for him the plot of the movie, in which she played a femme fatale. The movie could be her big break if it was produced properly. If money was spent on promotion. The script was not bad at all. What are you doing here, by the way?

Taking pictures of shipyards and boats, he said.

It's winter, she said.

The shipyards and boats don't care, he said.

And where do you live when you're not photographing shipyards and boats?

Washington, he said.

I lived in Washington for a while. My father is a congress-man.

You're kidding me.

I'm not kidding you.

Mine is a senator.

I loved politics, Annalise said. My father used to take me cam-paigning when I was little. Held me on his shoulders when he made a street-corner walk-by, all the matrons oohing and aahing. Good symbolism, my dad said, attentive father, family man. His opponents said he was exploiting a five-year-old. I loved it. "Ju-dah Jones is on your side." That was his campaign slogan. Bal-anced budget, that was his signature issue. They loved it in Win-netka where everyone's budget was so large it never had to be balanced.

So he's a Republican, Alec said. Mine's a Democrat.

He ever take you campaigning?

No, Alec said. I was not an adorable child.

Hah, she said. I was.

I can believe it.

Then I didn't like politics so much. I liked boys instead. We only lived in Washington a few years. My mother didn't like it. She had work of her own. So we moved back to Winnetka and my father commuted. He still does. Commute.

Later on, the bar almost empty, Annalise confided that she had been married but the marriage hadn't worked out. Her hus-band was not in the entertainment business and that was difficult because the business was all-consuming. You didn't want it to be but it was. Her husband was the only lawyer in Los Angeles who had nothing to do with the entertainment business. He special-ized in patents, so at the end of the day they had nothing much to talk about and drifted apart as people tended to do when the eve-nings were marked by silence. Alec said he understood about drift. He had been married but was no longer. His wife had left him for a Hungarian layabout. His daughter lived with his ex-wife and the layabout in Switzerland.

Did she meet him in Washington?

Yes, she did.

I didn't know Hungarian layabouts lived in Washington.

This one did, Alec said.

I met a British layabout once. Never a Hungarian.

You probably didn't live in Georgetown.

Chevy Chase, Annalise said.

Well, that explains it.

What do you suppose attracted your wife to the Hungarian?

That's a good question, Alec said. I'm damned if I know. I'm sure it was an affair of the heart.

There are lots of those in Washington, Annalise said.

Evidently, Alec said.

My father had an affair, a girl in his office. My mother put a stop to it. She put her foot down. And so the affair went away and they continued as before. Annalise smiled devilishly and finished her cognac. I'm free tomorrow, she said. What are you doing?

Sailing, Alec said. Come along. We'll have a picnic.

I'll bring my mittens, Annalise said.

Alec parked the car a block from his house and walked slowly up the brick sidewalk. The night was warm, seasonable in April, and no one was about, though he thought he heard music in the vicinity. He passed Admiral Honeycutt's old house and Ronald di-Antonio's next to it, both men long, long gone. The count and countess's grand house was sold years before by the lawyers and had passed into other hands twice more before the sale, last year, to an oil man who did something important in the present administration, Alec had forgotten what it was. There was a time when he knew the names of every cabinet member in the government in order to successfully complete his father's dinner table decathlon. He had never met his important neighbor but he did often see the Vietnamese houseman carrying dry cleaning to and from the shop on the corner. The first thing the oil man did was tear up the tennis court and replace it with a gazebo surrounded by hedges and magnolia trees and, implausibly, a giant cactus; the cactus reminded him of Paul d'An's stag's head. Alec had come to think of the house next door as emblematic of the change of administrations. Each new owner put his stamp on the property. A fountain and a giant cedar made way for a tennis court as years later the tennis court made way for a cactus. Idle aristocrats made way for foulmouthed lawyers who made way for Republican oil men. Next year or the year after the cactus would yield to a state-of-the-art lap pool so the new owners could keep fit. In the old days everyone stayed on, lured by the capital's hospitality and sense of occasion and unquestioned authority. And if all you knew was politics and government, where else would you want to make a life? The exceptions were the ex-presidents, who felt obliged to go home to Johnson City or Atlanta or some address of convenience like Palm Springs or San Clemente, returning to Washington for funerals of statesmen like themselves. Johnson, Nixon, Ford, and the elder Bush had all known the capital as young men and could not fail to remark on the changes. The grandes dames were gone. The elder statesmen were gone. The small town of their youth was now a metropolis spilling over into the Virginia and Maryland countryside, farther each year. When you looked at the downtown, with its barriers and snipers on the roof of the White House, you could believe you were living in a garrison state. Alec noticed that his street was crowded with German automobiles, the large versions.

Alec had lived on this street for more than half his lifetime, a fixture now like the vanished grandes dames. That came at a price. Now and then a neighbor would pause in front of his house, the neighbor's voice audible through the open windows, explaining the charm of the surroundings, the sense of continuity and history.

That little place belongs to Alec Malone, the photographer. He's been here practically forever, at least since the Kennedy administration. I believe they knew each other well, Alec and the president. Played golf together. Went cruising on the *Honey Fitz*. Was a guest often at Hyannisport and Palm Beach and Glen Ora. Went girl-chasing together. There isn't anyone in this town that Alec Malone hasn't photographed, though for many years he's worked mainly abroad and on the West Coast. Private man, keeps to himself. That's what's good about Washington, the links from one generation to the next. In Washington the past is always prologue, you see. Malone's father was an important senator, friend of FDR. Why, you could say that Alec Malone goes back to the New Deal.

Live long enough in Washington, Alec thought, and they give you bells on your clothes and a false face, like a jester or a Kabuki dancer. They made you a legend.

His house was ablaze with lights. Alec always left the lights on believing they discouraged burglars. And to think that in the sixties he and Lucia never locked the front door day or night. Alec paused by the table in the hall and leafed through the mail, half a dozen bills and circulars and a letter from Mathilde, a long one judging from the weight of the envelope, postmarked London. Alec put the letter aside to read over dinner. He always gave her letters his closest attention. He walked into the kitchen, made a drink, and in seconds was settled in his wicker chair in the back yard. His roses were coming into bloom, especially lovely this evening. Next door the oil man was giving a noisy party complete with fiddle and guitar ensemble playing southwestern music. The very air seemed to vibrate with it. Alec heard the rattle of glassware and women's soprano voices. He listened for foreign accents but heard none, unless you counted the southern accents. And then, quite distinctly, he heard rapid Spanish. A sudden pause in the conversation told him that someone important had arrived. The pause was short, no more than a beat or two, then conversation resumed louder than before. There was a musical term for it, ostinato, a phrase or rhythm repeated again and again.

Alec looked at his watch, bringing it close to his eyes in the darkness. Eight o'clock. The count's menagerie was always gone by a little after eight. Charles removed the champagne and the party ended. All those guests-of-many-languages were either dead or returned home or living in Switzerland. The captive nations were no longer captive, unless you considered global capitalism a kind of captivity. That, apparently, was Nikolas Janos's view, according to Mathilde. Nikolas and Lucia had only recently moved to Prague after living in Zurich for so many years. They also kept a small apartment in Berlin. Alec sipped his drink thoughtfully and listened to the party next door.

Someone fluttered a knife against crystal and the southwestern music stopped. Conversation tailed away and then ceased. The oil man was introducing his special guest. It was an honor having him there, a man of strength and commitment, a very great American, a man of faith, a man who took no prisoners, the government was lucky to have him and didn't deserve him, a man willing to sacrifice so much including the precious gift of privacy . . . And then someone began to clap and the others joined in. Applause gathered, here and there a cheer. The special guest apparently declined to answer his host, for in a moment normal conversational ostinato resumed. Southwestern music resumed. Alec slipped into silent thought once more. The Morocco trip was definitely off. He would call Annalise in the morning, attempt another plan. He missed her, missed her easiness, her jokes, her repose turned abruptly to bird-on-the-wing. Perhaps they could meet somewhere else, New York or Los Angeles, when she finished her shoot. She was at her most irresponsible after finishing a film. Alec believed his father had weeks left, maybe more than weeks. But he deserved company in the time he had left. There was little enough Alec could do, but the old man deserved his best effort. Alec slowly sipped his drink and looked through his reverie room, this time giving himself over to the meaning of the red thread and where Annalise fit in.

PART TWO

ANNALISE

THEY FINISHED SHOOTING a week early, leaving Annalise at loose ends. Alec was delayed in Washington, waiting with his father for the long-nosed man who did seem to be taking his own sweet time. The senator mostly slept, unresponsive except for a grunt or nonsense word. Alec was subdued, remarking only that the old man's spirit was somewhere between a snowflake and nothing. When Annalise asked if he would like her to join him, he thanked her and said no; surely they would be together in a week, perhaps less. She did not press him.

Annalise went to Marrakech for three days, staying at the good hotel near the souk. The heat was unbearable. She rented a car and drove to Agadir for the weekend but the beach was uninhabitable owing to the desert wind. She read during the day and at night dined alone in the hotel restaurant. Her last night she was joined by a young couple from Chicago. Annalise knew the city well and they stayed at table long after the room had cleared, talking of Chicago and its colorful politics and adventurous theater. They were lawyers who specialized in environmental issues; they majored in the environment but had a minor in political law, grand jury work and matters of that kind. When they asked her what she did, Annalise replied that she was a fashion consultant. Strange, the young woman said, you really resemble the actress — and she could not remember the actress's name.

Annalise Amiral, Annalise said.

That's the one, the young woman said. You look so much like her, Judy.

It happens all the time, Annalise said.

The next day she flew to Tangier, a city she had first visited in the late 1960s. She had never seen a place like it. The Bowleses and William Burroughs more or less led the expatriate community, remarkably louche and unbuttoned. Everyone drank all day long and the nights were wild and without restraint of any kind. She was on the fringes of a crowd that went from café to café and then split up into groups of three or four to finish the evening in someone's apartment, smoking hash and playing strip poker. When you woke in the morning you had no idea who you were with. Everyone was obliged to reintroduce themselves so there would be a name to go with the body. Tangier seemed to exist outside the normal rules, the rules not so much ignored as forgotten. Certainly there were other cities like Tangier elsewhere in the world but Annalise had never seen one; she carried the memories her whole life.

Almost forty years later Tangier seemed to her to have grown sedate. Of course the Bowleses and Burroughs were gone. Tennessee Williams was gone. There seemed to her fewer Americans and more Germans. She saw a busload of Asians in straw hats and sunglasses. The cafés were lively and the streets crowded and, as always, you avoided the noonday sun. The odor of hash was present but not ubiquitous and now seemed self-conscious; and then Annalise had cause to reflect that she was no longer young, and what seemed so lurid to her then was the norm today. Tangier had not receded. Other cities had caught up, the sex trade as much a part of GDP as dates or olives. She called Alec and left a long message on his answering machine describing Tangier and its white light and Asian tourists, the somnolence of midday, the crystal blue of the Mediterranean. She called the city Babylon in aspic. How is your father? Call me at the hotel. She told him that she thought it was time for her to return to America.

She put in at a small hotel near the port and spent her first day revisiting old haunts. The next morning she bought the American newspaper and settled in at the café around the corner, the one she remembered from her first visit. She ordered a croissant and a café crème, looking around the café to see if there was anyone who looked interesting. When she opened the paper she gave a start. Ingmar Bergman was dead. She put the paper aside and when the waiter came she asked him for a pony of cognac on the side. She looked again at the paper with its grainy photograph, the great director with his left eye screwed into a camera's lens. He was gaunt, probably about forty years old when the shot was made. Annalise sipped her coffee and read the obit all the way through. So many films. So many liaisons, wives and girlfriends, multiple children from the multiple liaisons. She wondered if the two went hand in hand. In Bergman's case they seemed to. She stared again at the photograph and thought that it was as if one of the world's great languages had disappeared from the repertoire, vanished like the dialects of central Europe and the steppes of Asia. No one would ever speak it again. It was mothballed in film.

More coffee, she said to the waiter.

Her one regret in her professional life was that she had never made a film with Ingmar Bergman. Of course such a thing was impossible. Bergman had his own Swedish repertory company, von Sydow, Ullmann, and the others, and rarely used foreign actors, especially American actors. She had seen *The Seventh Seal* as a child and understood very little but seemed to feel it all; the enigma of the film reached to her very soul. She believed enigma was at the heart of both art and existence. She wished to understand the essence of enigma and thought Ingmar Bergman could point the way. Annalise tried a dozen ways to meet him and never succeeded. Once she saw him at a restaurant in Cannes, Annalise quite openly staring as he sat talking to a friend. She looked away a moment, and when she looked back he was gone, and a moment later she imagined him magically transported to that island he lived on, Faro, the place in the Baltic near Denmark, treeless and windswept, forlorn, the one place in the world where, he said, he felt safe. Years went by, her film career prospered, and she knew she would never meet Ingmar Bergman, let alone make a film with him. The one regret became part of her private personality, an invisible wound. It was her secret, which she shared with no one except Alec Malone. Her husband would not have understood. Invisible wounds were not in his inventory of useful patents. He had even less interest in enigma.

When Alec said he understood completely, that most everyone had something of the sort, Annalise smiled and said, Did it ruin your life?

Of course not, Alec said.

Bergman didn't ruin mine, either.

But it's there, isn't it?

Yes, she said. Yes, it is.

Annalise sipped her coffee and read the newspaper, news of Iraq and the unstable stock market; it seemed that many Americans were encouraged to buy houses for more money than they could afford to pay and now the payments were coming due. Surprise all around. Bergman had had a tax problem and exiled himself from Sweden, a move so painful that he suffered a nervous breakdown, and it was the Swedish government that apologized eventually. She dipped in and out of the newspaper all the while keeping an eye on the comings and goings in the café. Business was slack. In a far corner, at a table near a potted plant, someone was being interviewed. He did not look like an actor — more likely an athlete, a footballer or tennis star. He was talking and the reporter was transcribing every word, her pen racing across the pad. She had an avid look that Annalise recognized, having been interviewed often over the years, in the beginning milk-and-honey pieces in *Screen* and the other fan magazines. But as movies began to be taken more seriously the actors began to be taken more seriously too, and the questions became more pointed and intrusive from reporters who took themselves equally seriously. To Annalise the salient question was put delicately because in Hollywood it was seen as fundamentally insulting — and in Washington so insulting it would not be put at all, if the reporter wanted to remain on good terms with his source. But Annalise did not take reporters seriously, so when she answered it was often with a wisecrack or a confounding and unhelpful Darned if I know. The question was a variation on the following: Do you think you would have gone farther if you had been more ambitious? Fought a little harder? Demanded more? Did your temperament hold you back? Onscreen it seemed you were always out of range of the brightest lights. Everyone predicted great things — and here there were references to reviews in the national newspapers and newsmagazines — but the great things never quite materialized. One Oscar nomination. One Golden Globe. Or have I got the wrong end of the stick?

And that was when Annalise replied with her easy smile, Darned if I know. Had she felt inclined to enlighten her interviewer, so svelte, so British, leaning forward in her chair, her pen beating a little tattoo on the blank page of her notebook, her expression professionally sympathetic (she had aspirations in the business herself, it was obvious, and thought she might hear something of value, some insight that she might put to her own use somewhere down the line), Annalise would have added:

The perfect performance does not exist. For a few moments an actor could hold fire in her hands. But her fingers would open and the fire turn to embers. The audience might not be aware. The moment was fleeting. And there were so many externals, the lighting, the dimensions of the frame and what occupies the frame. The pentimento of the frame. It's an enigma, you see.

I have had an extremely enjoyable life in the movies.

I liked the work. The work liked me.

The camera liked me. I have made a very good living.

Perhaps there could have been more. But it is as likely that there would have been much less.

Had my temperament not, as you said, held me back.

Now scram.

Still — she thought of this as she watched a flutist attempting to coax a cobra from a wicker basket, tourists gathered on the sidewalk — there were things that might have been done differently. Her given name was Judy Jones, but when the studio put her under contract her agent insisted she change it. Her looks were so unusual that he thought something European was apt, so he suggested Annalise Amiral and she agreed at once, not without misgivings. An unwholesome precedent, she thought. If you surrendered your name so easily, what else would you surrender? Yet wasn't it all make-believe? You played a made-up character in a made-up story, the product of a dozen typewriters. What difference if your name was made up also? Later on, when the Renée Zellwegers and Parker Poseys came along, she realized she should have objected. She should have pushed back. Pushing back gave you respect. Pushing back signaled that you were one tough customer, not to be trifled with or condescended to. And she knew her agent's reply: in the history of the motion picture industry there has never been a star called Judy except for Garland, and that's very bad luck. She also knew in her heart that she wasn't an especially tough customer. She was Judy Jones from Winnetka, high school cheerleader, president of the drama club, field hockey captain, backstroke champion — and the stands surrounding the pool were near full at the girls' meets because that Jones girl looked superb in a tank suit. She was an adored only child. Her mother was a buyer of women's fashions at Marshall Field's. Her father was a popular congressman, a moderate Republican, no stranger to compromise; for that and for other reasons he drank more than was good for him and died at fifty-five after ten terms in the House of Representatives. Judah Jones objected to the agent-supplied nom de théâtre — for crissakes, Judy, you don't look any more European than I do — but never failed to come to the opening of her films, no matter the city. He was tall and broad, so tall and broad that when she was a little girl and walked with him she could not see his head when she looked up, only his long arms leading to his shoulders. His voice, a congressional tenor, seemed to come from the heavens. Her mother remarried a year after his death, but by then Annalise was living in Los Angeles. She did not care for the man her mother married, a property developer with houses in Florida and Phoenix. Her mother took up golf and quit her job with Field's. So they grew apart.

When Annalise was with the young Chicago couple in Agadir she mentioned her father, asking if they had met him in their political work. No, they hadn't. Republican, wasn't he? Yes, she said, he was, and mentioned his committees. An apologetic smile: We're Democrats. As if that mattered.

The flutist had managed to charm the cobra to the edge of the basket, its head swaying drunkenly to the music. The half-dozen tourists took a collective step back. Annalise thought the poor creature looked exhausted, as if it had been roused from a siesta. On cue it collapsed again into the basket. The flutist gave a little push with his shoe, nudging the basket an inch or two. He produced a long single note from the flute, evidently the signal to dance, but he was unsuccessful. The cobra continued to lay doggo. The tourists waited a minute more before moving off to the next sidewalk entertainment. One of the women dropped a copper coin into the purse next to the basket and the flutist frowned, most disappointed.

Annalise paid her bill and rose. Her cognac sat where the waiter had put it, untouched. In the corner the reporter was talking into a cell phone. The athlete had disappeared. She thought she had made a mistake remaining in Morocco. She knew no one in Morocco; all the old crowd had moved away. Many were dead. That was a part of her life that was amusing to look back on — hilarious, really, everyone so footloose and ardent, unafraid. Tangier was a parallel universe with its own language and code of conduct. Now they call it living in the moment. But where else were you supposed to live? And when you had had enough you went back to the other. Annalise left the American newspaper on the table after one last glance at hypnotic Ingmar Bergman. He had seduced all those others and surely he would have seduced her, too; and if he didn't, she would have done the honors. But there would have been no children because she was badly wired. Probably that would have been a disappointment to him.

She walked into the street. The snake charmer was gone. A breeze had come up and blew dust in her face. She felt the heat of the desert. Annalise thought the buildings were shabbier than they were those many years ago. The interiors were still closed to the street, and now and again there was movement behind the latticed windows; that was where the women watched after things. The glare of the sun on the whitewashed stone caused her to avert her eyes. Tangier, so exotic and febrile then, was just another rundown North African seaport, not much coming in, even less going out. In the street nothing moved except dust. The cafés were empty. She stepped into the store on the corner to look at jewelry, bracelets and rings, brightly colored pins. The proprietor rose heavily to his feet and offered to open the case, so many exceptional values at reasonable prices, authentic Moroccan craftsmanship. Please, madame, to try on whatever pleases you. I give you tourist discount. So Annalise bought a bracelet, a souvenir of a Thursday morning in Tangier.

When she returned to her room at the hotel on the port she found a message from Alec, his voice subdued, long pauses between thoughts. Annalise stood at the open window and watched the boats turn at anchor while she listened to Alec.

His father had passed away on Tuesday night, an unquiet death. Alec and the nurse were with him but he was not aware of that. His eyes were wide open and filled with terror. He did not speak but raised his hands as if to ward off an intruder. Alec apologized for telling her this but he had no one else to tell it to and felt the need to describe the old man's last minutes. Hours, actually. Whoever said "Do not go gentle into that good night" didn't know what he was talking about. After a long pause, so long that Annalise thought that he had rung off, Alec said that his father made a cry deep in his throat, then he closed his eyes and after a convulsion he died. The nurse was in tears because she was so fond of him. The funeral would be Friday, family only, meaning just him and Mathilde. Mathilde was arriving from London on Thursday. He had tried to get the Senate chaplain to officiate but the chaplain was vacationing in the Ozarks or the Poconos or somewhere and was unavailable, and the task now was to find a clergyman who could say a few words at the grave. Alec had no idea where such a man would be found. He planned a memorial service for the early fall when the Senate resumed session. Music, a dozen or more eulogies.

Alec went on about plans for the memorial service. Annalise thought he sounded disoriented, his voice unsettled; at the same time his tone was flat, as if he were reading from a prepared text. She continued to watch the boats turn lazily at anchor. A beautiful yacht was moored in the inner harbor, sixty feet long at least, flying an Italian flag aft. A steward, immaculate in white, served drinks in long glasses to three girls sunning themselves on the foredeck. When the girls raised their hands to receive the drinks, their arms curved like swans' necks. The steward carefully placed a long glass in each hand and backed away, a priest at the altar. Annalise remembered a midnight sail from Tangier that began well but ended badly, unpleasantness from one of the older men who had drunk too much and thought he was owed something because it was his boat, his liquor, his hash. Eventually he fell asleep and she and her friend Susanna sailed the yacht back into harbor as dawn broke, the surface of the water a vivid pink. That was when she knew her time was up in Morocco. The parallel universe lost its allure when the sea turned pink. The next day she packed her bags and flew off to Madrid and then Chicago and not long after that to Los Angeles, where her agent had arranged for a car and driver to take her from the airport to the studio, where a contract awaited her signature, Annalise Amiral.

The old man put up a mighty struggle, Alec said.

He didn't want to give it up.

Did I mention the obituaries? They were respectful, without errors so far as he could tell. All the facts were in order, trees concealing the forest. The obits spoke of the senator as an inside man, more a figure of the cloakroom than of the floor. Friend of presidents, FDR, Truman, JFK, Johnson. LBJ once said that Kim Malone was a better raconteur than he was. Untrue but a generous remark. One of the papers mentioned the bitter 1968 campaign when there were allegations of dirty tricks. The allegations were never proved, though they were widely believed. Alec said, It's disorienting to read an account of your father's public life summed up in a thousand words. They called me for quotes and anecdotes but I couldn't remember a damned thing. My mind went blank. You must have felt the same thing when your father died and you read the notices.

No kidding, Annalise said aloud.

She continued to watch the yacht with the Italian flag, much commotion along the rails. A deckhand slipped the anchor chain, the mainsail rose, and the yacht was abruptly under way. Flat on their backs the girls watched the sail billow. They toasted the sail with their long glasses. On the fantail two men played cards and did not give the sail so much as a glance. Annalise watched the boat exit the outer harbor and gather speed, its sails full. It was bound east through the Strait of Gibraltar and then — probably Marbella for a few days before continuing along the Spanish coast and into the Mediterranean, to Capri or wherever the boat was berthed. Well, it could be bound anywhere. Annalise remembered that her father's obit contained a sneaky sentence in which he was described as a most convivial after-hours House colleague. Everyone knew what that meant.

I'm tired, Alec said finally. I'm tired in my bones. As tired as I've ever been in my life. After the funeral I'm taking a week in Maine, two weeks if I want it. I've rented a house, and the house comes with a boat. Annalise raised her eyebrows at that, watching the Italian yacht bend into the breeze. The men were still playing cards but the girls were watching the water fly by. I'll be out of touch for a while, Alec said. I'll call you in Los Angeles. Thanks for your ear, darling. Then he rang off.

Annalise watched the yacht a few minutes more, then went to the telephone to call the airline to book her on the first available aircraft to New York via anywhere — Casablanca, Madrid, Paris, London. She'd wait a day to call Alec, to see if he wanted company in Maine. She had no plans and she hadn't been to Maine in years and years. Maine would be the opposite of Morocco.

The grave was on the downslope of the cemetery, within sight of Rock Creek Parkway. Alec had placed the urn on a green baize cloth and now waited patiently for Mathilde, making small talk with the Baptist minister recruited for the occasion. The day was warm and threatening rain but the Reverend Willis appeared cool and composed in his heavy black suit and shiny white shirt, bow tie. Alec thought it was strange that his father, always surrounded by people, feeding off them, had at this last moment only his son and a stranger. Alec explained that his was a small family. His parents had no brothers or sisters. He was an only child and his daughter was an only child. Such situations often ran in families, a combination of genes and attitude. Mathilde was in her forties but unmarried and likely to remain unmarried. She was extremely attractive and had a fine job with the State Department. She was said to be an able diplomat, good with languages, good with her counterparts. She took the Foreign Service exam and her grandfather saw to it that she would be accepted and receive a good assignment — a clear case of senatorial interference, but it worked out very well all the way around. You couldn't do that today. There'd be a leak to the newspapers and all hell would break loose, a scandal. Mathilde's had, I don't know, three or four serious boyfriends but marriage was never in the cards for her. She told me that once in just those words, but did not explain why, or whatever explanation she gave was not convincing. They were nice boys, too. One was English and the others American. Still, I think she has had good fortune in her life. She's close to her mother, closer than she is to me, but they both live in Europe so that's logical. Mathilde travels a lot for her work, which she loves and is good at. Alec was conscious of talking too much, speaking on automatic pilot, saying whatever came into his head.

She told me she thought marriage was a kind of trap.

She liked men but she also liked her own company.

I suppose she's what you would call a modern woman.

Do you have children, Reverend Willis?

I have five children, he said. Boys, he added with a brief smile to indicate that he would say nothing further.

The Reverend Willis was a middle-aged black man with a stoop, watery eyes, and a sympathetic smile. He listened politely but said little, his reserve suggesting a family retainer whose personal life would remain forever mysterious. Alec said he envied him his boys, always a handful but insurance that his line would continue. Alec's family name would die with him. Hell of a thing, isn't it, a family name disappearing like one of those remote stars that burn up, never to be seen again. Alec reached down to brush leaves from the surface of his mother's gravestone. Many of the nearby graves looked to be untended and unvisited like his mother's. He thought of the cemetery as an enormous battlefield, the dead scattered helter-skelter: he and the Reverend Willis were the only survivors. Black clouds gathered in the west and in a moment the distant shudder of thunder. Alec wished Mathilde would show up. She had left at nine on some errand and promised to meet him at the gravesite at eleven. Now the time was eleven-thirty. Alec said, The name Malone used to mean something in our state but it's mostly forgotten now except in political circles. The local paper gave my father a fine obit with a picture and a two-column headline below the fold on page one. Someone called me yesterday, a condolence call, and said they were surprised that he was being buried here instead of the state. But my father and mother were Washingtonians. They were from the state but they lived here, and Washington was where they wanted to stay. Back home was where the voters were. This was where politics was. Their life was here, you see. They loved Washington, both of them. It's a personal thing. The father of a friend of mine was a ten-term congressman from Illinois. Died too young. But they took him right back to Winnetka for burial. Maybe that's the difference between the Senate and the House.

I don't know where Mathilde is, Alec said.

We'll give her another few minutes if that's all right with you, Reverend.

The Reverend Willis said of course and looked at his watch. He held his Bible in both hands against his stomach.

She's often late, Alec said. She gets that from me.

Will anyone want to speak? the reverend asked.

I don't, Alec said. I'll ask Mathilde if she wants to.

I'll only read the one psalm then, the reverend said. If that's all right.

Yes, that's what I want.

And I will put the urn in the grave and, if you and your daughter wish, you can cover it yourselves. They've provided a shovel.

Yes, that's fine.

Later on today the cemetery personnel will smooth it over.

Yes, good.

The Reverend Willis looked over Alec's shoulder and smiled. Hello, Alec.

When he turned he saw Mathilde and Lucia, both dressed in black and carrying bouquets in their arms. Alec had not seen Lucia in years and did not expect to see her now. He had not recognized her voice. Mathilde was wearing a hat and veil; he had never seen her in a hat and thought it added years to her appearance. Lucia put out her hand, he took it, and they shook hands formally, as if they had just then been introduced. She said, I'm sorry, Alec. I know how close you were.

Mama wanted to come, Mathilde said.

Well, fine, Alec said.

I wanted to say goodbye to him, Lucia said. I remember his funny stories and his hats, the fedora in the fall, winter, and spring, and the straw boater in the summer. His seasonal hats.

Mathilde kissed her father. She said, We got lost trying to find the grave.

I hope he had an easy time of it, Lucia said.

He didn't, Alec said. Then Alec introduced Mathilde and Lucia to the Reverend Willis, and when that was done he said, Let's get started.

They moved close to the urn and the mound of dirt next to it. Lucia and Mathilde placed their bouquets to either side of the urn, a sudden splash of color. Rain began softly and Lucia opened an umbrella; she and Mathilde stood close together. Alec thought they looked like sisters. The Reverend Willis spoke beautifully and the service was completed in under two minutes. Alec explained about the shovel and they all threw in a ration of dirt. The Reverend Willis said a few more words and wished them Godspeed. Alec handed him an envelope and he moved off slowly through the gravestones to his car, parked somewhere over the hill in Georgetown. The rain eased off, only a few drops now at intervals. Alec stood alone looking at the grave and his mother's headstone next to it. She had had a church service and more than two hundred people were present at the graveside, the Senate chaplain speaking at length, a psalm, a brief eulogy, and another psalm. Halfway through it his father began to cry silently, great tears spilling from his eyes. Alec took one arm and Eliot Bergruen the other and he remembered now that his father seemed to sag, near collapse, and then he gathered himself and pulled the brim of his fedora over his forehead so that no one could see his tears, and he remained with his head down until the chaplain had completed the last psalm and the coffin began its slow descent into the ground, whereupon he looked away, up the hill. God, it was cold that day, snow in the air, everyone in mufflers. The chaplain went on and on about Gawd, Gawd this and Gawd that, Gawd's grace, Gawd's mercy, Gawd everlasting, his plains accent as flat as a drum. The chaplain had the voice of a senator, of a timbre commonly called sonorous but still flat as a drum. After the service the old man went home and poured himself a double Scotch, drank it off, and made another. That was twenty years ago. Alec was suddenly lightheaded and placed his hand on his mother's headstone to steady himself. He closed his eyes, thinking that the service had been too brief. The old man deserved more. But of course in the autumn would come the memorial service, all the ceremony anyone could want.

Alec?

He thought of Maine and the boat that went with the house. He reckoned about eleven hours door to door, and he had no reason not to start tonight except he didn't have the energy for an eleven-hour drive. And it would be good to have a quiet meal with Mathilde. At least this was over with and the Baptist had done exactly what he was asked to do, done it correctly and with formality. But what was Lucia doing here? He had no idea she was in the country or knew anything of the old man's death.

Alec?

When he raised his eyes he saw the Reverend Willis pause to catch his breath, then resume his slow pace until he was over the hill and lost to view. The moment of vertigo passed but Alec remained with his hand on his mother's headstone, the marble gritty on his fingers. He became aware of the thick silence behind him.

Lucia said, Are you all right, Alec?

Yes, he said. I'm fine.

A beautiful service, she said.

Reverend Willis has a wonderful voice, Mathilde said. I bet if you asked him he would have sung a hymn.

Yes, Alec said. He did very well.

Where did you find him? Mathilde asked.

He came recommended, Alec said.

I'm sorry we were late, Lucia said. We lost our way —

It's all right. No harm done. Alec noticed two young men in blue overalls standing under the big oak on the hillside, evidently the Reverend Willis's cemetery personnel preparing to tidy up. There was no reason for him to stay but he was not yet ready to leave. However, he did not wish to witness the tidying up.

Mama has an idea, Mathilde said. She wants to take us to lunch.

Only if you want to, Alec.

The new place on Connecticut Avenue, Mathilde said.

What place is that? Alec said.

It's quiet, Alec. French.

French restaurants are never quiet, Alec said.

This one is, Mathilde said.

All right, Alec said. Just give me a minute.

The two women walked off arm in arm and Alec remained. He thought he would say a few last words but no words came to him. He thought that his father had led a fine life, spoiled only marginally by his struggle at the end. Lord knows he did fight and that was a surprise because he was no friend of lost causes. "Show me a lost cause and I'll show you a loser." He won nine terms in the Senate either because of or in spite of his view of lost causes. Alec bowed his head a moment, then looked across to the workers waiting patiently under the big oak. He gave them a signal and they collected their tools and advanced down the hill with their wheelbarrow.

Mathilde and Lucia were watching him from under the umbrella, causing him to reflect again how much they looked like affectionate sisters, arm in arm, their heads almost touching. They walked away in slow steps up the path. Lucia's limp seemed more pronounced. When they were married Alec found the limp sexy. Her left leg was a mess, long vertical scars, the knee shapeless. That was sexy, too. Looking at her it was easy to imagine her splayed on the mountain, her limbs every which way. Easy to imagine her pain and her helplessness, her ski cap gone, her hair in her eyes and damp from snow. But no such thoughts came to him now.

The restaurant was not crowded. The maitre d' showed them to a table next to a window in the rear. Alec and Mathilde declined drinks and Lucia ordered a bottle of Sancerre. Mathilde began to talk about the Iraq War and the administration's hostility to diplomacy. Diplomacy was a sign of weakness. Not that diplomacy would solve much; the war was a tragedy brought about by hubris, ignorance, and carelessness. Events were in the saddle. Whirl was king. Perhaps diplomacy was useful at the margins but the consequences of the war would be terrible and affect everyone. These consequences could not be avoided. No one could say this out loud, Mathilde said. To say it was to suggest that nothing could be done and that the situation was hopeless and in the hands of the Fates. The Fates were indifferent. They played no favorites owing to their affinity for chaos. The Republicans were terrible and the Democrats not much better with their platitudes about benchmarks and deadlines. The Fates had no interest in benchmarks and deadlines. So if you are trained as a diplomat, spend your life at it, you feel like a fool. You're wearing white gloves and a flowered hat in a garbage dump. Still, you do what you can. I've had some contact with the Iranians but I'm not allowed to talk about that.

A zone of silence settled over the table. A light rain fell outside. Neither Alec nor Lucia wanted to discuss the war even though their daughter was, as they heard now, somehow involved. Alec could think of nothing to say to her.

After a long pause he said, Be careful.

It's not dangerous, Papa.

Be careful anyhow, Alec said.

Listen to your father, Lucia said.

It's just a thought, Mathilde.

You're infantilizing me, Mathilde said. I never should have said anything. It's always a mistake with you two.

Alec was watching a smoker lean against a lamppost and light up. It had been years since he had had a cigarette but he wished he had one now. But society had infantilized cigarette smokers, irresponsible hedonists threatening their own health and the health of others. This smoker seemed content enough despite sharp looks from passersby.

He said, Where are you living, Lucia?

We've left Zurich. Nikolas wanted to and I agreed. Now we have a house in Prague and a small apartment in Berlin. But we are spending more and more time in Berlin because the mood in Prague is foul. I suppose the word is "flat." Nikolas believed that

Zurich had lost its savor also, and this is why we moved to Prague. I do not think it is wise to move house when you are of a certain age. But it is certainly true that in Prague the oxygen became thin. It was as if we were living high on a mountaintop somewhere. The snap went out of things, do you know what I mean? There is greed and materialism in Prague and it is not good for Nikolas's work. Also, it is not good for sales.

I can imagine, Alec said.

Berlin is quite exciting.

It is?

Yes. It is avant-garde. Of course there is materialism in Berlin also.

The one often follows the other, Alec said.

Did you read Nikolas's last novel, Papa?

No, I'm afraid not.

I gave it to you for Christmas, remember?

Yes. I never got around to it.

It was very good, Mathilde said. A generational novel set in Poland. The father is an old socialist and his son is an entrepreneur. He imports Japanese wristwatches into Kraków. Makes a fortune. The son bribes people in the government. So there's a natural conflict between the old values and the new.

Yes, I can see that.

It's a sort of natural history of the new Europe, Mathilde said.

And about time, Alec said.

I don't see why you have to be sarcastic about it, Papa.

Nikolas wants to come back to Washington, Lucia said.

Alec looked at her blankly. Why would he want to do that?

I don't know if I want to but he does. Nikolas says Washington is where the tension is. He thinks America is beyond Rome in its decline, overextended, a debtor nation, its resources exhausted. It no longer controls the capital markets. Nikolas specializes in declining civilizations. He believes that only a European can write successfully of the American situation, its pathos, its inner contradictions, its strife. It's the European who has the authority to make such assessments, given our direct experience of the burden of the previous century. It's history from the point of view of the victims. However, Nikolas rejects the idea that the CIA controls American politics as the KGB controls the Russian. The Russian situation is a different matter entirely, a Slav thing. Nikolas has thought it through, you see. And he believes it's necessary for him to assess the American crisis firsthand. He loves America, actually. He particularly wants to visit Chicago.

Alec nodded sympathetically while he looked out the window at the middle-aged smoker, who took a last drag and flipped the cigarette Bogart-fashion into the street and strolled off. The sprinkles had ceased, and the sun shined dimly. Alec wondered how you would go about photographing a civilization in decline, choosing the correct subjects and the milieu and how the light fell. Not the whore in the gutter or the banker lighting a cigar with a hundred-dollar bill. What? Beckmann, Kirchner, and Grosz did a beautiful job with Weimar but they were artists. Alec was uncertain how to classify Beckmann's self-portrait in a tuxedo, decadent or not decadent. The face was not a decadent face but the truculent posture showed signs of incipient corruption; and then, thinking it through, Alec decided that the self-portrait revealed a glum satisfaction on the part of the artist and they were of course the same person, another thing surely. Contemporary American artists did not seem much interested in decline. Warhol would be an exception, though Warhol's work always came with a wink. Drawing his swine-faced men and feral gap-toothed women, George Grosz would slit his throat before he'd wink at his subjects or his audience. Winks were not in George Grosz's repertoire or Beckmann's or Kirchner's. Perhaps Bacon or Hockney, but they were British to the spine. Perhaps contemporary artists had too much invested in the decline. They would be ungrateful, perhaps naive, to bite the hands that fed them except in ironic ways that could be disowned later or laughed at. Sincerity was not in their repertoire either. Irony ruled. It would be difficult for them to look at the subject expressively and paint the results with sincerity, meaning savagely or with pity. Of the photographers Alec was even less certain. He himself had never thought of decline as a subject.

Lucia said, Nikolas has concluded that people do not believe in fiction. They do not have the time for it. They are impatient with it. They read fiction as a form of the author's autobiography. He is wondering if a new form must be invented.

Alec did not hear Lucia. He continued to look out the window at the quiet street and ponder decline. Weegee was dead. Diane Arbus was dead. Alec faltered there. The superb Walker Evans was dead, but Evans was always more interested in resilience than decline. Some of the *Vogue* photographers would qualify, all those dark portraits of louche women in dishabille. Fashion photography generally offered splendid opportunities but the results did not approach Beckmann, Kirchner, and Grosz, and Otto Dix also, even Man Ray and his sleek-bodied blank-faced nudes. "Decline" would not be the word for Steichen or Karsh. Alec reflected that decline had never much figured in his own work and wondered if his long-ago missed opportunity to photograph Vietnam was the reason, or anyway one reason, since there was always more than one reason for choosing one project instead of another. He certainly had plenty of time on his hands if he wanted to take it up now, although there was every possibility that through-thinking Nikolas was correct that only a European could do the subject justice owing to direct experience of the horrors of the previous century. Alec watched a cat slink from the alley next door and scoot across the street, tail high.

He's in a reverie again, Mathilde said.

He never changes, Lucia said.

The first time I noticed I was five, six years old.

Reminds me of the old days, too.

It's weird. But no harm done.

No, I never thought it was harmful.

Disconcerting?

Most disconcerting, Lucia said. Whenever I asked him where he was when he went away like that, I always got a false answer.

How did you know it was false, Mama?

I don't know. I knew.

The waiter arrived with the wine and made a show of pulling the cork and pouring a splash for Alec, who looked up with a start. He nodded at Lucia; hers to taste. Lucia sipped, said the wine was fine, and in a moment the three glasses were full and the wine bottle was in its bucket. They listened while the waiter recited the specials of the day, then stood with his pad, pencil poised. We will order in ten minutes, Lucia said, and the waiter went away.

What were you thinking of, Alec?

When?

Just now, looking out the window.

I was watching a smoker and thinking how much I'd enjoy a cigarette about now.

You haven't smoked in years, Mathilde said.

That's why, Alec replied.

Anyway, Lucia said with a smile, that's enough about Nikolas.

Perspective, Mathilde said. The European angle of vision.

I'm sure he's on to something there, Alec said.

Nikolas is exceptionally hard-working, Mathilde said.

That's what it takes all right.

He's published twenty books, Mathilde said.

Say a prayer for the forests of Canada, Alec said. He swallowed some wine and said to Lucia, Does your leg still give you trouble?

No more than usual. They want to do another operation since the first one was botched, they say. I don't know about it, though. I don't know if it's worth it at my age. But they tell me I'll be able to ski again without it hurting all the time.

That's something, Alec said.

Not enough, Lucia said. But thank you for asking.

I noticed your limp, he said. It seemed a little worse.

I go back and forth on the operation. One day I think I'll do it, next day I won't. Today is one of the won't days. Tomorrow I'll say what a great thing it would be to ski again without it hurting all the time. What do you think?

I don't know, he said.

No, really. Nikolas is against it.

I never liked any sport well enough to get cut for it.

Sailing?

You don't need to get cut to sail. Anybody can sail.

So you still do.

Not much, he said, neglecting to add that he did not see well enough to sail. Bad enough driving a car. Alec imagined closing his good eye during a regatta and seeing half a dozen Munch-boats coming at him and commencing a reverie about the Norwegian forests and piling into a pier.

Why are you smiling, Alec?

I like the wine, he said.

If I may ask. What are you going to do now?

Nothing new. What I've always done.

No trips?

I'm leaving for Maine tomorrow.

An assignment?

No. There are fewer and fewer of those each year. I get older, the magazines downsize or go out of business. I mostly photograph for my own pleasure.

You always did, Alec.

Not always, he said.

Mathilde drove me by your house this morning. It hasn't changed much, at least from the outside. The dry cleaner is still on the corner. The Alhambra's the same, too, at least the façade is. Lucia turned to Mathilde and remarked that the house was much smaller than she remembered it. Alec ceased to listen because of the commotion at a table in the corner of the room, the one that promised privacy. A very old man was struggling to his feet assisted by a gray-haired woman and the waiter. Upright at last, he swayed a moment then ambled from the restaurant, much stooped, the woman at his side. He turned at the door and Alec got a clear look at him, the secretary of defense of so long ago. Alec remembered Lucia's mischievous wave and the secretary's answering smile. It was said that when he departed from his post at last, neither he nor Lyndon Johnson could say for certain whether he had resigned or was fired. Kim Malone called it a true Washington whodunit. Those years were laden with mysteries.

Then the waiter was at their table with omelets for Lucia and Mathilde and steak-frites for Alec. Alec asked the waiter for a glass of red Bordeaux and listened to Lucia and Mathilde talk about the changes in Georgetown, fancier cars on the street, showier people on the sidewalk. And the dress shop on Wisconsin Avenue, still there, Alec. Where I bought my dress for the party at the d'Ans', the first time we were invited. I was so excited.

Where was I? Mathilde asked.

Not born, Alec said.

She was too. I remember the babysitter.

Yes, the nosy Russian woman, Mathilde said.

She was observant, Alec said. Through the window he watched the former secretary of defense cross the street, walking arm in arm with the gray-haired woman. Alec wondered if he thought often of those days when he was a prince of the city; now he was a former prince with a mournful countenance. Alec said, Where are you staying, Lucia?

Who is that man in the street, Alec?

Nobody you know, Alec said.

Lucia shrugged. I'm staying with Gretta. She lives at the Watergate. Since Charlie died. I couldn't be more surprised. I thought she'd return to Sweden where her family is. I've visited her several times over the years. Gretta's a different person in Sweden. Of course — a bright laugh from Lucia — she's older now and not so much of a hell-raiser. She did love Swedish men. She said that once she came to know Washington she liked it. Gretta always took a month each year in Sweden, though. You were a puzzle to her, Alec.

I was?

Yes.

Alec did not inquire further. He bent to his steak-frites, perfectly cooked. The meal could only be better with a glass of red wine, which at that moment arrived in the hand of the waiter. Lucia and Mathilde began to talk about the State Department. Mathilde said she was afraid she had made a religion of work. She worked all the time. She had no social life to speak of. Of course she enjoyed the work, otherwise she wouldn't do it, but she had the feeling also that she was missing out. Because she was unmarried and footloose they gave her traveling assignments. She loved the pace and the variety. She was good at what she did. She knew there was a reward at the end of the line, a small embassy somewhere, she hoped not too small. Not Africa, unless it was North Africa or South Africa. Probably she was too old for a family but she wouldn't mind a permanent man in her life, and he would have to be a very special character to put up with her odd hours and traveling. Whoever he was, she hadn't met him yet. Mathilde lowered her voice, speaking directly to her mother, Lucia nodding in agreement with whatever her daughter was telling her. Something in Mathilde's tone and bearing reminded Alec of his father. He saw Mathilde touch her mother's elbow, something his father habitually did when he had a secret to impart. But all she said was something about her fitness routine, a long jog in the morning, the gym whenever she could fit it in. That made Alec smile, thinking of Mathilde and her grandfather. She had no idea how much she owed the old man.

Alec?

He would never again make the trip to the hospital as he had done once or twice a week for five years. He would never again visit the cemetery with the effigy of the Confederate infantryman, young Timothy Smith. The journey had become the organizing principle of his life and now it was gone. In a few days he would be in Maine and in a few weeks back in Washington, unless he and Annalise went somewhere. His calendar was blank. He wouldn't mind a vacation abroad if Annalise would go with him. He didn't feel like working, though. Alec decided that when they finished lunch he would walk back to Rock Creek Park and stop at his father's grave, say whatever words came to him. He was suddenly very tired. His arms felt as heavy as anvils. He had barely touched his wine.

Alec looked up when Lucia said something to him.

I wonder if I can ask you a favor, Alec.

If I can, he said. Depending. He tried to keep his voice free of suspicion but suspected that he failed.

Lucia gave a little pro forma laugh and said she had a confession. She had not come to Washington for Kim Malone's funeral. She had arrived three days ago on another mission altogether. Most unexpected, most unsettling.

Yes, Alec said.

My father is here, Lucia said.

Living in Washington, Mathilde said.

Where is he living? Alec asked.

It's a kind of retirement home, Lucia said. Way out northwest.

He sent word to Mama, Mathilde said. He wants to see her.

I have no idea how he knew my address, Lucia said. I mean where Nikolas and I live in Prague. The letter came out of the blue, unfamiliar handwriting. I can't imagine why he's here of all places. My father never had anything to do with Americans or Washington. All these years I've believed he was dead. My mother assured me. She was quite positive about it. Lucia poured some Sancerre into her glass, her hand trembling when she brought the glass to her mouth and swallowed. She looked bleakly at Mathilde. The pale light of the afternoon sun touched her face in such a way as to highlight the freckles that had faded with age. Quite suddenly she looked years older. If Alec had passed her on the street he would not have recognized her.

Mama's upset, Mathilde said.

How do you want me to help, Alec said.

I want you to go with me when I meet him.

Please, Papa, Mathilde said.

I don't want to see him but I feel I must, Lucia said. His letter was courteous but abrupt. He said he wanted to see me and that I could come any time, he wasn't going anywhere. He gave me his address and a telephone number and said he would expect my call. All these years, now this, out of the blue. I don't know what he wants of me but he wants something. Money, a reconciliation, a jolly chat about how cute I was when I was three years old. That was the last time we saw each other. I don't know what he looks like. I don't know what he'll say or do.

It's important, Papa.

He's very old, you know. He and my mother married when they were teenagers. Or he was a teenager. My mother was a little older. My father has been missing for — I suppose it's near seventy years. I have no idea how he's lived or where. I have no idea what this is about or why he's here of all places. But when I got his letter I had to come. Nikolas was against it.

Why was that? Alec asked.

He didn't see what could be gained. But the point isn't gaining or losing. The point is getting it over with. I have no idea what sort of home it is. I have an address and a telephone number. That's all. I know it's a lot to ask of you today.

Please, Papa, Mathilde said.

All right, Alec said. When do you want to do this?

I want to do it now, this afternoon.

Now? He thought of his father, the visit he had planned, the words he intended to say at the old man's grave.

I don't want to wait. I want to get it over with.

Surely you understand, Papa.

Alec looked over Lucia's shoulder to the street outside, deserted, no pedestrians, no traffic. The washed-out sun cast no shadows. Alec thought the street as blank as the pages in his calendar, the current page and all the pages that came after. He had much to look forward to because the long-nosed man had come and gone. He had no obligations, nothing to detain him. Still, the city looked as if it had gone into hibernation. Alec took a swallow of wine and his great weariness seemed to lift. He had always been curious about Andre Duran, the ghost at Lucia's elbow. Alec was aware of the silence at the table. He gave Lucia a considered look and said at last, All right. I'll go with you.

The waiter arrived with the bill and Lucia put a credit card on it without looking at the total. When the waiter went away she put her hand on Alec's and left it there. She said, I don't know anything about him. I don't know what he wants. I feel I need protection.

ANDRE

THEY SAID GOODBYE to Mathilde on the sidewalk under the washed-out sun. She had an appointment at the State Department with her boss and his deputy, unusual for a Saturday afternoon. They were coming in from their homes in the suburbs specifically to discuss the Iran mess, to see Mathilde and learn what she had picked up during her recent rendezvous in Paris. Mathilde smiled apologetically. She really, truly wanted to meet her grandfather but her duty called. Alec listened to this with a sunny smile. His daughter reminded him of his father, always tending to the public's business, scurrying off on weekends to his Senate office for urgent meetings with briefcase-bearing officials, Harry Hopkins or Cordell Hull, and later with Dulles or Herter, and later still with Rusk or Mac Bundy, returning home mildly befuddled and smelling of whiskey. The talks were always urgent. During the Nixon drought he continued to go to his Senate office on Saturday afternoons although he never described the meetings as urgent. Whiskey was involved, however.

Isn't she wonderful? Lucia said when Mathilde ran off to hail a cab.

Superb, Alec said. No question.

Always so full of pep, Lucia said.

A dynamo, Alec said.

She thinks she might get an embassy next year.

Which one?

She doesn't know. I think she wants Czech Republic or Hungary. Anyhow some country in central Europe. She wants a country that's struggling with its identity and national purpose. She believes the U.S. has a role to play in those situations. I wanted her to try for Switzerland but she wants no part of Switzerland. She says Switzerland's reserved for political appointments. Moneybags, she calls them.

Wise child, Alec said.

Wouldn't it be wonderful, our daughter an ambassador?

It certainly would be. But she should have gone with us to see her grandfather.

I don't mind, Lucia said. She has work to do.

She might learn something about struggling nations.

I don't like it when you're insincere, Alec.

Alec looked at the address and directed Lucia out Massachusetts Avenue to Wisconsin, and up Wisconsin to Military Road. It's a few blocks from the intersection, he said. Traffic was heavy and their progress slow. Lucia was silent, lost in thought. The car was warm and Alec yawned, drowsy in the heat; he was unused to wine at lunch. He closed his eyes and wondered if Mathilde had a chance at an embassy. She was overdue for one, though the Czech Republic and Hungary were usually reserved for very senior diplomats or very brilliant younger ones. Well, for all he knew Mathilde was very brilliant. Dealing with the Iranians would be a challenging experience, as you would be obliged to deploy all the witchcraft of diplomacy. You would need a sense of prophecy also, what you would want at the end of it beyond the Iranians' crying uncle. Alec felt himself drift off, aware of the starts and stops, exhaust fumes in the air, not asleep but not awake either. His head was thick with wine, his stomach heavy with steak-frites. If everything went well between Lucia and her father there was no reason for him not to slip away, allow them some privacy. Alec opened his eyes then, aware that someone was speaking, asking him a question. He felt a light hand on his shoulder.

We're at the intersection, Alec.

Turn right, he said.

You fell asleep.

Wine at lunch, Alec said.

Are we almost there?

Turn right again, he said. It's the next block.

Lucia turned into the curb and stopped.

It's the next block, Alec said.

I know, I want to wait a moment. Collect myself.

Alec was silent, then grunted a laugh. Damnedest thing, he said. I've forgotten your father's name.

Andre, Lucia said, Andre Duran.

I remember the Duran part, Alec said.

I have no recollection of him at all, Lucia said. If he poked his head in the car this minute I'd have no idea who he was, I don't know why he's called, all these years. What does he want with me? She drummed her fingers on the steering wheel and stared straight ahead. What does he have in his mind?

They were parked in a residential neighborhood, large Victorian houses with detached garages, shade trees either side of the road. Alec did not know the neighborhood, and looking at it now he thought it belonged in a small town somewhere, Iowa or Indiana. Doctors and lawyers lived on the street. You could believe the prairie began beyond the next street, section after section of soybeans or corn. The houses were well maintained and several had old-fashioned TV antennas fixed to the chimneys. The sidewalks were empty. When Alec rolled down the window he heard swing music coming from one of the houses. He listened appreciatively for a moment, then realized it was sound-over for a commercial. He closed his eyes once more, waiting for Lucia.

He would be a little over ninety years old, she said.

I think we ought to get on with it, Alec said.

Give me just a minute.

I'm surprised your husband didn't come with you.

Nikolas was busy. A lecture in Budapest.

Even so, Alec said.

He has his work, Alec. Just as you used to.

Alec opened the car door and stepped out.

Where are you going? Lucia said, alarm in her voice.

Nowhere, Alec said. I need some air.

Lucia's hand went to her mouth. I thought you were fed up with me, she said, and decided to jump ship. Have done with all this.

I just need some air, Lucia.

I wouldn't blame you, she said.

Don't worry about it.

Thank you for helping me, she said.

Sure, Alec said. He looked up, focusing his bad eye on the telephone wires that split this way and that as he looked at them. Munch-lines, he thought of them, getting worse each time he checked. But his head was clearing and his stomach was settled nicely. He surveyed the street once more and checked his watch, three-thirty. In the big house on the corner an upstairs curtain moved, someone worried about strange cars in the neighborhood. He heard the bark of a dog.

I'm ready now, Alec.

Let's go, he said and got in the car.

They parked across the street from number 1007, a stone pile three stories high with a square-cut widow's walk with a railing on top. It was the house of a banker or a newspaper publisher, perhaps a merchant prince of the previous century or the century before that. The house looked to have eight or nine bedrooms at least — they had large families in those days — each bedroom window fitted with its own slatted shutters. Lucia said the house looked like something you might find in a suburb of Prague or Berlin, solid, built to last. The shutters were painted flat black. The widow's walk was white and even from a distance it was evident the structure was in bad repair, dangerous footing for a widow or anyone else who ventured there. Alec explained to Lucia that it was a design of the sort found in whaling villages like Edgartown or Nantucket, a place for the woman of the house to stand staring out to sea, expecting her absent captain from his voyage to the South Seas or the North Atlantic.

They'd be gone two, three years, he said. Often they didn't come home. That's why it's called a widow's walk.

But the sea isn't anywhere near Washington, Lucia said.

It's a decoration, he said. Either that or the merchant prince had it built for his wife, expecting her to wait there each evening for his return from the countinghouse downtown. A round of applause when he drove up in the Pierce-Arrow.

Please. What is a Pierce-Arrow?

Expensive car, Alec said.

Two giant oaks stood left and right of the sidewalk leading up to the porch steps and the front door. The covered porch ran around the front and sides of the house, a glider positioned to the right of the front door. Wisteria clung to the porch railing. No one was about. It took Alec a moment to notice the small sign on the front lawn. Grass had grown up around it. The sign read, in Gothic script, *Goya House*.

They walked slowly up the sidewalk and the steps leading to the porch. There was no bell to push or knocker to rap. He told Lucia to wait and he walked from one window to another, looking inside at a large room filled with chairs and a sofa and tables piled high with newspapers and magazines, many of them from abroad. When Alec turned the corner he stopped short and signaled Lucia to join him.

Alec said, I think that's your father.

He was dressed in dark slacks and a white tunic, leather sandals on his bare feet, smoking a cigarette in an ivory holder, the ivory stained brown by nicotine. He was seated in a rocking chair, gently moving back and forth while he smoked and watched a squirrel collect acorns on the lawn. Andre Duran — for it was indisputably him, his features a rough cut of Lucia's, his tight smile identical to his daughter's when she was in repose — did not acknowledge their presence. The resemblance ended there. He was built like a wrestler and looked like one, with his crew-cut iron-gray hair, gnarled forehead, and heavy hands and arms. For all that he presented an air of authority, some combination of civil and military rank, accustomed to issuing orders and having them obeyed. He looked younger than ninety years old, but that did not imply that his life had been easy. Alec noticed that the hand that held the cigarette holder was missing its little finger. Andre Duran had not heard them approach and Alec thought that odd until he saw the hearing aid in his ear. Behind him, Alec heard Lucia's quick intake of breath.

She stood in front of him and said, Hello, Papa.

He looked up sharply, annoyed at being disturbed. But his face softened at once and he said, Oh, Lucia. You've come to see me.

He took her hands, smiling broadly, and began what seemed to be a speech. He spoke in a deep voice that rose and fell with emotion. He was moving his hands up and down, her fingers disappearing into his fists. He talked on and on, all of it in Czech. His expressions went from high delight to despair and back again. Andre Duran was evidently telling a story, some version of his life, how he had lived his days, where all the years had gone, the places he had lived and how he had thought all this time of his daughter but was unable to communicate with her. The incomprehensible words flew by. Lucia moved once to interrupt him but he was having none of it, shaking his huge head and speaking in a kind of growl, struggling to condense and intensify his life's journey. All this time he was looking at Lucia as if she were some miraculous incarnation of a fairy princess, come to rescue him from his own memory. She opened her mouth to interrupt him again but he paid no attention. His eyes were far away, back somewhere in his youth or early middle age. He went on and on until at last he rapped his knuckles on the window, releasing her hands as he did so.

Papa, I don't speak Czech.

That can't be true, he said.

I did speak it. But I lost it after Mama died.

You speak no Czech?

Only a few words, she said.

I was saying how happy I am to see you.

I understood that, she said.

I have wanted to say those words for a very long time.

I understood that, too. We can speak German if you wish. Or French.

No German, he said dismissively. No French. His eyes moved sideways to make a quick glance at Alec, ignored these many minutes. Alec was not certain he had been noticed at all, so rapt was Andre Duran in his daughter.

This is Alec, Lucia said.

They shook hands, calluses on soft flesh.

Alec is Mathilde's father.

Who is Mathilde?

Your granddaughter, Papa.

He looked around him. Where is she? Is she here?

She had an appointment, Lucia said. She works for the State Department —

The American State Department?

— and she is there now for a meeting.

What meeting?

I don't know. A meeting of the sort diplomats have.

Is she talking about me?

You? No, not you. I think it has to do with the Iranians.

Andre considered that a moment and turned to rap once more on the window.

Please, he said. Sit.

There were wicker chairs at the far end of the porch. Alec fetched them and he and Lucia sat. Lucia began to speak of Mathilde, where she had gone to school and university and what she did for the State Department. Lucia spoke slowly so her father could fully understand. Mathilde had had postings in Europe and Africa and was now in the political section of the London embassy. She was hoping to be nominated ambassador next year. She wanted a central European country, Czech Republic or Hungary. But if not central Europe then farther east, one of the breakaway republics of the former Soviet Union.

And what is the attraction of these countries?

Mathilde calls them serious countries, Lucia said. They are countries struggling with their identity and national purpose and how they organize themselves, and in these circumstances America has a role to play, advising. How to write a constitution. How to organize a judiciary. Formulate a foreign policy. Control the military. She looked to Alec for help but Alec said nothing. This was the first he had heard of the breakaway republics of the former Soviet Union.

Andre grunted a mirthless laugh.

Mathilde was unmarried, Lucia said, taking the conversation in another, theoretically safer, direction. She was a wonderful student as a child and now she was married to her work, an excellent diplomat, gifted with languages, wonderful at negotiation. People speak so highly of her, Papa. We are very proud that she works for the government. Alec's father was a senator — here, Andre turned to look quizzically at Alec — so it is a family affair. Alec watched Lucia as she spoke, leaning forward, moving her hands like an orchestra conductor. She and her father had the same gestures, though neither of them seemed to notice; the effect was of a nervous companionability, two friends striving to catch up and not knowing where to begin. Lucia was talking rapidly, her words tumbling one after another. She had stared intently at her father when they met, and Alec knew she was remembering her mother's photograph of the young man at the café table in Prague wearing a Borsalino and smoking a cigarette, the best-looking man in the room. She was trying to fit the portrait to the aged man in the rocking chair, the one listening hard to each word she said. Alec wondered where he found the ivory cigarette holder, an accessory as well worn as a billfold or a pair of slippers.

Andre turned to Alec. Do you think she will be ambassador to Czech Republic?

No, Alec said. That's a post for a senior diplomat.

Hungary?

I would say the same.

But we're hoping, Lucia said brightly.

Be careful what you hope for, Andre said. And now we will have coffee.

A sullen teenage boy arrived carrying a brass platter of tiny cups and saucers and a pot of Turkish coffee. Andre rapped on the window and said something to the boy, who shrugged and put the tray on the floor and departed. He returned in a moment with a wooden table, placed the tray on it, and went away, this time for good. Andre's eyes were on him the whole while, as if he expected the boy to pilfer a spoon. At last Andre sighed and poured Turkish coffee, the consistency of mud but aromatic. Alec took a cup but Lucia declined. Andre nodded and with great concentration lit another cigarette, screwing it into his ivory holder. He carefully balanced the tiny cup of coffee on the arm of his rocking chair and sat back watching the squirrel forage for acorns on the lawn. Alec had the idea that this was an afternoon ritual, no hurry because Andre had no place to go. Conversation was suspended while Andre watched the squirrel, the picture of bourgeois contentment. A wire of cigarette smoke rose in the heavy air.

Are you comfortable here, Papa?

Oh, yes. Quite comfortable.

But — can you tell me. Why are you here?

It was arranged for me.

This place?

Yes, it's run by people I knew at one time. It's a boarding house for refugees, stateless people or people who consider themselves stateless. People who have no place else to go. Goya House is a kind of way station, a port of call, quite comfortable and agreeable except for that lad who brought the coffee. He wants a good whipping, insolent little beggar. They have no manners, the young. But he makes good coffee.

And have you been here a long time?

At least two years, he said. More than that, I think. It's easy to lose track of time in America.

Alec smiled at that, suddenly enjoying himself, listening to Andre dole out his precious bits of information. Alec liked listening to his antique English, *insolent liddle beggah*, inflected with Czech and God knows what other languages from middle Europe and beyond. Andre had begun to rock again, the cigarette holder clamped between his teeth and his fingers securing the coffee cup, an untroubled ship's captain in full command of his vessel.

It's a very large house, Lucia said.

Yes, well. Andre smiled. The money came from an industrialist who made a fortune in the war. Dry goods, I believe. He died a very pleasant sinner's death in the south of France. He and his son were estranged but he left the boy his fortune nevertheless, and the boy gave it away to these people I knew at one time. They wanted to name the place after their benefactor but the son would have none of it. He insisted they call it Goya House, having in mind *The Disasters of War.*

Goodness, Lucia said.

The young man hated his father but he did have a sense of humor. Goya has another meaning, popular in the American army. Get Off Your Ass.

The industrialist was American? Alec asked.

German, Andre said. Through and through.

Lucia said, You certainly look well.

I am in good health, Andre said. Against all odds.

But Papa. Where were you before? Where have you been living? All this time we thought you were dead.

No, I wasn't dead. Where did you get that idea?

That's what Mama said.

Your mother was a romantic. I imagine she was repeating something she had been told.

She believed it. And so did I.

Loose talk, Andre said. People talk too much.

And we heard nothing to the contrary, Lucia said.

Conditions were not ideal, Andre said after a long pause. Those were terrible times. Hard to make sense of them even now. They are hard to describe. There was confusion, a mare's nest of half-truth and innuendo. Andre raised his head and made a tick-tick-tick sound, looking at the squirrel, which froze, an acorn between its busy teeth. Neither Andre nor the squirrel moved for a heartbeat or two. Andre took a sip of his coffee, a motion that seemed to break the spell, if that was what it was. Andre blew a series of smoke rings and the squirrel returned to its acorn.

We had no reason not to believe it, Lucia said. In the absence of other news, Mama believed it.

Communication was difficult, that's true.

I met a man years ago at a party in Washington, Lucia said. His name was Kryg, an ambassador —

Kryg! Andre said, and began to laugh, this time with sincerity.

He told me he had seen you in Trieste.

It was not Trieste. I have forgotten where it was but it wasn't Trieste.

Kryg was also vague about the date. He was vague about everything, and I believe he regretted saying he had seen you. But he said you were in business. I told him he didn't know what he was talking about, you alive and in business in Trieste. He was quite taken aback. He apologized. He said he had to speak to me because we, you and I, looked so much alike. He knew I was your daughter before he knew my name.

Kryg was always unreliable, Andre said.

So you did meet him.

Kryg and I met on and off for years, Andre said. I'd see him here and there. Andre paused a moment, lost in thought. And strictly speaking he was no more unreliable than many ambassadors. He was a shrimp. Came up to my shoulder. But he was not a fool. By no means a fool. The time was difficult, as I said. Difficult for me and for everyone else. So we had a conversation. I needed money and he gave me the money I asked for. It wasn't much.

Why didn't you let us know?

Know what? Andre seemed genuinely puzzled by the question.

That you were alive, Papa.

The time was not convenient, dear Lucia.

I don't understand, she said.

Andre smiled sympathetically. He said, Now I would like it if you would tell me what happened after you left Prague, all the details. I know you and your mother lived in Zurich and she taught at the university. Tell me of your life there.

Alec rose then and asked directions to the men's room. Without taking his eyes off Lucia, Andre said it was on the first floor, second door right. Knock first. Alec wandered off as Lucia began her Zurich saga, events familiar to him. He found the men's room unoccupied and pissed for what seemed a minute or more. In the living room once again he glanced at the foreign newspapers and magazines and the framed posters on the wall, posters of Budapest and Sarajevo, Kraków, Sofia, and New York. They were ordinary travel posters of the sort found in airport waiting rooms, cheerful scenes of picturesque squares and cathedrals, cafés in bright sunlight, the Statue of Liberty. Alec looked through the window at Andre listening to Lucia. From the few phrases he could hear, he knew she was telling him of her mother's salon, who was there and what was discussed, the arguments, her mother a kind of impresario of intellectuals. She was so beautiful, my mother, Lucia said. Everyone admired her. She believed in socialism until the very end. I think everyone loved her and when she died Zurich was a poorer place. Of course she always considered herself Czech.

Andre hardly moved during this recitation. By now he had lit a fresh cigarette, and when Lucia waved her hand to deflect the smoke he seemed not to notice, for he immediately took a deep drag and released it in a thin stream. Alec was conscious of the thick silence inside Goya House and wondered whether Andre was the only tenant and the liddle beggah the only worker. He moved quietly to the doorway and took his seat on the porch as Lucia was winding down her tale, her years in Washington and her subsequent move to Zurich and then to Prague with a new husband. She stopped there because she was much more interested in her father's story than her own story, and she had not gotten far with him.

Nikolas Janos, Lucia concluded, and fell silent.

Why do I know the name? Andre asked.

He writes novels, Lucia said. Wonderful novels.

Oh, yes. I read one of them.

He is very successful, Lucia said.

He is of the new generation, Andre said.

Lucia smiled at that. Not anymore, Papa. There are two generations behind him. And one still in front.

I used to have a beautiful library.

What happened to it, Papa?

It was lost, he said. He turned to Alec and said, Did you find the toilet?

Yes, thank you.

We are very quiet here today. Everyone has gone to the soccer.

But not you, Alec said.

I have never cared for sport except skiing.

Do you ski, Papa?

I have always skied. I started skiing when I was six.

Lucia was a skier, Alec said.

And then I broke my leg, Lucia said. I still ski but not seriously. When I broke my leg I thought my heart would break. I thought my life was over so I came to America.

Alec gave her a look of surprise. He had never heard that.

And you, Alec, Andre said, what is your sport?

Alec said, Sailing.

I myself am an inland man, Andre said. I do not care for the sea.

It can be a dangerous place, Alec said.

I'm sure, Andre said with a smile. If I may ask, what is your business?

Photography, Alec said.

There are many sides to photography. What is your side?

Alec was silent a moment. He never knew how to answer the question. He supposed by "side" Andre meant "subject." But Alec had many subjects. He said, I suppose I prefer photographing actors onstage, preferably in rehearsal. I believe they are most natural when playing a role. Also, I like their company. He explained that he favored repetition, his garden and sailing vessels in the Chesapeake Bay. Over the years he had photographed landscapes, seascapes, cityscapes, bowls of fruit, baseball infields, and the heavens, along with the actors.

I started out with news, he said.

Automobile accidents? Andre asked.

Once or twice, Alec said.

I watch the television in the evening and they seem most interested in automobile accidents and murder.

No murders, Alec said. We weren't that kind of paper.

Politicians?

Oh, yes, many politicians. The paper was interested in politics above all else. The politician with his wife, the politician with his children, the politician campaigning. But never asleep. The politician never sleeps. Andre was looking at him with a sly smile and Alec saw at once that he had misunderstood the question. He returned the smile and said, Of course a murdered politician would be news.

Andre considered that, and then he said, War?

The paper was interested in war, Alec said. Vietnam and the wars that came after. Andre looked at him with an amused expression and Alec felt that he was being led into troubled terrain. He said, I mean Somalia and the Balkans and Iraq One and now Iraq Two. One of our people was badly wounded just last year. He wondered at his use of the word "our" because he had not worked for the paper for almost forty years. He said, The Iraq War is the biggest story in the world.

Andre said, Did you go?

I was out of the newspaper by then. They asked me to go to Vietnam but I said no. Lucia and I were still married then. We had Mathilde. I didn't see the point. I told them that photography glorified the war. Vietnam was not my business.

Yes, Andre said mildly, I can see that.

I think he did it for me, Lucia said.

Not entirely, Alec said.

Yes, I'm certain of it, Lucia said, looking at her father who did not appear to be listening. His face seemed set in stone. His eyes were closed. I remember the conversation, she said.

Very different, Andre said, and fell silent, extracting another cigarette from the pack at his elbow and screwing it into the holder. He struck a match and resumed contemplation of the squirrel, now burrowing near the privet hedge that bordered the lawn. The sun was disappearing and lights winked on in the houses around the neighborhood. An elderly couple strolled by and they and Andre exchanged waves. The woman said something and Andre laughed and gave her a thumbs-up. My favorite time of day absolutely, Andre said, and blew a fat smoke ring.

I remember the conversation very well, Lucia said.

Hush, Lucia, her father said.

My opinion, Lucia said.

In error, Alec said.

You two, Andre said, stop bickering. Enjoy the evening.

What difference does it make? he added.

A moment passed, the sky continuing to darken. Alec said, You were in the war.

Yes, of course. Everyone was. You had no choice. Even if you wanted to make a choice there was no choice.

Lucia asked her father where he had fought.

Central Europe, he said. All over.

Whose army, Papa?

The partisan army, he said. We operated in Yugoslavia and beyond. I suppose you would call us irregulars. We were not under normal military discipline. We fought where we felt like fighting, mostly in the mountains. It seems to me in those years that it was always winter, snow, frostbite. You would wake up in the morning and the water in your canteen was frozen stiff. I have no memory of the summer or spring. I have no memory of the month of May or the month of July. We went where the opportunities were. A bridge that needed to be taken down, a section of railroad track, a munitions depot. When we came upon a German patrol we would engage it and we were usually successful. We chose carefully. The fascists chose carefully also in their reprisals, whole villages taken out and shot without pity. A mayor hanged. A farmer's wife raped in front of her children and her husband. There is an obvious abnormality here, an imbalance I should say, but we chose to ignore it. For the most part they were not our villages, our mayor, or our farmer's wife. As a consequence we were not admired by the local population. Instead we were feared, even hated. So we moved as often as possible, fighting on the run. And we took many casualties but there were always young men prepared to join up. I daresay among the young men there was a romance about us. The romance was at a distance. Up close we were not the young woman of your dreams but the witch of your nightmares. Our idea was your Lincoln's idea: save the Union. And that was reduced to a single mission: kill the fascists. Nothing else mattered. So we did what we could, badly equipped until the end. At the end, there was plenty of German ordnance to choose from. The Germans were beautifully equipped. Leather boots and gloves, warm greatcoats, superb weapons. Snow gear. Even their skis were professional quality, made in Switzerland as I remember. We looted the dead. And then we moved in a direction we should not have moved in. Our intelligence was faulty and it is all but certain that there was a betrayal. In any case we outran ourselves. It's often the way with an irregular army, filled with confidence and the elation that comes with it. We thought the fascists were finished. We thought we were untouchable. So we got careless. We did not take elementary precautions. We heard rumors of an Allied landing in North Africa so we believed we were at the endgame. By God we had given them a bloody nose, but that's all it was, a bloody nose. In our confidence and elation we decided to attack one of their headquarters and they just beat the hell out of us with tanks and heavy artillery and more infantry than we thought possible. Fresh troops, well trained, disciplined. Where did they come from? I don't know. They were waiting for us and it was all over in under an hour.

But you escaped, Lucia said.

Captured, Andre corrected. I was sent to a fascist prison camp in Poland. We were there two years. We were liberated, if you want to call it that, by the Red Army. And then we were sent to a camp in the Soviet Union. Andre was silent again, the only sound the creak of his rocker.

The German camp, Lucia began.

I will not speak of the German camp, Andre said.

Oh, Papa, Lucia said.

They were swine, Andre said.

Yes, Lucia said.

There has been too much talk already of the German camps. I can add nothing to what has been said and written. I have no interest in going over it again. Do you understand?

Yes, Papa.

Good, Andre said. But I will tell you about the Russian camp if you wish.

Yes, Lucia said. Of course.

We were sent to a camp in the Soviet Union. It was south of Murmansk. I wasn't sure where it was located precisely. I'm still not sure. My papers, such as they were, had been lost. They had no idea who I was, only that I was not Russian. I tried to tell them that I was one of them, a loyal communist. Had been a communist since the Nazis overran Sudetenland. They didn't believe me. They thought I was a fascist trickster and the unit I led, the one that was not strictly speaking under discipline, a gang of hooligans. Bandits. And it was true, we lived off the land while we fought the Wehrmacht. We took what we wanted when we wanted it. We tried never to lose sight of our Lincoln ideal, kill the fascists where they stood. That was in first position and everything else in second position. So they took us for bandits or maybe only revisionists. I never knew for certain. There was no trial. There was no due process, as the Americans like to say. The commissars made a decision and the decision was final. Three men and a woman in one small room in the headquarters section of the German camp. Fifteen, maybe twenty minutes. They allowed a one-minute statement from me, in Czech, which none of them spoke. One day I was in Poland and a few months later I was in the Soviet Union, in the camp south of Murmansk. By then I was separated from my commando. We were transported in cattle cars, Hungarians, Bulgarians, some Czechs, even a Swiss, all charged with various crimes. Or simply "detained." The train never reached a speed of more than twenty kilometers an hour, with long stops along the way. Food and water were short. Men fell sick and died. Everything stank. During the long stops the guards dismounted and stood along the siding, jokes, laughter, the smell of tobacco.

I can't listen, Lucia said. I can't hear any more of this.

But Andre did not hear her. Still, he said, it was spring. A cold spring but spring nonetheless. It was an improvement over what we had. In due course we arrived at the camp. There, it was not yet spring. Snow was on the ground and I remember thinking that it would be there forever. Snow as far as my eye could see, gray snow, snow the color of a dirty sheet. Andre shook his head heavily. Well, he said, enough of that.

He rose suddenly, surprisingly agile for so large a man. He stretched his arms wide as if embracing the night and pitched his cigarette on the lawn where it bounced in a little shower of sparks. He looked around him and then he rapped again on the window. The boy appeared at once.

Schnapps, Andre said. Three glasses. Have one yourself.

Right away, the boy said, and hurried off.

He's better at night, Andre said. His manners come back to him at night because he knows very well that I'll give him a glass.

Bring the bottle, Andre said loudly.

Thank God you're here, Papa.

Yes, I'm comfortable.

It's a nice house.

Adequate, Andre said.

I didn't know what to expect, Lucia said. But Papa, what do you do here?

Do? I don't understand.

Your life, day to day.

Andre shrugged. The question had no meaning for him.

I mean, Lucia began.

I am happy to be alive. In good health. I enjoy my Turkish coffee, my schnapps. In the evening I often play cards. He smiled broadly. I suppose I have always looked for the absolute, Andre said.

Night came in a rush. The street was suddenly busy with arrival and departure. Somewhere nearby a dog barked and an infant began to cry. The tray that held the coffee now held a bottle of schnapps and three delicately etched glasses. Lucia was certain the glasses were Czech made, the works at Železný Brod. Andre poured three glasses of schnapps and sat back again in his rocking chair, another cigarette in the ivory holder. Lucia watched her father fill the schnapps glass in his hand, the one that was missing the little finger. He appeared the picture of contentment, a man at ease in the world, lost in thought now. His thoughts, whatever they were, looked to be pleasant, for he was smiling.

Lucia had the idea he was thinking of her mother, dead so many years. They must have had a tremendous romance before he went away and disappeared, dead in her mother's eyes. She wondered when his birthday was. She would ask him the date and buy him a Borsalino as a present. She would invite him to Prague and take him to a fine café for lunch. Nikolas, too. They would have a sumptuous lunch with wine and schnapps to finish. He and Nikolas would like each other. She heard them discussing the literature of central Europe, Zweig, Kafka, Walter Benjamin. Perhaps Nikolas could get him to talk about the camps and how he survived. She wondered if there were any women in his life. Andre looked twenty years younger than his age. Everyone said she did, too. Alec looked exactly his age, seventy years old; or was he now seventy-one? She couldn't remember. Alec didn't look well. His face had a kind of pallor and he shuffled when he walked, like an old man. His eyesight was failing and he still wouldn't answer a direct question. Lucia wondered if he was still seeing his Hollywood star, though "star" was far too generous a term. She had never been a star, merely a competent second lead. Mathilde told her that whatshername mostly acted in made-for-television movies of the policier variety, cops-and-robbers business. Well. Whatever made him happy.

Lucia had so many questions to ask her father. She didn't know where to begin and she didn't want to sound like an inquisitor giving him the third degree. So far he had been forthcoming. She had hated telling him that she no longer spoke Czech or enough Czech to follow a complicated story. She saw the dismay on his face and heard it in his voice. She remembered her mother telling her she would never lose her essential Czechness. But it seemed she had. She couldn't imagine what was in her mind when she told Alec she needed protection. She didn't need protection, and if she had needed it Alec was not the man for the job. She had been with her father only an hour and she felt as if she had known him her entire life. Now she watched him roll the schnapps glass in his hand and take a swallow, still smiling at whatever thought or memory was occupying his mind.

When did you lose your finger, Papa?

Years ago, he said.

In the war?

Andre looked at the stump. He said, When I was a child. My father and I were chopping wood. I lost control of my ax. It was only a child's ax but sharp all the same and I wasn't paying attention. Instead I was watching my father to see how he used his ax. My father was a fine woodsman and knew all the tricks. I remember that he went chalk white when he saw the blood, but he picked me up and carried me the mile or so to our house. My mother was furious with him. There was a terrible row between the two of them, my mother yelling at my father like he was trash. She ordered him from the house while she wrapped my hand. My mother took me to the doctor's office herself in our horse-drawn cart, refusing to allow him to come along. Of course I felt responsible for their argument. All the way to the doctor's office my mother repeated over and over again, Idiot, Your father is an idiot, your father is an incompetent. I knew that wasn't true. He only turned his back at the wrong time. And I was careless. I promised myself never to be careless after that. A valuable lesson, Lucia. It saved me much grief later on. A small price to pay, one finger, for the lesson.

Does it bother you now?

Sometimes when the weather is clammy it aches, he said and resumed his watch of the street.

Lucia wanted to ask him how badly it hurt at the time. Probably his wound was worse even than her ski accident. She remembered the pain coming in waves, each wave larger than the one before until she passed out. She took his hand then, so heavy, heavy in her palm. She turned it this way and that, looking at the finger stump. The stump skin was waxy, slippery to the touch. She said, It's hardly noticeable. If that happened today they'd find a way to sew the finger onto your hand. And then you would be whole again.

I never notice it, Andre said. You learn to live without.

I never got over my leg, Lucia said.

Andre nodded in the darkness, then turned to Alec. Have you ever been injured?

Alec thought a moment and said, No.

No broken bones ever? No wounds?

I have led a fortunate life, Alec said.

I would say so, Andre said.

But I am losing my eyesight. Would that qualify?

I don't think so, Andre said.

Why are we talking about injuries? Alec asked.

Lucia mentioned them, Andre said.

Losing one's eyesight is a painless injury, Alec said. Even the effects of it are painless. Inconvenient, but painless. It's painful thinking of the future without eyesight but that's not pain of a physical sort. Alec finished his glass of schnapps and poured another. I have never been in prison, either. I have trouble imagining what it's like locked up, one day following another without much distinction between them.

The distinctions are small, that's true, Andre said.

The weather, I suppose. The task at hand.

The monotony, Andre said.

Trying to imagine what's over the horizon?

I suppose so, Andre said.

Alec sipped schnapps and wondered aloud if one single thing from the experience was — and he could not summon the correct word. Elevating? Convincing?

The disappearance of one's friends, Andre said, often without explanation, and then days later the rumors begin. So-and-so was transferred. Had a heart attack. Was found dead in bed by his own hand, or another's hand. Was taken away and shot. The Stalin years were the worst. Later on, discipline relaxed a little. The food improved. The weather never improved. Andre screwed another cigarette into his holder and lit it, allowing the match to burn down to his fingertips. It was difficult keeping one's senses in such an atmosphere. You became unnaturally aware of your own body, the lost weight, your bones visible beneath the skin. Rotting teeth. Obscure pains that came and went. Sexual desire went into hiding. It had to be there somewhere but you could not locate it. The absent-minded man lost the keys to his car and no amount of wishing or recollection brought them back. Your situation was ludicrous. Absurd. And unfathomable. In a sense inscrutable. Of course those were not the words you used then.

They came later when nutrition had improved and you were able to think clearly, relatively speaking. Make an assessment of where you were and how you had come to be there and what might happen next. That is to say, think about the future. I cannot tell you what a luxury that was, conceiving the future. It was the equivalent of imagining yourself in a wonderful café somewhere in the company of close friends, everyone laughing. Someone is telling a story. A policeman walks by and smiles because everyone is having such a good time. You begin to wonder if at some unspecified date in the future they will let you out. Decide that you are harmless after all. Not a threat to the state. Not a threat to anyone. Perhaps conclude that a mistake has been made, a bureaucratic blunder, understandable in wartime. No hard feelings.

I don't want to hear any more, Lucia said.

Andre filled his glass and Alec's. Lucia's was untouched but he poured a little anyway, absent-mindedly, minding his manners.

Please go on, Alec said.

Lucia doesn't wish it, Andre said.

I don't like to think of you in prison, Papa.

Well, he said, I was released. Many weren't.

What did they tell you when they released you? Alec said.

That I had served my sentence and that I was free to go.

No explanations?

None asked, none given. They gave me some money and put me on a train to Prague. When the train reached its terminus I got off. That was all there was to it. End of story.

Just like that, Alec said.

I had been ill, Andre said. They had finally allowed me to see the camp doctor, who said I had pneumonia and must enter the hospital at once. Except there were no unoccupied beds so my admittance was delayed, and when they found space for me I was hallucinating. My fever was high. Tremendously high. The drugs on hand were few and not altogether potent. I don't know how long I was in the hospital. Weeks certainly, all that time either comatose or hallucinating. Sweating, then chills. In my delirium I conjured fantastic visions, the gardens of Bosch and Dalí's melting clocks. And when I woke it was to the solemn colorless interior of the pneumonia ward. My God it was cold in the ward, only one small brazier fire at one end of a long dark room, cots along both walls. One sheet and one thin blanket. But I refused to die. That was what the doctor told me — he, too, was a prisoner so he knew what he was talking about. The offer was made and I refused. I have always had a strong constitution. So I improved, and as I improved I began to think about the world I had made for myself. I knew I had fallen behind in life, all those years in camps, and my own actions had brought me there, no matter how unjustly my actions were judged by the authorities. I had to account somehow for the lost years and began to rationalize them in this way. They were like one's infancy and early boyhood, call it the years from birth to age six or seven. One has scant memory of those years, and the memories one does have are trivial unless there's drama of one sort or another, a death in the family, an earthquake, something of that nature. Of course I had been in prison a very long time but still I could think of the years as childhood years when not much is recollected. God knows there was little enough to recollect from the monotony of captivity. Prison is more a process of forgetting than remembering. I was not ashamed of the acts that had brought me first to Poland and then to the Soviet Union. I would not change anything except naturally there were acts of cruelty and indifference during the war. I regret those acts but I am not ashamed of them. They are war's signature, cruelty and indifference. War has its own rules, handed down through the centuries. So I lay in my hospital bed and improved and improved some more and when I had improved enough they released me. And a month or so after that I was let go altogether, given some money and a train ticket and another man's suit of clothes. *Do svidanya*. No hard feelings.

Now you must excuse me a moment, Andre said, setting aside

his schnapps and stepping inside the house, leaving Alec and Lucia alone in the darkness and neighborly silence of a suburban street.

All those years in prison, Lucia said. I wonder if he ever thought of my mother and me. Wondered what had happened to us.

I'm sure he did, Alec said.

He didn't say he did, Lucia said in a small voice. He mentioned Bosch and Dalí. His pneumonia. Many other things. Not us.

An oversight, Alec said. But he was not interested in what Andre did or did not recollect of his wife and daughter, safe in neutral Switzerland. Andre had said, I knew I had fallen behind in life. What did that mean? He had fought bravely in the war and been imprisoned first by the Nazis and then by the Soviets for what appeared to be decades and his assessment was that he had "fallen behind in life"? That was true as far as it went but it did not go nearly far enough. Andre seemed to bear his captors no real rancor, and that was hard to believe. History had swallowed him up, then spit him out. His voice was gruff but colored also by irony, a psychic detachment, as if the appalling events had happened to someone else. In a literal sense he seemed to stand apart from his own circumstances. Alec was all but overcome with admiration for Andre Duran, whose endurance seemed to him all but superhuman. He was a courageous man. Andre had regret, he said, but no shame over what he had done. He had merely obeyed war's rules. "Merely." Alec was in no position to judge. He wondered if there were photographs of Andre in the war and later in the camps, and if the photographs, if they existed, would add anything important to the story. Certainly they would not add glamour.

It would not have been an oversight, Alec.

That was a joke, Alec said.

I don't like jokes at this time, Lucia said. Jokes have no place here. I would like to think that my mother and I were remembered if only for a minute. She turned away from him and stared into the empty street. She said, You would never understand. That was never your métier, Alec, understanding the situation of others. I am sorry now that I asked you to come with me.

Alec did not reply but thought to himself, You forgot him. Why would he not forget you?

All this time we thought he was dead. We had no idea where he was. We had no idea how he died and where he was buried.

And then Andre was back, slamming the door behind him, humming some unfamiliar melody, standing at the porch railing inhaling the night air, searching his pockets for his cigarettes and ivory holder, his matches, absently rubbing the waxy skin where his little finger had been. He reached down suddenly to pat Lucia's knee, three taps and a gentle squeeze, smiling all the while.

I am so pleased you have come to see me, he said.

Papa, she said, and for a moment Alec thought she would break down.

I wasn't certain that you would, Andre said.

Of course, Papa. What did you think?

One never knows, he said.

I admit it was a shock to me, hearing from you.

It could not be avoided, he said. Andre said nothing more for a moment, looking fondly at his daughter. He said at last, I see a little of me in you.

She smiled and said that Kryg had remarked on the resemblance.

Kryg was not stupid, Andre said.

I didn't like him, Lucia said.

He was harmless. I think Kryg never found his true place in the world. He did not want to make enemies. He spent most of his life staying out of harm's way and then harm came to him in Corsica.

Sardinia, Lucia said.

Corsica, Andre said sharply. He gave Lucia's knee a final pat and sat down in the rocking chair. For a moment no one spoke. Kryg had been disposed of.

So you arrived in Prague, Alec said.

Yes, Andre agreed.

What happened then?

That's enough of my story, Andre said.

No, Papa, Lucia said. Please go on.

Old war stories are boring, Andre said.

Not to me, Lucia said.

I went looking for friends, Andre said with a sigh. I needed papers. I needed some proof of identity, it didn't matter whose identity. Nationality didn't matter. The papers mattered. I had friends who managed that sort of thing. But it took me a while to find them. So many were dead or moved away. I had been out of touch for a long time and only my closest friends knew where I had been. They had been sworn to silence and they were not eager in any case to reopen the book. It had been a long time. I was not certain and they were not certain whether I was wanted in some other jurisdiction. At last I found a friend, the one I needed. He and his wife and your mother and I used to see each other in Prague in the old days. Quite the surprise for him when I showed up at his door. He made the necessary inquiries, which did take quite some time. There were no outstanding warrants. So he fixed me up with an identity card and a passport and I went away to the mountains. End of story.

But — where in the mountains?

Andre laughed. A small resort in Yugoslavia. Nobody ever heard of it. One chairlift. I got a job operating the chairlift and giving ski lessons on the side. I had my own chalet, quite comfortable. Living was cheap, a happy interlude for me. My health came back quicker than I expected, no doubt the result of mountain air, downhill skiing, a decent diet, and anonymity. An average life, I would say. And as I told you, I have a strong constitution.

Andre paused here, his expression resigned. He took the cigarette pack from his pocket, looked at it, and put it back. Also, he said, I was able to ignore politics. Politics was not a part of the mountain air. Politics was elsewhere, vanished along with Hitler and Stalin. Yugoslavia was restless, but Yugoslavia is always restless, so little space, so many tribes. Yugoslavia is an unnatural state but it is beautiful all the same. We had no television and no newspapers. I was done with politics anyway. But you cannot remain incognito forever, Andre said. There are too many people in the world and they are always traveling and eventually an acquaintance arrives at the resort. She doesn't recognize me but I recognize her because I make it my business to look closely at our travelers. She is the wife of an old comrade. She is alone. I'm the sort of fellow, as I'm sure you understand, who is naturally curious. When I have an itch I scratch the itch. So when she arrives at my chairlift I say to her,

How are you, Sonja?

She looks at me, bewildered.

It's Andre, Sonja.

Of course she thinks she has seen a ghost. I thought she would faint.

Andre?

Yes, Andre.

I heard a rumor —

That I was alive after all?

Yes, that was the rumor. I didn't believe it.

As you can see, Sonja. Here I am.

Unchanged, she said.

Yet you did not recognize me.

Do you always wear your ski mask, Andre? Indoors as well as out?

So I closed the chairlift and we walked in the cold to the village for lunch, a lunch that lasted most of the afternoon as Sonja brought me up to date. Her husband, Rolf, my old friend, is dead. Two of her three sons have said goodbye to her and immigrated to America. They went to Detroit to work in the auto industry. She does not know the whereabouts of her youngest boy but she fears he is involved in the Prague underworld. He sends her money every month, she says, and as she talks I remember this child — now a middle-aged man — as sweet-tempered and shy, everyone's favorite. Sonja asks me if I know about the Prague underworld and I say I do not. She tells me that Prague now is worse than it was under the Soviets, and then she paused and said that hers was a generational attitude. Young people seem to thrive in Prague, the films, the music and the dancing, the sex. We had sex, too, but not so much music and dancing. We did not have the money for music and dancing and if we did have the money music and dancing were not permitted or at least not permitted to excess. Amusement generally was discouraged, but we found a way, didn't we, Andre? I would say we reached a separate peace, Sonja said. She brought me the news of all our mutual friends, many of them gone, most of the rest living here and there on the margins. She herself lived in a village in Bohemia. There are still a few around who would love to see you, Sonja said. Your name comes up all the time. They say you were the best, Andre.

I'm retired, I told her.

What are you retired from, Andre? She said this with a smile.

Politics, I said.

Did I mention politics?

You were about to, I said.

I heard you were in Russia, she said.

I was, I told her.

She nodded, an expression of sympathy, and did not inquire further. The details of the camps were well known and my story did not differ in any important way from the other stories. She said, I would like to tell our friends that you're back among us. That the rumor is true. That you live here. Allow me to do this. It would mean a great deal to them to see you again. You look well, by the way.

I lead a healthy life, I told her.

How long have you been here?

Years, I said.

Living alone? she said.

Oh, yes.

That's not like you, Andre.

I told you, I said. I'm retired.

Retired from life? she said.

Something like that, I said.

So I may tell the others?

I would appreciate it if you didn't, I said.

You're content, then, with your chairlift and your skiing lessons.

For the moment, I said.

Very well, she said. I understand.

Of course she didn't understand. There's a limit to understanding. Extreme situations do not yield to understanding. She sympathized and that was enough. We seemed to have run out of conversation. I am sure that if a stranger had stepped into the restaurant he would have taken us for an old married couple, together so long we did not have to speak to make ourselves understood. Coffee grew cold in our cups but still we did not move. Sonja was staring out one window, I out another. The waiter dozed at a table in the corner. Something remained to be said but I did not know what it was. Finally Sonja looked up.

Do you remember Dusko? Of course you remember Dusko, she said, everyone knows Dusko the busybody. She went on and on about Dusko, leading up to something, I couldn't imagine what. Then she said that Dusko was back on the battlefield, our battlefield, the one her husband Rolf and I occupied during World

War Two. He had been at it a year or more investigating the killings. The word Sonja used was "atrocities." Dusko was methodically driving from village to village collecting evidence, searching for documents, interviewing everyone in sight. A number of villagers remembered the German occupation very well and that was the focus of Dusko's inquiry. They were eager to tell of their privations, the cruelty of the Germans and the atmosphere of violence everywhere in the district. And in the course of his interviews, Sonja said, he turned up evidence of atrocities committed by our commando, Rolf's and mine. You know Dusko, she said, he's tireless. He'll go to the ends of the earth if he has to.

Who's paying him? I said.

A writer, Sonja said.

What kind of writer? I asked.

An American historian, Sonja said. The historian is writing a book on forgotten atrocities of World War Two in Europe. He's compiled quite a list, mostly Nazi atrocities. But Nazi atrocities are a dime a dozen, they're not news. But he thinks he's on to something fresh with your commando, your international brigade doing the Lord's work in Yugoslavia. So he and Dusko are retracing your line of march, your orders, where you went, what you did, and who you did it to. A neglected episode, the historian calls it. That's according to Dusko.

I looked at my watch. Time to go.

It would be good if you would have a word with Dusko, Andre. Your word would carry weight with him. It's monstrous, what he's doing.

I have no interest in Dusko, I said.

That's not the point, Andre. Dusko has an interest in you.

And poor Rolf, she added.

I can't bear it.

Andre smiled into the darkness, poured schnapps once more, and lit a cigarette. Alec leaned forward in his chair, rapt, waiting for the rest of the story. But Andre had said all he was prepared to say. The story hung there like the smoke from his cigarette, slowly dispersing in the balmy air. Lucia nervously turned her wedding ring and stared at her father.

What did you do, Papa?

Hush, Andre said. Enjoy the evening.

I can't enjoy the evening, Lucia said.

I'm tired, Andre said. I've talked too much.

I don't know what to think, Lucia said.

Andre shrugged and began to rock in his chair. He blew one smoke ring after another and took a swallow of schnapps, shuddering. All the houses round and about had lights burning, television's electric glow visible in every living room. A settled community, Alec thought. What must they think of the inhabitants of Goya House? From far away came the bleat of an ambulance siren.

Did you find Dusko? Alec asked.

It wasn't hard, Andre said. It was like following the tracks of an elephant. Dusko and his historian were not careful. Nor discreet. They made enemies wherever they went because they excited suspicion. No one knew what they were after really. The American had an unfortunate manner. I had never met anyone like him before until I came here and began to watch American television, news programs and quiz shows. He seemed to think he was bringing enlightenment to these peasant communities and they were somehow obligated to tell him whatever they knew. And a few did. There were many scars from the war and the scars have not healed. They will never heal. I believe Dusko and the historian were in some danger owing to the indiscreet way they went about things, their brusque questions and insistence on answers. Dusko should have known better. But he was being very well paid and I think in some sense he was seeking absolution for his own actions in the war. Or, I should say, his inaction. So they were in a spot of trouble when I arrived. I don't think they knew how much trouble. When Dusko saw me he nearly collapsed. He pretended not to know me. He pretended not to know my name.

Dusko has had a loss of memory, I told the historian.

No wonder, so many years ago. But I'm sure, on reflection, he'll recall our long and complicated friendship.

I bring regards from Sonja.

Sonja told me of your project and now I'm here to help.

After you, I said, ushering Dusko and the historian into their car, a green Land Rover piled high with expensive luggage, food in tins, and a case of whiskey. The American historian was quite young, I would judge not yet fifty years old, too young to have known the war. I directed them to one village after another, describing the actions of my commando. I spared nothing. I told them everything in my memory. Along the way I helped them interview the old people who had been present. Once or twice my name came up, not always in a flattering way. I did nothing to prevent them telling their stories nor did I disclose my identity to them. Once or twice I was able to help them along, innocently asking questions about this bridge or that rail line. The farmhouse where the Nazi headquarters was. Many times the old people answered falsely or incompletely, at least according to my memory of events. We drove from one district to another with the aid of a map someone had given the historian. I was with them for almost half a year and at the end of that time they had a fairly complete picture of our orders, where we went, what we did, and who we did it to. Also, they had a fairly complete picture of the Nazis, what they did, and who they did it to. I wanted them to know the war in the round, the atmosphere at the time, the hatred we felt one to the others. How the cost in lives diminished year to year until at the end of the war the cost was negligible. Hardly any cost at all. There were so many dead that the battlefield seemed to us like a bonfire, and the dead so many stray twigs fed into it. They had no more significance than that. We killed anything that moved. So did they. We both did terrible things. They killed many more because they had many more men and heavy weapons. But that was the only reason. I walked Dusko and his historian through each action, where we were, where they were, how the matter progressed, and the results. I described our tactics, their tactics, and the advantages and disadvantages of each. I described also the civilians who were caught up in it. They had nowhere to go. For them we were like a great natural disaster, a hurricane or a flood, except there was no high ground. And at last the fascists caught us. They killed most everyone in the commando. We had nowhere to run. But five of us survived and the other four died in the prison camp in Poland. We five were greatly surprised that they did not shoot us where we lay but I think they wanted us to experience a German prison camp. The camp would be the great punishment. I wanted Dusko and his American historian to understand the world we lived in, its limits and its excesses, how things went day to day, and the kind of man you became. But in the end they did not understand any more than Sonja understood. Any more than you understand. So I was left with sympathy. I wanted them to know that no one could judge us. No one had the right. No one who was not there with us day to day. Perhaps God will judge us. But we doubted that God would take the trouble.

Andre fell silent again and gave an enormous yawn.

Lucia said, Was the book ever published?

No. It was never written.

The historian took your advice, then.

Andre shook his head. No. He died. When Andre saw the look on Lucia's face he smiled fractionally and added, Natural causes. He worked and worked on the book, worked on it for years. But in the end he could not write it. In any case, he didn't. From time to time he would pass me a letter via Dusko, questions about this or that event. Trivial questions, I thought. Dates, times of day, the nutritional value of the rations we ate, the color of a man's eyes. Then the letters stopped. Dusko sent word that the historian was dead. A little after that Dusko died and the matter was closed.

All this time Andre had been talking directly to his daughter, watching her reactions to his account.

The silence lengthened. Alec said, What was the historian's name?

Andre said, Holder.

Jimmy Holder, Alec said. I knew him. He was one of the foreign correspondents on the paper I worked for. He went to Vietnam, one tour after another. He couldn't get enough of it. He was one of those who was unable to forget the war. He quit the paper to write books, military histories. Successful books.

That was his name, Andre said. He continued to look at Lucia, whose eyes were downcast. He was uninterested in the biography of Jimmy Holder. As he said, the matter was closed. Yet one fact of Andre's tale was in error. The historian did not die of natural causes. He took his own life after his wife died. He himself was in poor health and could not manage without her. That was the explanation that went around.

I knew him quite well, Alec said. Lucia did, too.

Andre shook his head, tapping his earpiece; evidently he did not hear Alec clearly. He turned to Lucia and asked some question about Nikolas. Alec slipped off into reverie, remembering Jimmy Holder. Everyone liked him, a hard-drinking raconteur who did not approve of Alec's refusal to photograph the war. Such a refusal gave all journalists a bad name and served only to fortify the right wing, and he implied that Alec's reputation would suffer also. Everyone had to pay his dues. When Alec quit the paper Jimmy Holder said he had made the right decision. Despite the disagreement they remained friends, though they saw less and less of each other as time went on. Alec was bemused at the co-

222

incidence and had difficulty imagining Jimmy, overweight and hung-over, charging around Yugoslavia with Andre. Coincidence seemed epidemic in the news business, friendships replicating the news itself, so often repetitive, reductive, and inclined to formula.

Thinking of Jimmy Holder, Alec thought now of his father and resolved to visit the grave in the morning, say a few last words. The service had been perfunctory, though the reverend — and he had forgotten the reverend's name. Wallace? The Reverend Wallace had done a fine job, a touch on the pompous side but his father never minded pomposity so long as it was kept within bounds. Kim Malone once said that in the United States Senate pomposity was a sacrament. You didn't necessarily treasure it but you missed its absence. Pomposity resembled the intentional walk in baseball, tedious and action-slowing but vital to the integrity of the game. Integrity was necessary in the news business also. Alec supposed that if he had gone to Vietnam his life would have taken a different turn, driven by the one experience so drenched in the atmosphere of violence. Jimmy Holder had taken his own life by gunshot. Yet war service had not diminished Andre. Alec remembered Andre deep in thought when he and Lucia had come upon him on the porch of Goya House. Was he remembering the war? His daughter? A café in Prague? Andre Duran had as much vitality as any man Alec had ever met. He thought again of twigs into the bonfire. We did terrible things. We killed anything that moved. No one could judge us. No one who had not been with us day to day. God himself would not take the trouble. Alec thought his father would probably agree. He believed the legislative craft was beyond the ken of outsiders. The apparatus of it was mystifying. The rules often contradicted themselves. No one outside the field of combat could appreciate the personal and political loyalties of members of Congress. Even the bribe was ambiguous. One man's bribe was another's campaign contribution. Of course every election cycle the voters had their say and that verdict was final, ill informed as it was bound to be, yet another burden of democracy. Alec looked up to find Lucia and Andre staring at him, Lucia saying something.

We should go now, Alec.

And then they heard a wild commotion at the curb, cars thundering up the street and parking in front of Goya House, men spilling from the doors, shouts and bursts of conversation. Lucia recoiled from the sudden noise; the neighborhood had been so quiet. Andre was on his feet at once, waving his arms and giving a kind of lupine growl. Alec rose also, alarmed, watching the men gather on the sidewalk, shouting at Andre. A few of them gripped beer cans. All of them were wearing Basque berets and leather jackets of various colors. They rushed across the lawn to lean against the porch railing, everyone talking at once, their arms around one another's shoulders, Andre grinning, his hands flung wide in welcome.

They loved the soccer game, Andre said to Lucia.

These are my housemates, he added.

Andre signaled for quiet and introduced Lucia and Alec, the conversation subsiding at once. There were eight men, all of them older but not so old as Andre, and they all extended their hands in greeting. Alec could not identify the language they spoke. There were several languages in any case. They were all tipsy and a few of them were frankly drunk and having difficulty with their footing. But they were in very good humor and now began to explain something to Andre, evidently an account of the soccer match. Their team, whatever team it was, had won. That was obvious. The conversation went on and on, a din. Across the street someone opened her front door, looked out, and retreated back inside. More beer was produced and Andre poured schnapps once again, happily listening to their accounts of the game, winding down now. And after a while the men made their goodbyes and drifted away, stomping up the porch stairs and through the front door, dispersing to their various rooms. The downstairs toilet flushed and flushed again. In a few minutes the house was quiet and the street silent as before. Andre, Lucia, and Alec took their seats once more on the porch in the darkness. A sudden chill was in the air.

Soccer, Andre said. The one thing that reminds them of home. They are boys again when they go to the game. They become very excited. The neighbors are used to it. I hope you weren't bothered.

Not at all, Alec said.

They are good boys, Andre said.

Mostly Czech? Alec asked.

They are from all over middle Europe, and not only Europe. They were very surprised. They did not know I had a daughter.

We must leave now, Papa.

Will you come to see me again?

Yes, of course.

Tomorrow?

In the morning, Lucia said. I leave for Zurich in the early evening.

So soon?

Yes, I'm afraid so. But I'll be back.

The morning will be fine, Andre said.

I'll bring Mathilde, Lucia said. And sometime you must meet Nikolas. You and Nikolas will have much to talk about.

I am eager to see Mathilde, Andre said. My only grandchild. And then he smiled broadly and added, That I know of.

She wants very badly to meet you, Lucia said.

I'll be here on my porch, Andre said.

I am glad I came, Papa.

I, too, Andre said.

Goodbye, Andre, Alec said.

Goodbye, goodbye, Andre said.

Tomorrow, Papa, Lucia said, and kissed him on his cheek.

Lucia drove slowly back to Military Road, turning at Wisconsin Avenue. Traffic was light, the rush hour concluded. They were silent in the car until Alec asked Lucia the name of the minister who officiated at his father's graveside. Willis, she said. Oh, yes, Alec said. The Reverend Willis. I do that all the time now, forget names. He was looking out the window at the familiar street, the department stores and hardware stores, movie houses and liquor stores and restaurants. He searched and searched for the Chinese restaurant he knew so well but it was not where it should have been, and then he remembered that it was on Connecticut Avenue, not Wisconsin. It was years since he had been there, the last time with Mathilde when she was a teenager. My God, he thought, that would have been the Carter administration, conceivably Reagan One, somewhere in there. Alec remembered that he and Mathilde had Peking duck, amusing themselves with the fortune cookies that came with dessert. They went to the movies later, one of the James Bond epics. The star was one of Connery's successors, the one with the smirk, Roger Moore. Mathilde was taken with him. Maybe his memory wasn't going to hell after all.

Tell me something, Alec said. Was he what you expected?

The Reverend Willis? Lucia said, puzzled.

Your father, Alec said.

I didn't know what to expect, Lucia said. I had no image of him in my mind. I mean, nothing specific beyond a handsome man in a Borsalino hat. But that image went away when I saw him.

You spoke of him very seldom, Alec said.

I know. He was not part of my life. I remembered nothing of him. Only what my mother told me, and I am pretty certain that she made revisions. Perhaps made things up. I never knew why they split up. I mean, something I could believe. Something that made sense. That's why, when Mathilde was old enough, I told her everything about us. The life we had together and the advent of Nikolas. I didn't want her to be in the dark, as I was. I didn't want her living with a mystery.

Nothing wrong with mysteries, Alec said.

I don't like them, Lucia said.

Sometimes you have to learn to live with them.

Not me. Not if I can avoid it.

They drove on in silence, one stoplight after another. Finally Lucia said, Do we look alike?

Absolutely, Alec said. You must have seen it. His eyes. The set of his chin. His laugh. His gestures.

I suppose I did, Lucia said. Didn't want to admit it.

He is very masculine and you are very feminine. Still, two sides of the same coin.

I admit it was strange, seeing him.

He knew it, too, Alec said.

Thank you for coming with me, Lucia said. I was — nervous.

I'm glad I came, Alec said.

You are?

An interesting man, your father.

I suppose so, she said.

A twentieth-century life, Alec said. Every inch.

I cannot admire his life, Lucia said. A life of violence, a life that seems to me to have been dictated by history. I wish he had turned his back. I wish he had found a way to stay with my mother. She had an empty place in her heart because of him. I do, too. He does not recognize that. He does not appreciate the wreckage he left behind. That was his achievement. I cannot admire it.

You, too, Alec said.

What do you mean?

You, too, have led a twentieth-century life. Every inch.

They were in Georgetown now, on his street, then at Mrs. Wheatley's old house, a stretch limousine, bone white in color, at the curb, delivering two couples in evening dress. Lucia waited behind the limo until the passengers were on the sidewalk and the chauffeur eased away. A butler opened the door and stood aside as the guests swept through. Beyond the open door Alec saw the others, women clutching little black purses, men with their hands in their pockets. White-coated waiters passed drinks and canapés. Alec recognized one of the women as a television commentator of liberal slant, in earnest discussion with an army general in fullest fig, about one square foot of decorations on the left side of his dress jacket, stars on his shoulders. From the look of things the television commentator was doing most of the talking, not that the general appeared to care; she was an attractive woman, almost as tall as the general. And then the front door slammed shut. Lucia continued on down the block, and when she pulled up in front of Alec's house the interior was dark. Mathilde had yet to return.

Alec said, Do you remember Jimmy Holder? Your father's historian.

Vaguely, she said.

He quit the newspaper because they brought him home and made him an editor. He hated editing. He missed the battlefield and all those countries he visited. Mostly he missed his byline. So he took a buyout and wrote books instead.

Lucia rolled her eyes. She was drumming her fingers on the steering wheel, impatient to be off. Those reporter friends of yours, she said. They all blend into one. It was so long ago.

Give my best to your father when you see him tomorrow.

I will, Lucia said.

And if you get the chance, ask him how he got to Goya House.

If I get the chance, she said.

It's a strange setup, Alec said. A bit of a mystery.

Lucia said, In case you're interested, I don't look on my life as a twentieth-century life. I look on it as a normal life. She spat the

228

words as if she could not get rid of them fast enough. And I don't think you admire my father. I think you're envious of him. Envious of the wreckage.

No one envies wreckage, Lucia. I do admire fidelity. Alec stepped from the car and she drove away without another word. He fumbled with his keys a moment; when Mathilde had gone out she had forgotten to turn on the lights. He stepped inside the house, collected the mail from the floor, and leafed through it as he pressed the button on the answering machine. One message, Mathilde announcing she was spending the night with a friend and would call in the morning. Alec dropped the mail on the hall table and ambled into the kitchen, intending to pour a glass of wine until he thought better of it and poured Scotch instead. He stood on the steps leading to the garden, sipping whiskey and sifting through Andre Duran's crowded biography. But he quickly tired of that and wandered back inside. Nothing of interest in the refrigerator except a carton of eggs, enough for an omelet. He wasn't hungry. Alec looked into the living room and sat in the big wing chair, facing the west wall where his photographs were clustered, more than fifty years of work, his pleasure and his livelihood, what he liked to think was the organizing principle of his life. The ones on the wall were not necessarily the best photographs but his favorites, having to do with the circumstances of the shoot or the personality of the subject, and as he looked at them he thought he would go to his father's grave in the morning, shoot something in black and white. He stared now at the Jefferson Memorial at dawn and the façade of Mrs. Wheatley's house, the grille of a Buick poking through the right edge. All the photographs were set in simple black frames. Next to Mrs. Wheatley's house was a shot of Jimmy Stewart, nonchalant in a dinner jacket, a flute of champagne in his hand, homespun Mr. Smith as worldly as any Georgetown gigolo. Mathilde at a tender age concentrating on a chessboard, her index finger touching the queen's crown. Annalise on the beach at Malibu, delicious in a yellow bikini, balancing a red beach ball on her nose like a trained seal. His father asleep at his desk on the Senate floor. The Japanese houseman Charles, a faint smile at play on his mouth, holding someone's overcoat. There were a dozen others — his garden in the moonlight, his mother smoking a cigarette on the terrace of the Chevy Chase house, Duke Ellington shaking hands with the chairman of the Federal Reserve, Henry Fonda brandishing a nine-iron, Oleg Cassini, the Countess d'An, Joseph Alsop, Admiral Honeycutt, the Confederate infantryman, Jacqueline Onassis, and the newsroom of the paper late at night, no one in sight, identical desks with identical typewriters, the big Westclox on the wall reading midnight. Finally, the long-ago Georgetown students, on book, giving *Lear* everything they had.

The telephone rang but Alec did not rise to answer it. He sipped his drink and looked carefully at the photographs, one after another, up and down and left and right. He realized that none of them were of recent vintage. He remembered the circumstances of each shoot, the location and the time of day, the solid feel of the miraculous Leica in his hand. Cassini and Admiral Honeycutt were caught unawares, Cassini in a bathing suit on the terrace of a villa in the south of France, the admiral taking his afternoon constitutional. Jimmy Stewart and Mathilde were more or less posed. Annalise was pretending not to pose. The unseen figure was himself, the man behind the camera, the mechanic at the engine; and then he saw a sliver of shadow on Annalise's red beach ball, his own. Naturally all the photographs had his signature, though Alec was hard put to say precisely what that signature was, its specific stamp, its tone of voice. Alec wondered what it was that bound the photographs together or if anything bound them together. They were his favorite shots so somewhere ran a common theme, the extended imagery of a poem or a song's ostinato. Alec rose and stepped forward until he was a foot from the wall, looking at the photographs again each in turn. He closed his bad right eye so that he could see more clearly, judging the light, the boundary of the shot, the feel of the material. He finished his whiskey and put the glass on the sideboard. Now he closed his good eye, moving from one photograph to the next so that all the photographs were in motion, variations on Munch's *Scream*. But that was not the common theme, far from it. Alec stood staring at the wall of images for many minutes and realized finally with the most open dismay that the common theme was the absence of conflict.

THE THICK OF IT

ALEC WENT TO BED TROUBLED. Before sleep came he was reading the African book of the great Polish correspondent Ryszard Kapuściński, his observation that ordinary people searched for normality. The search was instinctive. In Africa the brutality of political events — coup d'état, rampage, revolution, conflict of every color and shape — was seen as a function of nature, natural phenomena to be endured and waited out as one would endure and wait out a storm from the heavens. In time the storm passed and normal life resumed, even if that normal life consisted of nothing more than sitting in the sun or enjoying a morning cup of coffee. Such people had no interest in pushing the envelope of human experience. Envelope-pushing was not in their nature. Envelope-pushing got you into a world of trouble, perhaps dead. Envelope-pushing was another word for vanity. But Alec was not certain that the slow-moving sun-drenched furnace of central Africa was applicable in the century of the American empire, where war was always waged in a distant country and affectless unless you knew someone who was there, a soldier or civil servant. Otherwise it was experienced as a photograph in the newspaper or a film on television or on the Internet. A good question for Kapuściński, but Kapuściński was dead and unavailable for questioning. They said that wherever Kapuściński went in the world, and he went most everywhere, his true subject was Poland. Iran, Congo, China — only Poland written in another tongue. Alec had no idea whether what they said was true. It sounded true, and if it was, then Poland was a fabulous country.

Alec showered and dressed and drank two cups of coffee while he scanned page one of the newspaper — more of the same, with a well-balanced photograph of an Iraqi child perched on the knee of a GI, stock footage except the child was smoking a cigarette, as world-weary as any café intellectual. Alec looked at the weather report, cloudy with rain later in the day. When he looked at the date he gave a start. Today was his father's birthday, an occasion that meant a great deal to the old man. Last year Alec had bought him a bottle of single-malt Scotch with an unpronounceable name, and when he died there was still a half-inch in the bottle. Alec stared at the date for a long time, then went to his desk and wrote a note to Mathilde, telling her where he was going and when he intended to return. Then he set out for the cemetery, the Leica snug in his pocket, strolling up the street past Admiral Honeycutt's old house and Ronald diAntonio's until he came to Mrs. Wheatley's, all the shades drawn and a faded white carnation in the gutter. The morning newspapers were stacked neatly on the front stoop. His mother had told him once that Eleanora Wheatley read six newspapers a day, cover to cover except for the sports page. She enjoyed catching her guests in errors of fact, Joseph Alsop a favorite target, Kim Malone not far behind. He wondered if Ryszard Kapuściński had ever visited America. Certainly he had, everyone came to America sooner or later. But had he ever written on the subject? Probably not. America was not

Kapuściński's material, since it bore no conspicuous resemblance to Poland.

Alec entered the cemetery grounds at R Street and took the path that wound down in the direction of Rock Creek Park, past gravestones high and low, plain and gaudy, old stones side by side with new ones. At nine in the morning the cemetery was deserted, and then he noticed a woman setting up her easel near the Saint-Gaudens monument to Clover Adams, Henry's wife, who died in circumstances mostly unaccounted for, except it was known she drank from her own darkroom's developing chemicals; toward the end of her life she had become a passionate photographer. And decades later Eleanor Roosevelt came to sit by the hour beside Clover Adams's grave after she learned of her husband's affair with Lucy Mercer. Alec's father had told him the story. He called the gravesite hallowed ground.

Alec walked awhile, uncertain where he was in the cemetery. He was slightly winded moving down the undulating path. The distant parkway was thick with rush-hour traffic, carbon monoxide heavy in the chilly air, now and again the sound of an auto horn. He remembered the Reverend Willis walking uphill and pausing beside a tree, and now he tried to locate the tree. His father's grave was on the downslope not far from the parkway. Alec rested a moment on one of the benches placed at intervals along the path. Traffic was at a standstill now and he heard programs from a score of radios, Snoop Dogg and Puccini and news talk joined in a mighty cacophony, two hos and Rodolfo making their way arm in arm along the dangerous streets of Baghdad. Alec closed his eyes and when he opened them he saw his father's grave not fifty feet away. He sat very still, the Leica inert in his hand. A fat black crow was poking at the grave soil, its head jerking violently.

There were no known photographs of Mrs. Roosevelt at the grave of Clover Adams.

Those days, his father said, they let people alone.

Alec stood and sidestepped down the slope. The bird flew away. He picked his way down, sliding here and there on the damp grass. The Leica was still in his hand but he had forgotten about it. Standing at the graveside he tried to summon his father's presence but was unsuccessful. He had thought of a few words to say, so he said them without confidence that they would be heard by anyone except himself. He asked for repose of his father's soul and happiness in the afterlife. He wished him happy birthday and hoped that someone had remembered to bring a cake and a bottle of Scotch. No one should have to celebrate alone. Alec stepped back then and squeezed off two shots of the grave and the wilting flowers beside it. They would be flat shots, for there were no shadows on this milky spring morning. The grave soil was cold to his touch and damp but he picked up a fistful anyway, crumbling it in his fingers. Alec stood stone still, aware of the stalled traffic behind him. What a lonely figure he must look to the commuters on the parkway and the joggers on the path next to it. He stepped back two more paces and put the camera in his pocket. Upslope he saw the gravediggers, the same two who had attended his father. One of them pushed the wheelbarrow and the other strolled alongside. They were talking companionably and when they saw Alec they gave respectful salutes and Alec saluted back. He thought suddenly that gravedigging must be the oldest profession. He watched them continue on their way over the hill for the day's work. Alec made a last shot of them as they disappeared over the brow.

He had done what he came to do and now it was time to go back home, visit with Mathilde. Yet Alec did not move. He listened for his father's words but heard nothing except the sound of traffic. He tried to summon conversations from years past but was not successful. His father was lodged in a region of his mind but that region was not accessible. He could not at that moment even recall the sound of the old man's voice, its tone and timbre. Alec bent down, knees creaking, and made another shot. He thought of the urn under the earth and the ashes inside the urn. Something paltry and incomplete about it, not equal to the occasion — and Alec thought then that he was feeling not grief but loss, unless they were the same thing. He and the old man were fundamentally estranged, had been estranged for decades, a question of temperament, differing ideas on how a life might be usefully lived. What counted, and the reckoning. They saw the world through opposing lenses. He wondered if the same schism occurred between mothers and daughters, and then he remembered Lucia and her mother, married to socialism. In his father's life there seemed no separation between the public and the private, each locked in death's grip. Alec wondered if his father saw his son's life as a rebuke. Probably he did. Ryszard Kapuściński's father must have felt the same rejection. What was his boy doing flinging himself all over the world, the Asian continent, Africa, the Middle East. What was wrong with Poland? Except the whole world was Poland, and when he died Kapuściński was the most admired foreign correspondent in all Europe. His father would have known that and, dime to a dollar, would have been proud. Surely that was the case.

Time to go. But Alec did not move.

The old man had led a satisfactory life, a life of consequence to a very great age where he could look back with satisfaction and some wonder and amusement. The Senate was no doubt a better place with him than without him. He had been on the right side of things generally, moments of accomplishment and some courage along with low comedy and the usual disappointments and compromises and feuds, the blowback of a political life. Kim Malone liked being in the thick of it. He often said there was no reason to live in Washington if you were not in the thick of it. If you didn't want the thick of it, go back to Dubuque. Alec remembered Timmy James chain-smoking and threatening to piss on a Republican. The evening calls from Franklin Roosevelt, his high Hudson Valley squire's accent instantly recognizable, wanting help with this or that piece of legislation or a judge or cabinet member he wanted confirmed at once without delay. Can you help me with this? Calls every night from colleagues and lobbyists, constituents, now and again a vice president, but the call that counted was the one from the White House. None was savored in the way that the Hudson Valley squire's calls were savored. Kim Malone believed himself indispensable to the civic life of the nation. Nothing else mattered in quite the same way as a war resolution, a tax act, Social Security, Lend-Lease. Ordinary life was a version of frivolity, redundant, and in that way he and Andre Duran were kin, one holding a floor and the other a sword. Against that Alec had a camera, used for peaceful purposes. Against that was the thought that life was not a competitive race. In life, as in golf, you played against the course, not your opponent. Courses came in infinite varieties of shapes and sizes and degrees of difficulty. Success depended on the shots you had and how creative you were with them, and always a requiem at the end of the day. Alec supposed he could be described as having had a sidelines sort of life, peaceable for the most part. Wasn't it Orwell who observed that pacifism was a respectable idea so long as you were willing to accept the consequences?

He heard a step behind him and wheeled about to see Mathilde.

She said, I knew you would be here.

To say a few last words, Alec said.

I have to say goodbye, Papa. I have a noon flight.

So soon? Well, I'm glad you were here.

Me too.

When will I see you next?

Mathilde gave an inconclusive shrug. Probably a few months. Certainly before the end of the year.

You should make an effort to meet Andre. You'd like him. He's — unusual.

Mama said the reunion went well. She was nervous before-hand.

I think it did, he said.

She's with him now, Mathilde said.

The reunion meant quite a lot to Andre, too.

I'm worried about you, she said.

Don't be, Alec said. He raised the Leica to his left eye and made two shots of his daughter. For the second shot Mathilde offered a wide grin — a reluctant grin, Alec thought. He said, I'm driving up to Maine for a week or two. I'll call you in London.

Will you take care of yourself? You should get more exercise. And watch your diet. Mathilde went on in that vein and when she finished they embraced, and with a wave she was gone, walking back up the hill with an athletic stride. Alec waited a few moments before he, too, began the climb up the hill.

Home, Alec stepped into the kitchen and brewed a pot of coffee. He was winded from the walk back from the cemetery and now paused to take stock of his surroundings. The pot was decades old. The refrigerator and stove were decades old, as were the chairs and sofa in the living room. The carpet was threadbare. The digital wall clock was new, a Christmas gift from Mathilde. He could donate the ensemble to the Smithsonian for one of their exhibits, "The Way We Lived Then." Minus the wall clock. Minus the Bose radio, also a gift from Mathilde. Probably the time had come to give the place a shave and a haircut, a makeover for the twenty-first century. Alec made a mental note to call Bloomingdale's in the morning. Bloomingdale's was his mother's department store of choice. Two chairs and a sofa — his mother had called it a davenport — and new end tables, and lamps to go with the end tables. He heard a sound somewhere and thought it was his father laughing.

Pouring coffee, he remembered the telephone call from the

night before, the one he had left for the answering machine. He touched the button and heard Annalise's breathy voice. She was arriving in New York at four in the afternoon, staying at the Algonquin. I've been thinking about you and hope everything went well with your father. Are you going to Maine? Please call.

Alec drank his coffee, killing time for an hour, paying bills and thinking about Bloomingdale's. A dozen or more bills had collected over the past fortnight. He made a mental note to call his bank for a fresh supply of checks. He noticed another ten percent increase in his health insurance premium. Heating oil was on the rise. The American Express bill was negligible because he hadn't been anywhere. The Democratic Party needed money. Alec put the mail aside and called the Algonquin and left a welcoming message for Annalise. At noon he set off in his car, up Wisconsin Avenue to Military Road, right on Military to the tree-lined street where Goya House was located. He sat in his car a moment listening to the engine tick. Andre was alone on the porch, looking as if he had not moved since the previous evening. He was smoking a cigarette and rocking gently in his chair and did not notice Alec approach.

Andre? Alec said.

Yes. Andre fumbled with his earpiece.

It's Alec, he said.

Lucia is no longer here. She had to catch her airplane.

I know.

She is returning to Europe, Andre said. She did not bring Mathilde. Apparently there were appointments at the State Department.

Mathilde left for London this morning. Via New York.

So much travel in your family. But we'll meet when it is time.

I wanted to see you again.

Why?

I enjoyed our conversation yesterday.

Andre made a sound somewhere between a laugh and a grunt

and in a sudden motion pitched his cigarette onto the lawn. The day had turned dark, heavy clouds building to the west, no breeze.

Your story interests me. I would like to know more. You see, I have never met anyone like you. With your background. The way you have lived your life.

Andre shrugged and shook his head.

I don't mean to intrude, Alec said.

Would you like Turkish coffee? Without waiting for a reply, Andre rapped sharply on the window and called for the boy to bring the pot and two cups right away. The answering shout was grudging.

Alec's Leica was in his pocket. He said, Would you mind if I took your photograph?

No photographs, Andre said.

As you wish.

Why do you want to know how I came to be at Goya House? It is no business of yours. Lucia said you were curious.

I am curious about Goya House.

It's an ordinary boarding house, Andre said.

Of exiles, Alec said.

Yes, of exiles.

Not ordinary, surely.

Andre sighed and did not speak for a full minute. Rain began to fall softly, more heard than seen. Leaves on the trees shivered with it, the sky lowering. Nothing moved in the street. At last Andre said, The historian Holder arranged it. He was very ill but he made the necessary calls. Goya House has a board of directors and one of them is a newspaper editor. Holder called the editor, who made the necessary inquiries. Quite simple, really. There is a Goya House in the suburbs of Paris and another near Toulouse and a villa in Italy. Mostly for the casualties of fascism but not only fascism. This house had a vacancy and I filled the vacancy. End of story.

I see, Alec said.

There's nothing underhanded about it, Andre said.

I didn't think there was.

Yes, you did.

I was only curious, Alec said.

Andre was silent again, smiling to himself, watching rain leak through the trees. He said, We had a death last month, an old comrade. We had met briefly in Spain in 1938, the Catalonian front. We were on — I cannot say opposite sides but sides that were distrustful of each other, most suspicious. A feature of the Spanish war, a matter of control of tactics and strategy. Who has possession of the genie in the bottle. He was an anarchist and I was on the communist side, of course. It is the nature of anarchists to cause trouble. Anarchy is their way. *Qué lástima*, as the Spanish say. What a pity. He was still full of fight, that one, and he was even older than I am. Hated us, hated the priests, hated the fascists, and at the end of his life hated the king most of all. He mourned Catalonia his entire life. He insisted there be no funeral. No formal notice of his death. He did not want to give them satisfaction. He only wanted his ashes returned to Catalonia and scattered in his native village near Gerona. He was a man of the mountains. He left us money for airfare, though he hated doing it. He hated money. Money was the antichrist even more than the priests. So we have this money and now we have to decide who is going to Catalonia with Salvador's ashes.

Not you, Alec said.

Not me. I will spend the rest of my days here, however many days remain to me. Someone will volunteer. We try to look after one another. We are a community after all. We have responsibilities, even toward someone as disagreeable as Salvador.

Andre rapped the glass again. Where is the little shit?

I have a question for you about Mathilde, he went on. Is she one of those responsible for your interventions here, there, and everywhere.

No, Alec said with a smile. I think those decisions are taken at a level higher than hers. The president, the secretary of state. God. God apparently has a role in the administration's statecraft.

She has no part in them?

She is one of those who carry them out, the decisions.

An apparatchik, Andre said.

A Foreign Service officer, Alec said.

Isn't it strange? Time was, America refused to intervene anywhere. Spain, Czechoslovakia, Poland. Now it intervenes everywhere. Asia, Central America, the Middle East, even Africa. No corner of the globe is immune. Do you have an explanation? I mean other than God's hand.

You could say we learned our lesson.

Is that what you would say?

No, Alec said.

One of our group here is Polish. He, too, was in Spain, though we did not know each other. He fought the Nazis and then the Soviets and ended up in the Gulag. In due course he was released, drifted for a time, and ended up here. He has a nephew who lives near Kraków. The nephew calls himself a squatter. He does not work but somehow he gets along. He is forty years old, this nephew. He says he writes poetry but refuses to show his poems to his uncle. My Polish friend does not know what to make of his nephew, who seems to have made nothing of his life. He has a wife but they have no children. He lives day to day with his poetry, which he does not publish. Well, who is to say? Kafka published almost nothing in his lifetime. But my friend does not think his nephew is Kafka. Lately his letters have taken a fresh turn. He has identified his enemies. They are, along with the Americans and the Russians, the state, the church, the gangsters, the drug dealers, the skinheads, and the police. They are destroying Poland. Destroying him. This is the thrashing-about of the powerless. People who have no investment in anything. Their morale breaks. They turn their scorn on anyone and anything outside. Never themselves. They lose their ability to think critically. Therefore they cannot make a life for themselves.

Andre paused and added, I do not know why I tell you this story. But it was what I was thinking about when you arrived.

Then the front door slammed and the boy was at their elbows with the tray of coffee cups and the spouted pot. He said something to Andre, who grunted noncommittally. The boy departed at once and Andre poured, the coffee thick as lava. They sat quietly waiting for the coffee to cool. From somewhere in the house Alec heard Russian music, a balalaika.

Alec said, Do you miss soldiering?

Andre said, Of course. Soldiering was something I did well. Did very well. I was often beside myself with fright. But my fright did not prevent me from acting. Only once or twice was I frozen in place, unable to move forward. This is not a good feeling. Breathing is difficult. Yet it goes away. I am too old for soldiering now so it is just as well that I spend my days here on this porch, drinking my coffee during the day and schnapps in the evening, thinking about the nephews of friends and anything else that occurs to me. I sleep well at night. And you. Do you miss photography?

I still photograph. Mostly for my own pleasure. Now and again I take a job if the job interests me. But the jobs that come along interest me less and less, so I find myself marking time more than I would like. Until very recently I was caring for my father but he is gone now.

You did not marry again after Lucia left you?

No. Once was enough.

Nor I after I left Lucia's mother. It has to be said that I did not have many chances. Spain, then France with the Resistance, later on in Czecho and Yugoslavia. Then the camps. After the camps I was not romantically inclined. I had opportunities for mercenary work in Africa but that did not interest me. I had no interest in Africa. There was nothing in Africa worth fighting for except money. I knew a few women when I was working at the ski resort but they were only tourists and not interested in anything permanent, and I suppose in that way the liaisons suited us both. I did not have the sort of background that lent itself to sharing. Isn't that the word in use now? Sharing? I hear it on television. One time I told a woman about my early life and when I woke up in the morning she was gone, not even a note left behind. And we were fond of each other. I think I frightened her. I know I did, Andre concluded, and gave a shrug.

It's the opposite with me, Alec said. Women love hearing my stories about shoots here and there, particularly Hollywood. They like hearing about movie stars. They want to know what the stars are really like, and when I tell them that what you see in the photograph is all you're likely to get, they don't believe me. They think I'm holding out on them.

And are you?

I don't know the stars. I only photograph them.

That sounds like a pleasant way to make a living. Pays well, doesn't it?

Yes, it does.

The locations are pleasant.

Most of the time, Alec said.

Did you ever photograph Gary Cooper?

He died before I got into the business, Alec said.

I liked watching Gary Cooper. His films were everywhere in Europe before the war. I always thought Cooper represented a kind of ideal American, resolute but with an amusing side to him. Sympathetic to the underdog. Not a city man but rather a man of the West. A mountain man, I would say. Also a man of action, sure of himself but never a bully. A man of few words.

Alec nodded in agreement. Gary Cooper had been dead for decades.

Alec said, Did you ever meet Tito?

Andre laughed and said he had met Tito once during the war. Not a pleasant man but one with great personal force. Andre said, He wanted to bring my commando under his control, his orders, his objectives. I said I would think about it. He said I shouldn't take too long; too much thinking could be dangerous. He gave me this, Andre said, and pulled the ivory cigarette holder from his pocket. He said that would cement our friendship. Our collaboration under his control, his orders, his objectives. I got out of there damned fast, I can tell you. I refused to be under his orders or anyone's orders. When I told that story to Holder, he didn't believe me. But it happened all right. There were witnesses. Andre screwed a cigarette into the holder and struck a match, exhaling a fog of smoke that seemed to hang in the air forever.

I admire your life, Alec said.

I don't believe you.

You fought the right battles, Alec said. And you didn't wait for them to come to you. You went looking for them.

I fought the ones I could fight.

And paid the price. How many years were you in prison?

Many, many years. Twenty years, I suppose. More than that, I think.

I imagine even prison was worth it. If prison was the price.

You don't know what you're talking about. Prison is a terrible experience. You lose track of the world and the world loses track of you. Do you know that it took one man nine hours to dig one-half a cubic meter through the permafrost? And you did this day after day without knowing the purpose of the excavation. Your daily patch, one-half meter of soil. Some days each swing of the pick yielded a finger-sized piece of Siberian soil. The war was a terrible experience, too, but at least you are free more or less. You conduct your business in the open, not in a cell. You have something to show for the struggle. You can believe that what you are doing is worthwhile even if it is but a small part of a much larger picture. Often it was helpful not knowing the larger picture. The larger picture was not your business anyway. I still think of my half-meter. In any case, I survived.

Yes, Alec said. How, exactly?

Andre moved his shoulders and did not reply.

I'm sorry I asked.

Luck, Andre said. And I have a strong constitution. Also, I was born at a particular time in a particular place. Life was always hard for my family. Later on the war was everywhere, inside and outside. I could not avoid it. No one could. The Nazis were a terrible cult and the Soviets not much better. Stalin was a gangster. Still, if you were forced to put your cards down, you'd put them down in Stalin's favor. That was the situation. The war was not an elective and a choice had to be made. That was how I saw it. I think I told you once that I have always looked for the absolute.

And were you disappointed?

Rarely, Andre said.

I had the belief that if I went to the war my photographs would make it beautiful. The very horror of it had a beautiful side also, the kind of beauty that's alluring. Bewitching I would say. It draws one in. Makes you larger than life. Did you ever read the *Iliad*?

Of course. Many times.

Such beautiful poetry describing such appalling events.

But surely, Andre said with a wolfish smile, surely we would not be better off without the *Iliad*.

Alec removed his eyeglasses and looked away in the direction of the street, his vision more fractured than usual. He ran his thumb over his lower lip as he often did when concentrating. But this time his concentration yielded nothing. Rain continued to fall through the trees and Alec did not see the visitor until he was a few steps away. The intruder wore a blue uniform and carried a heavy pack on his shoulder.

Andre said, Good morning, Vincent.

Good morning, Andre. Not much mail today.

Anything for me?

One letter. The postmark is smudged. I can't tell you where it came from.

Dubrovnik, Andre said when he looked at the letter.

Will you save me the stamp?

With pleasure, Vincent.

The postman nodded, handed Andre the rest of the mail, and went away.

Please, Alec said, read it now if you want.

I'll save it, Andre said. I know what's in it anyway. An old comrade wants me to send him some money. He is eternally in need of funds. He does not care to work and is too feeble to work if he did care. He doesn't have a trade in any case. Soldiering was his trade. So he writes me, and from time to time I send him fifty dollars, whatever I can spare. You were saying?

It gives me pause that the conditions of our world make the *Iliad* indispensable.

We are making progress, Andre said with a sour smile. Remember what Isaac Babel said. You must know everything.

It wasn't Babel who said it. His mother said it.

Andre thought a moment. Yes, that's right.

In order to survive the world. That's why she said it.

That is the sort of idea you get when you are born in Russia, Andre said. Your first thought is to pass it on to your children. He blew a fat smoke ring, evidently enjoying himself. What sort of photographs do you make?

I make still lifes, Alec said, except for the most part they are not arrangements of flowers or fruit but human beings and man-made objects. A doorway or a sailboat. A newsroom. I have photographed my own garden but readily confess that my garden is a sentimental subject. I have a knack for making beautiful pictures. They are pictures without obvious conflict and therefore I was miscast in the news. I have often wondered if I missed an opportunity when I refused to go to Vietnam.

I wouldn't worry about it. Your war was an elective.

I don't worry. I used to worry. And "missing an opportunity" is not exactly what I mean. What I did was not a business decision. Alec was silent a moment, and then he added, There's a sort of shame attached.

Andre rolled his eyes but said nothing.

That must be it. What else would it be?

That accounts for your — uneasiness?

You went, Alec said. You went without a second thought.

Andre sighed heavily. You refuse to listen, he said. I have been trying to say to you that we had no choice. I could not stand aside. My country was invaded. All the countries around me were invaded. Central Europe was disappearing. Try please to understand what that means. Your world is vanishing before your eyes without the slightest indication that anything you do will reverse the tide. Stop the rot. Make it cease. So you went to war and learned how to do it in the way that a carpenter learns how to make a chair. An artisan's work. But also you are free and whatever else your life may be, it is not still. I can see you are troubled. But I cannot help you.

So it was personal, Alec said.

Andre's reply was swift. What else would it be?

Alec had left his eyeglasses off all this time. Now he replaced them and reached into his pocket for the Leica. Andre was relaxed in his chair, gently rocking, watching Vincent the postman work the opposite side of the street. This was an untroubled neighborhood, mature shade trees lining the streets, the hum of the city inaudible, spring turning slowly into summer. Even the rain was benevolent. Alec thought the street with its picture-perfect plant life and settled houses had the aspect of a film set, something from the conformist 1950s, a balalaika from an upstairs bedroom, Vincent the postman bursting into song as he danced from lawn to lawn. Alec thought, Time to leave this neighborhood to itself. He was an intruder.

Alec looked around him, at the porch with its heavy railing and the empty room behind the window. Andre stirred and said something unintelligible; he was talking to himself in Czech. Alec took a last sip of Turkish coffee and rose heavily, his knees hurting. He looked at his watch and saw that he had been sitting on the porch for almost two hours. Alec turned to say something to Andre but the old man's eyes were closed, his hands flat on his belly, fingers linked. Whatever dream he was having was peaceful, and even in repose his body had the hardness and everlastingness of permafrost or one of those solemn statues of Stalin that once stood in the squares of middle European cities. And then it occurred to him that he was not the intruder in this peaceable neighborhood. Andre Duran was. Alec stepped quietly off the porch and came around the lawn to face Andre head-on. He made two shots with the Leica, the shutter's click as quiet as the tick of a clock.

Alec turned his back and walked across the lawn to his car. As he opened the door he looked up to the rooftop of Goya House. Someone was standing on the widow's walk, still as a statue, dressed in a yellow oilskin slicker and a gardener's floppy hat. Alec recognized him as one of the soccer fans, looking now for all the world like a distressed widow scanning the horizon for signs of a ship's sail. Alec gave a wave but the figure on the roof took no notice. He looked due east, his hands gripping the flimsy railing, his concentration complete. Rain continued to fall and somewhere behind it Alec heard the balalaika's song.

He was in no rush. Alec turned the ignition of his car but did not drive away. He sat quietly looking at the great mercantile hulk of Goya House, lights visible here and there from the windows of the upper floors. Alec thought of it as a cathedral, with all the dark places and mystery of a cathedral, empty in midafternoon. He was certain now that he and Andre would not meet again. Their conversations had reached a dead end, and there was this: Andre's voice had changed when he spoke of Spain, his tone softer, almost feminine. Alec wondered if the heroic wish had given voice to the thought, a feat of the imagination. For one of Andre's generation Spain was a grail, the ur-struggle of the previous century. To be present there was to be present at the creation. Of course there were gaps in Andre's memory, things omitted or forgotten, glossed over, redacted and invented. Memories bore the same relation to the facts as distant cousins to a common grandfather. Yet was it not also true that the myths one lived by were the real stuff of life, its romance and surprise? Certainly the way one saw a much-loved grandfather was not the way he saw himself. Every life was subject to misapprehension; people saw what they wanted to see. The dance floor turned as the dancers waltzed. So stories were told to give a context to things. To give voice to the unspeakable. The listener either believed the account or did not. Often you hid your own face to see clearly the face of another. Alec believed Andre, and if he had a reservation about Spain, the reservation was unimportant. And Alec was sure Andre would say the same of him, with a reservation of his own. But what that reservation was, Alec could not say. Either way, Alec knew he was finished here. He listened hard for the balalaika but heard nothing. The figure in the yellow oilskin had vacated the widow's walk. Evidently the ship was not yet in view, so he had given it up. No doubt he would return at dusk or early the following morning and for as many days as was necessary.

As Andre said, you do not have the luxury of being certain about things, least of all the context of your own life.

MAINE

IGH HOUSE WAS BUILT on a bluff that looked across Baylor's Harbor to a lighthouse. There were many smaller islands round and about, and at nine and twelve and three and six the high-bowed ferry arrived from the mainland; last boat off was at nine P.M. It had been years since Annalise had been in Maine and she had forgotten how green it was, everything green and black-green with spots of yellow in the underbrush and on the surfaces of rocks. Maine was untamed. The house was a decade old and built on the margins of a forest, clear-cut looking south to provide a panorama of Baylor's Harbor and the open water beyond. A lone spruce stood dead center fifty yards out for perspective. The branches were widely spaced and bare to the tips, where nests of needles flourished. In early morning the nests of needles resembled floating islands, islands of the sky because their branches were obscured by fog. Now and then a gull floated out of the fog to appear on one of the branches. Except when the wind died, Baylor's Harbor and the thoroughfare beyond was alive with boats, some large, some so small that from the house you could see only the wake, a string of white on blue. At dead calm there were flat stripes in the water, gray in color and steely white where the flat spots were, a function of hidden ocean currents. At dead calm the ocean did not move at all, the only sensation that of depth and tremendous weight. Then, the water seemed to have an ominous potential behind an uneasy truce, the sense that in an instant and without warning the water could begin to heave and swell with who knew what consequences. Annalise and Alec looked up often from their books to watch the unsettled motion of Baylor's Harbor, judging the wind and looking to the west and southwest where the weather came from. Alec remarked that John Singer Sargent claimed that when he showed his portraits to members of his family, one of them always observed, Well, y-yess, but isn't there something wrong about the mouth? Baylor's Harbor was like that. Something wrong about the lay of the water.

High House (as it was called by everyone on the island) had a bedroom and bath on the first floor, a kitchen, pantry, and dining room on the second, and a living room on the third. The ceiling of the third floor was twenty feet high. The wall facing south had six high windows and a door leading to a narrow deck. The other walls were windowless, lined with bookshelves accompanied by a ladder hung on a rail attached to the ceiling. The owners had no interest in the island's interior and did not want to look at it. Their passion was the water, Baylor's Harbor and the thorough-fare beyond. Alec estimated there were more than two thousand books in the room, books of a certain age and character: three full shelves of mysteries and thrillers, McDonald, MacDonald, Cain, Hammett, and Chandler; Erskine Childers, Maugham, le Carré, McCarry; and elsewhere, floor to ceiling, Wodehouse, Waugh, John Wheeler-Bennett, Carlyle, Gibbon, Laxness, O'Hara, Charles Bracelen Flood, Mrs. Wharton, Mrs. Gaskell, Trollope, Don Marquis, Austen, Dostoyevsky, Edmund Wilson, Robert Frost, Yeats. The bottom shelves were for the children, full sets of the Hardy Boys and Nancy Drew. The deck girdled the third floor but it was rarely used because the planks were not secure, well weathered with symptoms of rot, the ground forty feet down. On a low rise behind and aslant of the lone spruce was a squat cabin painted in now faded red and white stripes, a folly of the neighbors, transported log by log from Norway — Arctic Circle Norway, a fisherman's shack intended as a playhouse for the grandchildren until colonies of wasps nested. Heroic and continuing efforts to expel the wasps were unsuccessful. The interior of the cabin had not been entered for many years, so it sat untended and unoccupied, derelict.

In May the air was chilly, a biting wind most frequently from the west. The air was filled with seaweed and brine, bracing so long as you bundled up. The hills of the mainland were often obscured by low clouds that broke in the early evening, providing a spectacular sunset, a brief entertainment for the cocktail hour. Alec and Annalise took long walks in the morning and again in the afternoon; the rest of the time they read or played dominoes in the living room, conscious always of the weather and aware when a car or pickup truck motored by on the road to town. A Herreshoff came with the house, but Alec was wary of the tides and the unpredictable spring wind so he let the boat rest on its mooring, waiting for a sunny day with a benign breeze. Annalise thought the boat too small for two people, but Alec said it would be fine; the first good day they'd take it for a sail to the beach on the western side of the island, the one with sand instead of rocks and boulders the size of a small coupe. A good place to picnic, Alec said, a beach in the lee of the wind.

In the morning they walked the two miles into town for breakfast and it was then, on their third day, that Annalise announced that the script she was reading was junk.

Just awful, she said.

Send it back, Alec said.

It's work, Annalise said. I like to work. I enjoy the set. And the

255

director and cinematographer are old friends. Best yet, they're shooting in Key West. Next winter, even better.

Who are you playing?

A whore with a heart of iron.

You've been there before.

I know. But I've always had fun in Key West. You could come with me, make some photographs of the filming. You've been idle for too long. It's not good to stay away from your craft, you lose your touch.

Alec did not reply. He was watching a red-tailed hawk circle the lighthouse, making great wide circles, riding the wind. He took the Leica from his pocket and squeezed off a shot, knowing the hawk was too far away. He lowered the camera and took one of Annalise in full pout.

You're distracted, she said. You were distracted last night in bed.

I was, that's true.

Most unlike you, she said.

Too much wine, he said.

Nonsense. Your mind was elsewhere.

Goya House, he said.

What's Goya House?

Alec had not told Annalise of his encounter with Andre Duran. He had not mentioned Lucia, either, because Annalise did not like her and was vocal about it. They had never met but Annalise had formed her own stubborn opinion, a matter of loyalty to Alec. Most hesitantly he described lunch with Lucia and Mathilde and his visits to Andre. He confessed he had been fascinated and unsettled by their conversations. He and Andre had led utterly different lives, opposing lives, you could say. Andre's was very far from a normal life. His was a life you read about in books, the ones with lurid covers. Of course their circumstances were different but Andre's experiences had given him standing along with an ardent sincerity that in another setting — say, the men's bar of a downtown club or a political rally or pulpit — would have translated into smug. He had presence, Alec said, built like an ox, brimming with energy, behaving like a man thirty years younger. Andre Duran was startlingly forthcoming. And he had been through terrible times, committing, by his own account, unspeakable acts. Probably a clever prosecutor could make him out a war criminal and Andre would not be a convincing witness in his own behalf, contemptuous as he was of any jurisdiction beyond himself. Remorse was not in his nature. In that way, Alec said, he reminded me of my father. Those in the arena lived by the arena's rules, always opaque to outsiders. Of course Andre was on the right side of things generally, a righteous warrior in the common struggle. His own experiences were the only experiences he trusted. Your experience or mine was off-book, not quite real to him. They did not exist for him and in any case were more or less expendable or valueless, like civilian casualties, collateral damage. Hard to know what to make of a man who so completely lived inside himself. Whatever private sorrow that went along with such a life was unknown, at any event unexplained. I believe he felt himself driven by fate. He had no say in the matter, assuredly a convenience in assessing the life he had led; he did what he did because he could do no other and left the assessments to strangers who were, naturally, unequal to the task. He was handed an assignment and he completed the assignment, no questions asked. Andre Duran was a locomotive on rails and the locomotive was called History. Alec said that his encounters with Andre had caused him to look critically at his own life, where assignments did not figure. What he found there was puzzling, an enigma. When he tried to remember his ambitions for himself when he started out he found he could not except for a vague desire to record daily life, its fundamental stillness, its pauses and silences and unexpected rewards. "Vague" was probably the wrong word. The correct word was "incomplete." You could not know everything about your own life or the life of anyone else. Surely there was a lesson somewhere in Andre's life and everyone had a secret store, a habit, of sorrow. Alec regretted nothing. Regret was not in Alec's nature.

They had paused in front of the town cemetery, an acre plot bounded by a rusting wire fence, ancient gravestones tilting left and right. Many stones dated from the eighteenth century and a few from the seventeenth. Alec wondered aloud what promise could have drawn people to this remote island, with all of the American South and Midwest open to them. What was their reward? A growing season of two months maximum, appalling winter hardships, dangerous navigation, and hostile Indians. Perhaps hardship was the point. In colonial times such a place would be fundamentally lawless, and that, too, would be an attraction for a man who had a certain idea of himself and a cast-in-granite vision of the life he wished to lead. Alec looked again at the gravestones and saw that most of the names were effaced, eroded by weather. Here and there he could make out a date and an RIP at the top of the stone. The place looked haunted.

They resumed their stroll into town, Annalise silent.

At last she said, I don't know what takes us into one business instead of another. I could as easily have been a dress designer. If I had been born ten years later I could have gone into politics, followed my father. I always liked the atmosphere of the committee room and even the floor of the House, the wheeling and dealing, the sarcasm. I liked campaigning. My mother hated it, so I was the one who showed up on the street corner or at the candidates' debates with my father, shaking hands and giving them a big wide smile. My mother couldn't disguise her distaste for it all, the handshaking and air-kissing. It's all so insincere, she said. But that's what I liked about it, the acknowledged insincerity. I didn't have to disguise anything. But in my junior year I joined the drama club and found I was good at it. And I was pretty, and that was a big plus. I photographed well. So instead of politics I went into acting. I always thought that if I'd met Ingmar Bergman and seduced him, then my career would have been different. I coulda bin a contendah. I coulda bin somebody. But I never met Ingmar Bergman or Bibi Andersson or von Sydow or any of the others, so I never got to dance on the heath with the angel of death. I never ate wild strawberries. So my career was as it was. Is, I should say, because I'm still working, still in demand, and a lot of girls I started out with are retired and living with their third husbands in Palm Springs. God, I hate Palm Springs. So let up on yourself, Alec. You're an honorable man.

Andre was fundamentally lawless, Alec said.

Sounds like it, Annalise said.

I'm not, Alec said.

Annalise smiled. I am, more than you.

You're in a lawless business.

That's its charm, Annalise said.

I wish you'd met him.

He doesn't sound like my type, Annalise said. You're my type. But what I don't understand is, what are you disappointed about?

Maybe I didn't take advantage of things.

You mean the war, she said.

Not only that, Alec said.

But the war was the main thing.

I knew people who were suited to the war. They had a high appreciation of ambiguity, for one thing. They actually liked the atmosphere of violence. Lawlessness, really. That atmosphere suited them down to the ground. I never liked it. I was never attracted to it. I think they saw in it a kind of romance, some high-flown sense of themselves in a world where everyone was watching. And this was true not only of the men but the women, too, everyone at ease in the butcher shop. Wouldn't life hold an exaggerated importance in such a situation? I was damned if I was going to the war as a good career move. The truth is, I never found an Ingmar Bergman I wanted to seduce or who I wanted to seduce me. I wonder if I missed something.

Annalise gave him a long look but did not reply.

We'll never know, Alec said.

I think you know. You don't want to admit to it. Everyone misses something in life. Andre did. I don't know what it was he missed and I don't care, but I know it was something and my guess is, he knew it, too. I know I wouldn't be content spending my last days in — what was the name of that place?

Goya House, Alec said.

Drinking schnapps and arguing about the soccer match.

He seemed entirely content to me.

In full reminiscence about the camps, for heaven's sake.

He's entitled to it.

He certainly is. And welcome to it.

That's harsh, Annalise.

That's life, Alec.

They ate breakfast at the café and read the Bangor newspaper, two days old but full of surprise crises — North Korea, the bond market, the elderly in far Downeast Maine who were so poor they were convinced that many others were even worse off than they. Alec and Annalise walked to the boatyard and watched the shipwrights at work, caulking and sanding and painting. Alec felt in his pocket for the Leica but did nothing with it. He did not want to be seen as a tourist looking for quaint local color. These men and women were working hard because in little more than a month the summer people would be back, all of them expecting their boats to be shipshape, rails varnished, hulls painted, engines tuned, sails well stitched. There were half a dozen radios in the yard, all tuned to the same music station, Bruce Springsteen from the sound of him. The air smelled of brine, oil, and sweat. Nondescript dogs prowled the premises. The day was not warm but most of the workers were wearing T-shirts and shorts, even the women. Alec thought there was something attractive about the ancient art of boat maintenance. Intrinsic procedures would not have changed since the voyages of Odysseus. This Maine archipelago bore some resemblance to the ancient Aegean if you discounted the weather and the vegetation on the islands, not to mention the color of the sea itself. "Wine dark" did not describe the waters of the Gulf of Maine. Slate gray was closer to the mark, at least on this May morning. By this comparison the summer people would be Myrmidons, the ones who laid siege to Troy; except that the families who arrived here from New York and Boston were not at all warlike, unless they arrived to find their vessels still in dry dock, and even then their complaints would be muted because the islanders did not respond well to threats. In any case, a Leica was out of place, not that the shipwrights would have minded. They were concentrating on the special tasks at hand. Alec did not wish to take advantage.

Annalise sat on an old dory writing postcards, and when she finished they both walked to the post office to mail the cards. When Alec checked for mail, the postmistress handed him a letter that had arrived that morning, postmarked Washington. He recognized the handwriting as Lucia's but rather than open it right away he put the letter in his pocket to read later when they were home. The long hike up the hill seemed to Alec more arduous than it had been the day before. Eyes down, he did not pause at the cemetery, and farther on the hawk had flown away. Annalise tried to pick up the pace but Alec's step was slow and his breathing hard. His feet hurt. The wind had come up and the air was abruptly chilly and filled with the promise of rain. Clouds gathered in the west and the gulls had vanished. They were passed by one pickup truck after another. Alec was relieved when High House came into view, whitecapped Baylor's Harbor below it. The high-bowed ferry had embarked for the mainland, rolling a little now in the long swells, its wake a confusion of white water.

Home at last, Annalise put on a pot for coffee and Alec climbed to the third-floor room to read Lucia's hasty scrawl, long ragged lines, occasional illegible words.

Lucia wrote that her father was dead. He was sitting in his usual place on the porch, at dusk, drinking schnapps. Something in the yard caught his eye and he stood, his hands on the railing. When he fell he took the entire balustrade with him. He fell like a tree, causing the house itself to shudder. That was according to Mr. Halvesi, who had been sitting with him. And there was no question that Andre was dead before he hit the ground. A heart attack, according to the doctor's report. The next few words were illegible but contained the word "miracle." Alec could not judge the context. Andre and Mr. Halvesi had been talking about a visitor earlier that day. Something the visitor said perplexed Andre. Was that visitor you, Alec? Mr. Halvesi thought it might have been. Andre was laughing at something you had said to him. He was still laughing when he stood to look for whatever it was on the lawn that caught his eye. And then he grunted and fell forward as if frozen, a statue. Since you seemed to take a liking to him I wanted you to know exactly what happened, Lucia wrote. The next two words were illegible. I am glad I had the chance to meet my father at last and I was looking forward to meeting him again, perhaps even in Europe. I wanted him to meet Mathilde especially, and of course Nikolas. I don't know why it should be that he would be taken from me only as we found each other after all these years. This does not seem just. I looked forward to many years of — and the next word was illegible. I wanted to know how he and my mother found each other. I wanted to know what my mother was like when she was young. Now I shall never know. By the time you get this the funeral will be over and done with. We will have a service at Goya House. One of Andre's friends was a priest, no longer part of the church but willing to preside. It seems my father had no religion but was very fond of the priest. It would break your heart, Alec, to see the look on the faces of my father's friends, Mr. Halvesi, Mr. Minh, Mr. Magris, and the others. They are broken up. One of them told me that my father was the center of their lives, the one they went to when they were troubled or there was some community decision to be made. They trusted his word. They trusted his good will. It was as if they were an ancient tribe that had suddenly lost its headman and was without direction or purpose. They were dismayed when I said I must take my father's ashes to Switzerland. They begged me to reconsider and allow him to remain at Goya House, where he had been happy. But he left a note that stated he wanted to be buried next to my mother in Zurich, so I was bound to disappoint them. I am very pleased he still felt something for her, that after all these years she was not a forgotten episode. He asked me specifically to carry his ashes to Zurich, so I was not a forgotten episode either. Mr. Halvesi found the note in Andre's desk, in his room. Dated last year. He knew he would find me. So I have comfort in that, too. Thank you for helping out, Alec. You must tell me sometime what you and my father talked about that morning. Whatever it was, I am very glad that his last day contained laughter. I will let you know if Nikolas and I decide to move house to Washington. I doubt it will happen. Be good to Mathilde.

Alec sat in his chair tapping the letter against his thumbnail. Annalise was standing with the coffee pot at the top of the stairs.

She said, What's wrong?

He said, Andre's dead, and handed her the letter.

Annalise read the letter and said she was sorry.

It's hard to believe, Alec said.

He was a very old man —

Yes, but he was the sort of old man who looked as if he had ten, twenty more years left. Of course there were the cigarettes and schnapps.

Do you really believe that was what it was?

No, Alec said. It would take more than that.

The camps, she said.

Yes, definitely.

I'm sorry I never met him.

Yes, I am too. You'd be a match for him.

He was probably outside my realm, Annalise said. He was from another country altogether. I'm not sure we would have had much to say to each other. I'm pretty sure we would have been antagonists from the beginning.

Andre was outside my realm, too. But I liked him.

Annalise poured coffee and handed him a cup. She said, It's hard for me to be talking about someone I've never met. I know he's vivid to you. And you've made him vivid to me, but still. As I said, he's outside my realm. My frame of reference, I should say.

Sorry. I'll shut up now.

You don't have to shut up.

I think I'll shut up.

Are you sorry you missed the funeral?

No. Who do you suppose the priest was? A Central American, I'll bet, a liberation theologian. Maybe Spanish, a renegade from the old days. The service would have been conducted in Spanish, nondenominational in character. But I'll give you even money that incense was burning.

Did you ever photograph Andre? It would be easier for me if I saw his picture.

Alec tried to recall his last few moments on the lawn at Goya House. I think I did, he said. I don't remember clearly. I think I photographed him from the lawn. Not a formal shot, God knows. Two quick surreptitious snaps maybe, Andre asleep in his chair, breathing hard, lost to the world. But maybe at the last minute I didn't. I've never favored shooting people unawares. I had to do it when I worked for the newspaper. But I prefer not to.

I know, she said.

Invasion of privacy, he said.

Yes, of course.

Damnedest thing, I can't remember.

If you did, the film would be there.

That's true, he said.

By the way, I look on photography not as an invasion of privacy but a guarantee of it. It seems to me that I've been in front of a camera for half my lifetime. It's an old friend, just like you.

The telephone rang then and they both looked at it. Annalise was first on her feet and when she picked up her mouth broke into a wide smile. She said, Hellohellohello, how on earth did you find me here of all places? What's going on? She sat in the big leather chair, the phone to her ear, listening to whoever it was tell her how he had found her here of all places.

The foghorn had begun to growl at ten-second intervals, incidental music back of the wind. Alec rose with his coffee and moved to the glass door, stepping carefully onto the deck. The boards shifted under his feet and he avoided looking down. He stood staring into Baylor's Harbor, the boats straining at their moorings, wind whipping the water. The Herreshoff looked secure. There were six boats altogether, manacled like prisoners. Low scud came in on the zephyr wind and here and there Alec could see heavy black clouds above the scud. He had the idea that the wind was quartering and that could mean a three-day blow. Probably it would be smart to lay in provisions. Alec sipped his coffee and watched the sea turn and heave. Inside he heard Annalise's laugh, prelude to a change in plans; he knew it as he knew the effect of the quartering wind. The deck felt fragile to him and he stepped back into the doorway, out of the wind and drizzle. The weather disintegrated as he watched it. In a place like this your day was governed by the weather, the first thing you thought about in the morning and the last thing you thought about at night. In the city no one cared. On islands the weather was god-like and therefore inscrutable.

Alec remained in the doorway listening to the timbers creak and wondering what was next. He felt for the Leica in his pocket but did not take it out even though the striped Norwegian fishing shack was a wonderful flash of color amid the damp black and green, the more mysterious because it was uninhabited and had always been uninhabited. He thought of the interior as crowded with the ghosts of Norwegian fishermen tormented by wasps. Alec had a sudden hunger for his house in Washington, the familiarity of it, his wall of photographs and the rose garden in back, the former Alhambra next door. The garden needed tending. He had a tremendous urge to be in the garden at dusk, a drink in his hand, listening to the sounds of the neighborhood. The hell with Bloomingdale's. Behind him Annalise said something but a fresh gust of wind blew her words away.

Are you coming in?

In a second.

It's cold in here, Alec.

It's wild outside. Come look.

I can see from here, Annalise said.

Your kind of weather, Alec said.

It is not my kind of weather. Key West is my kind of weather.

He turned to look at her, her tousled hair and her face tanned by the Moroccan sun, her frown that threatened to break into smiles.

You've got to come look at this, he said. A schooner motored past the lighthouse and into the thoroughfare. Its sails were furled. Water crashed over the bow and the vessel heeled perilously to starboard. Annalise came to stand beside him, her arm around his waist. They could see the crew in bright yellow oilskins and the skipper at his big wheel in the stern, the skipper looking up to the rigging. By the set of his shoulders, the cock of his head and his raised right arm Alec knew the skipper was irritated, the storm at hand, the port a mile or so distant. The schooner flew behind one of the small islands and was lost to view. By the time Alec had counted to ten it was visible again and entering calm waters.

Alec thought he would give the island one more week, hope

266

the weather improved so he could make one sail in the Herre-shoff, a quick boat, responsive and reliable, wonderful to look at, lines as clean as a Matisse sketch. It had been a year or more since he had taken a helm. He would sail out of Baylor's Harbor to the western side of the island for a picnic with Annalise. And then he would return home to Washington to see what came next.

END OF STORY

ANNALISE'S TELEPHONE CALL was Los Angeles business, as Alec suspected when he heard her voice and the throaty chuckle that went with it. Hellohellohello was a producer who needed her urgently because the movie he was filming had lost one of its featured players to what appeared to be a nervous breakdown, although in these times, who knew? But the actress was out of commission, off the reservation as it were, and shooting was commencing the day after tomorrow in lovely Vancouver, and if Annalise would take his word for it that the part was a very good one and made for her would she please please get on an airplane at once, about three weeks work, top salary, nice bonus at the end. Easier said than done, Annalise said, and told him where she was. There was a one-minute silence while the producer's assistant fiddled with his BlackBerry to locate the island off the Maine coast and verify the ferry schedule and determine the distance to the nearest commercial airport — and, well then, this is a piece of cake. We'll charter a plane to Montreal where you can catch the ten o'clock Air Canada to Vancouver and plan to be on the set at noon for a run-through. Meet the cast. Meet Fred, who's directing. He's on board. Loves your work.

Do you have a fax where you are?

Annalise laughed. Of course not.

I'm faxing the script to the charter company. You can read it en route.

I don't know, Annalise said.

We're in a hole, honey. Just a hell of a hole. Help us out. I won't forget it. Fred won't either.

I'm on vacation, Annalise said.

We'll make it up to you.

All right, Annalise said.

You're a sweetheart, the producer said. You won't be disappointed.

Promise?

Cross my heart and hope to die.

Have you thought about wardrobe?

That won't be a problem, Annalise. This scene we're shooting the day after tomorrow? A negligee is all you need.

Don't forget to call my agent, Annalise said.

Annalise and Alec stood on the dock in the wind and drizzle waiting for the six o'clock ferry to begin boarding.

You should come with me, she said. A change of scene would do you good.

I need a few more days here, Alec said.

The weather's a mess. You won't like it.

Give it a few days. I'm sorry you're leaving, though.

I can never resist last-minute appeals, she said.

I'll bet you didn't count on the negligee.

Listen. At my age that's a compliment.

You are superb in a negligee, Annalise.

A sudden commotion on the ferry dock indicated boarding

time. There were only a dozen passengers, all of them in hats and heavy windbreakers. Annalise wore a woolen suit and high heels, a black beret, and an Aquascutum raincoat, a wheeled suitcase at her side. Alec noticed one of the passengers turn to a companion and mouth the words That's Annalise Amiral, the actress.

Alec said, You've been spotted.

Annalise said, It's about time.

They're going to ask for your autograph.

Not this bunch, she said. They're much too laid-back.

I'll miss you, he said.

Miss you, too.

We had fun, didn't we?

I'm sorry about the crack I made this morning.

Which one?

You distracted in bed.

You were right.

Never, Annalise said. You're the best, Alec.

I'll bet you say that to all the boys.

I certainly do. But I mean it when I say it to you.

The chain went down at last and the little group of passengers shuffled forward, a line of six pickup trucks behind them. Engine exhaust was thick in the damp air. Alec and Annalise took their time.

I'm awfully sorry to see you go.

Maybe I made a mistake.

Not a mistake. When there's a call, you take the call. But I'm going to miss you.

Me, too, she said.

Call me when you get there.

If it's not too late.

Call anyway.

You'll be asleep.

I'll wake up.

Take care of yourself while I'm away.

You, too. There's mischief in Vancouver.

Stay out of that damned boat.

Did you hear what I said about Vancouver?

She said, I'll be three weeks only and then we can see each other again. Of course you could come to Vancouver. You've never been. You might like it precisely because you've never been. Vancouver's a beautiful city, good food. The art galleries are good. The natives are harmless. The British Columbia coastline is a lot like this one except it's inhabited. Plenty of boats, though. And then there's the tremendous excitement of the set, four hours of gin rummy preparing for thirty seconds on camera. The romance of the making of a major motion picture and so forth and so on.

Maybe later, Alec said. Maybe next week.

She shook her head. It'll never happen, she said.

No, he said. I'll meet you in Vancouver.

I was having a fine time with you. And then they called because they were in a jam and I said all right, when do you need me. I do that all the time. I've done it my entire life.

Shucks, he said, and laughed.

Is Andre still in your head?

He was, Alec said. But he went away.

I don't mind, you know. I'm happier with my life when you're in it.

Don't worry about Andre.

Andre makes it a crowd, she said.

Annalise kissed him before stepping onto the ferry. People were watching them. Alec stood with his hands in his pockets as the pickup trucks eased onto the ramp. They were only a few feet apart but such distances were always deceptive. The last truck boarded, the chain went up, and the crew set about casting off. Annalise and Alec continued to look wordlessly at each other until she said 'bye in a small voice. He put out his hand and she took it, Annalise looking as sad as he had ever seen her, and he knew what she was thinking because he was thinking the same. He gave her hand a squeeze as the boat slipped its moorings, advancing dead slow into the harbor. Annalise did not move from her place in the stern and at last gave a little forlorn wave, an insincere theatrical gesture that dismayed him — until he heard her low laugh as she turned and walked between the trucks to the passenger cabin. She was imitating a hundred third-reel farewells, on railway platforms and in airport waiting rooms, at bus stops and army bases, bedrooms and city streets and ocean liners and dance floors, a Hollywood convention that went back at least to D. W. Griffith.

Alec watched the ferry motor slowly into the channel, its running lights dancing on the surface of the water. Two sudden blasts from the horn that in other circumstances could be mistaken for an orchestra's fanfare. Dusk was coming on and the wind softened. The drizzle ceased. Alec remained alone on the dock watching the ferry's lights recede. He raised his hand for a final wave even though there was no one on deck to receive it.

Annalise called that night, safe in Montreal; and the night after that, safe in Vancouver. The negligee fit nicely. The part wasn't bad, not bad at all. She had stolen one scene and if she was lucky might steal another. The screenplay had some weight to it and that was probably because the writer was even older than she was. The director knew his business. If you get out here quick there's a bit part for you, a barroom piano player with a heart of gold and a bad right eye. And you get to wear a tuxedo whereas I have to make do with the negligee. It's only a made-for-TV movie but it has some punch to it and the director is a peach, an old pro just like me.

The next morning Alec ate breakfast early and set off through the overgrown field to reach Baylor's Harbor. En route he looked in at the Norwegian fishing shack but the windows were so dusty he could see nothing definite. Wasps' nests hung from the eaves and he noticed a dry woodsy odor: the Norwegian planking and the paint that continued to fade and peel, a children's playhouse from the brothers Grimm. Alec continued to stroll in the direction of the harbor and the pier where a dinghy was stowed. It took him a minute to find it and another few minutes to upend it. Oars were underneath. The day was bright with a ten-knot wind from the southeast. Fair-weather clouds drifted by. Alec rowed through the chop to the Herreshoff, shackled the dinghy to the stern, and awkwardly climbed aboard. He had trouble with his balance. He banged his knee and then his elbow, drawing blood each time. He looked up to see the high-bowed ferry in the distance, the nine o'clock run to the mainland. The half-mile of water between the Herreshoff and the ferry was crowded with lobster pots, all the colors of the rainbow spread in a great fan like the glittering lights of a Christmas tree. He took the Leica from his pocket and focused on the pots, then remembered the film was black and white. He made a shot anyhow and returned the camera to his pocket.

The Herreshoff looked to be shipshape. Alec spent some time sorting out the mainsail and some more time getting it into position. He worked slowly, realizing he was out of shape and out of practice. The jib had been carelessly stowed and that took twenty minutes to unravel. Alec moved with economy in the small space, the boat tipsy in the light chop. When he finished, Alec poured coffee from the canteen strapped to his waist. Sunshine on the water was so bright it hurt his eyes, so he turned his back and drank coffee while looking at the Norwegian shack and High House beyond it. There were other houses along the shore but none of them looked occupied. Alec took his time about everything, no need to rush. The day was a masterpiece and could only improve. He finished his coffee and set about the sails, mainsail first, then jib. He untied the dinghy and walked it to the bow and shackled it to the mooring. Then he released the Herreshoff and was away, heeling gently. Alec had a chart but he would not need it except for marking shoals. There were plenty of those, even at high tide. He intended to sail southwest from the harbor, then north to the beach. He would decide when he got there whether to land or to come about and head for home.

Thirty minutes out, a lobsterman crossed Alec's bow, giving a casual salute. Alec returned it, happily remembering a conversation years before with one of the old island salts who had been describing the treachery of the Gulf of Maine, its changeable moods, now blithe, now sullen. The islander's accent was so thick Alec had trouble understanding. He said people from away had strange ideas. One of the summer people had a name for the gulf — Mare Nostrum. Our Sea. The old salt cackled when he said it and Alec laughed along with him. The Gulf of Maine was no one's sea. It was its own sea with its own laws and history. At the moment it was sparkling in the sunshine, benign as any sort of spring day. Alec set a course due west and then north, the sails full. There were few boats about. He dipped his hand in the water, heavy and cold. And then the sail commenced to luff, the wind dying. Alec pointed the boat closer to shore. He was watching the sails, now nearly limp in the sudden calm. When he turned he saw the island slowly disappear in the fog that had come from nowhere. That was one of the things the old salt had told him: the southeast wind often meant fog. A strange, unpredictable wind from the deep ocean. Alec had forgotten that part of the conversation, recalling instead Mare Nostrum, information of no practical value at all.

He moved the tiller in the direction of the island and the boat heeled slightly. All he could hear was the creak of the rigging and an engine's throb far to the west. The sound of the engine tailed away and he was left with the tick-tick of the rigging. He looked at the surface of the water, flat with a gentle heave. Here and there were sprigs of seaweed. Alec tried to remember whether the tide was coming in or going out but could not. The roll of the water told him nothing and his vision was good for ten yards only. There were no shadows in fog nor any sense of perspective, depth of field. Fog was its own closed world, a nation apart, sovereign, featureless, and primitive. Alec knew that high above the opaque surface of the water the sky was a crystalline blue, the sun so bright you had to avert your eyes; the sun at your back, you could see forever. From what seemed a great distance Alec heard the cough of the foghorn. The boat was drifting on its own motion. Alec thought of many things in a rush — the Norwegian shack, Annalise on her sound stage in Vancouver, his father in his Senate office, Andre falling like a tree, his beautiful garden at dusk, the guests-of-many-languages assembled at the Alhambra, the Count and Countess d'An making the introductions, Charles passing champagne. He hoped Mathilde was successful with the Iranians. The boat was overcrowded with so many people in it, but it continued to drift as Alec close-hauled the sails, waiting for the fugitive breeze that was certain to come. The fog made him lightheaded as if he were in thin air. Alec relaxed in the stern of the Herreshoff, his right arm draped over the tiller, and gave himself over to reverie in the spirit of an insomniac counting sheep. He lost track of time. In due course the breeze arrived and Alec made for shore — not an anchorage but a place to wait a little until the weather cleared.

By the time Annalise arrived the formalities were done with. She took the taxi from the ferry landing to High House, the driver close-mouthed but glancing frequently into his rear-view mirror at Annalise, who sat with her face averted, staring out the window at the endless expanse of firs and water beyond the firs. When he remarked that it was a mighty shame about poor Mr. Malone she nodded but did not speak. Seemed a nice fella, the driver said, a good enough sailor who had bad luck. The weather in these parts is hard on people from away, the driver added, but allowed his voice to trail off when Annalise pulled a pair of sunglasses from her purse and put them on even though the day was overcast, threatening rain. She gave him twenty dollars and told him to keep the change and not to bother about her bag; she'd fetch it herself from the trunk.

Mr. Malone was familiar with these waters, Annalise said.

Yes, ma'am, the driver said.

And he was a skilled sailor. Beautiful sailor.

But the weather was awful bad, the driver said.

Annalise nodded and dismissed him. She stood in the driveway next to Alec's Chevy, her bags at her feet, looking at the foolish house nestled among the spruces, higher than all of them, an assertion of temporal authority. She had never liked it, this willful, arrogant, hopeless house built by totalitarians. You were obliged to accommodate yourself to it. Concessions were not in its nature. Annalise stood in the driveway and grew angrier as she glared at it, wondering what it would take to burn High House to the ground. Burn it so that only ash remained, a conflagration that could be seen from the mainland, causing people to wonder what was happening on the island, no doubt some perverse maritime ritual. Islanders were strange in their habits. Their children were strange. Families intermarried. Dangerous drugs were epidemic and also disease. They disliked outsiders, and if you got into trouble God help you — the islanders wouldn't. They feared people from away. They were a sly, crafty, spiteful tribe without compassion — and then Annalise broke down. She thought there were no more tears left in her. She had cried in Vancouver, cried on the airplane, cried once more on the ferry. She had stood in the stern watching the lights of the mainland recede until she had pulled herself together, hunched against the bitter western wind. The crew seemed to know who she was and why she was there. They helped her with her bag and asked if there was anything she wanted. They couldn't have been nicer. When she walked to the stern they left her alone but someone was always nearby.

Annalise looked into Alec's Chevy. The keys were in the ignition. She put her bag on the rear seat and stood looking over the roof of the car to the preposterous house. She saw Alec's rain hat on the dashboard and almost broke down again but gathered herself and walked the twenty yards to the front door, unlocked as Mathilde promised it would be. Inside, she looked at the unmade bed, coins on the dresser, Alec's clothes on the chair. Annalise did not linger there but climbed at once to the second floor. The time was just before seven, dusk well along. In the refrigerator was a bottle of Montrachet that Alec had brought from Washington. The corkscrew was on the sideboard so she opened the Montrachet and poured a glass. She took it to the third floor. There was enough light to see by so she did not switch on the lamps. She noticed Günter Grass's recent memoir and a copy of the Bangor newspaper on the coffee table along with a stack of picture books relating to the state of Maine. The Leica was there, too.

The telephone rang but she did not answer. It would be Vancouver and she did not want to talk to Vancouver.

Annalise stepped to the window and then stepped back, conscious of the wall of books behind her. From where she stood the island looked deserted, undiscovered country. It looked as it must have looked to the Indians or the Norsemen or whoever found it first and staked a claim. Probably the island seemed hospitable, a natural anchorage on the southern side, ponds inland, acres and acres of timber, enough stone to build the pyramids at Giza had it occurred to them to build pyramids; and naturally all the fishes of the sea. Probably on a summer or autumn day it would look like paradise. Of course they would have to beware of weather, fair skies followed by long hours of fog followed by cold and then squalls. Even very experienced mariners lost their way. A compass was essential along with good nerves and an adventurous spirit; probably the two went together.

Why had Alec come to this place? Annalise had no satisfactory answer to that question. Blind fate, she supposed. Dusk continued to fall. There were no lights anywhere in her line of vision and no sounds, and then she heard the cry of a gull and the rattle of a pickup truck on the road. Annalise stepped forward, closer to the window, fearing very much what she would see, and her fear was realized at once: the Herreshoff swinging easily on its mooring. She watched it move in the breeze and the current, hardly more than a shadow now, sails safely stowed in the bow. Her dread eased as she looked at the Herreshoff, lines as clean as a Matisse sketch. Alec had said that. She missed his way of speaking, his turns of phrase, the look he had when in reverie, a hundred small things, and his fidelity. At that instant, in the quiet of the evening, time ceased and nothing existed for her except the room and the boat swinging on its mooring in the twilight.

Annalise switched on a lamp and looked around the room. She would collect Alec's clothes, as she had promised she would do, and the car and whatever personal items were about. His wristwatch, his reading glasses, his wallet, and the Leica. They were all that was left but they would have to do. Looking at Alec's private things, Annalise felt pushed back in time, to some earlier life, a long-ago time when she was young and the world mysterious and filled with possibility. The world was no longer mysterious but the possibilities, alas, remained infinite.